FLY AWAY HOME

FELICE STEVENS

Published by Good Man Press

Cover Art by Reese Dante
https://reesedante.com

Photographer: Rafa G. Catala
https://www.instagram.com/rafagcatala_13/
Model: Israel Martinez

Copyediting and Proofreading by Flat Earth Editing
https://facebook.com/FlatEarthEditing

Additional Proofreading by Lyrical Lines
https://www.lyricallines.net/

Digital ISBN: 979-8-88949-055-5
Paperback ISBN: 979-8-88949-056-2

DEDICATION

To my family.

ACKNOWLEDGMENTS

Thanks to my editor, Keren Reed, for always pointing me in the right direction. To Hope and Jess from Flat Earth Editing, for making my books shine and always going the extra mile. Thanks to Dianne from Lyrical Lines for those eagle eyes. And thanks to Reese for her art and vision in creating the most magical covers.

And as always, all my love for my readers. Whether this is your first book of mine or your sixty-first, thank you as always for making this the best damn job in the world. I couldn't do it without your support.

CHAPTER ONE

"Maybe I don't have to kill him. I could just choke him and stuff him in a garbage pail." In between sips of cold brew, he jotted a few lines in his notebook. "But I prefer murder."

Colson Delacourt sat in his neighborhood coffee spot, ensconced at a corner table. He chewed on his lower lip as he contemplated the plot of his new mystery while scanning the crowd coming and going in a steady stream.

Normally, he'd be at home in pajamas, sitting at the dining table he'd commandeered as his desk, the television on in the background for noise, while his fingers flew over the keyboard. No matter how many times he'd explained it to Evan, the man had never understood how Colson could write with so many distractions.

As it turned out, Evan hadn't understood a lot about him.

Colson's stomach cramped, but he couldn't be sure if it was from thinking about his broken relationship or the coffee on an empty stomach. Heartbreak and hunger didn't go hand in hand.

"Whatever," he mumbled to himself. "Hopefully the change of scenery will help." He closed his eyes for a moment, willing his swirling thoughts to coalesce into coherent words he could put on page. He couldn't sit and stare at a blank screen anymore, so he started writing longhand and it helped him.

Readers enjoyed not only the complex plots but following the lives of the detectives as they searched for answers. He had two *New York Times* bestsellers, several short stories, and a slew of awards. A beautiful house and a great neighborhood Chinese restaurant where they knew him by name.

Living the life, right?

Colson sighed. It had been almost four years since his first book had released to critical acclaim. Three years since the second was published and he and Evan had met and moved in together. The burnout had started soon after. It'd been eight months since the breakup. Forever since he'd felt whole.

Not today, Satan.

He reread what he'd written and rubbed his cheek as he pondered. "Dismemberment. *Hmm.* Haven't done that yet. Better check the ins and outs. So much blood. I hate a messy crime scene."

Colson flexed his fingers, took a look around, and met the gaze of an elderly man sitting a table away, who immediately turned his head. Colson frowned. He'd showered this morning and had made an attempt to tame his hair, although he needed to visit the barber. It had been a while. Okay, a long while. Probably his tattoos and the earring were a turn-off. Some people said he was intimidating. Guys used to think it was hot.

Maybe it was a bad-boy image, but his ink had been done more as a fuck-you to his tight-ass, cold-as-ice parents than to intimidate anyone. His stomach twisted again. Anger mixed with grief slammed into him, a common occurrence anytime he thought about them.

"Fuck it," he growled. "Let's do this." He closed his eyes, and suddenly, like a sunbeam breaking through murky clouds, it clicked. The names of the protagonists, their backstories, and the plot going forward. He could see the pages unwinding before his eyes like the fucking yellow brick road.

"Yeah, baby. That's it. Perfect. Love it." His cramping stomach forgotten, he let the words rush over him in waves, and when he finished, he grunted with satisfaction, oblivious to the pain of his almost-numb fingers.

"Finally. That's got to be three thousand words. That's two thousand, five hundred and forty more than I've been able to write in the past two years." He reviewed them, ecstatic to see they weren't merely words on the page but actual usable words. A great first chapter to hook the reader.

"Ha-ha," he crowed and banged on the table. At a sharply indrawn breath, he darted a glance and found the elderly man frowning. He then huffed and vacated his seat, finding one across the coffee house.

Colson didn't care. This book was a winner, and he was going to celebrate.

He picked up the phone and hit Hogan's number.

"Colson? That really you?"

"Yeah, it is. How's it going?"

"Better now that I've heard from you. What's it been, man? Four months, five? I tried calling, but you were kind of MIA."

"Make it eight. When...you know..." Colson shrugged. "And sorry about shutting you out. I wasn't in the right headspace for any conversation other than thanking my food delivery person."

"Shit, yeah. Sorry. You...okay?" Hogan asked cautiously—a far cry from how he would've done it during their hard-partying, beer-pong days in college.

"Yeah. I think so."

A whoosh of air filled his ear. "Thank fucking God." Colson heard a noise that sounded suspiciously like sniffling.

"Are you...crying?" A smile curved his lips. A bear of a man at six foot four and two hundred and fifty pounds, few knew Hogan was more teddy than grizzly.

"No, you asshole. I have allergies."

"*Mmhmm.* Sure. Anyway, I called because I got an idea for a book and I wrote the first chapter. Three thousand words. I feel it, Hogan. It's happening again. This is a good one."

"That's terrific. I knew the burnout wouldn't last."

"Three years is a hell of a long time." He chewed the inside of his cheek, his positivity beginning to fade.

"Nah," Hogan rushed to reassure Colson, as if he could sense the self-doubt beginning to eat away at him. "You're a talent. And quality takes time. Neither book is a carbon copy of the other. Trust me, your readers will be there when the time is right. You're unique because you put yourself in the head of the killer when you write. Scares me sometimes."

"Ha-ha. I remember when I told you I always think of myself doing the deeds, and you thought I needed psychiatric help."

Hogan chuckled. "I still do sometimes, but hey, what the hell do I know about creativity? I'm a numbers guy."

Colson snickered. "Numbers give me hives."

"Don't I know it," Hogan responded dryly. "Your tax returns are legend here at the firm. Good thing I'm your friend."

Guilt tugged at him. "Trust me, I know I'm the lucky one."

"It'll be okay. Evan turned out to be a shit, but you can't give up your life for someone who doesn't give a damn about you."

Ouch. Fuck, that hurt.

"Well, I'm out now. And talking to you." Irritated, he drank more coffee. "Do you want to hear more or not? Or does Bea have you on babysitting duty?"

"It's not babysitting when they're your kids, idiot. And of course I want to hear about the book. Even if I have to pretend I'm listening to a murderer talk to me."

Was it an unorthodox method? Maybe. But it worked for him.

"If I don't think of myself as the murderer, how can I make it real enough for my readers to immerse themselves in the story? Plus, when I shift to the procedural part of the story, I switch gears and put on my detective hat. Or shield, as it is. Realism is what I've always tried to give people. Hopefully they're still interested."

That was what happened when your personal life imploded, leaving you wondering why you even bothered to get up in the morning. If he had been so wrong to love Evan, who'd found it easy to cheat on him and leave without a backward glance, who was to say he understood anything? Maybe he needed to buy a cabin in the woods, get a dog, and become a hermit. Sounded good to him.

He put away his notebook. A trio of women in their midsixties had taken the space vacated by the grouchy old man. Good friends, from what he could see, as they were sharing pictures of children and grandchildren on their phones. A fourth joined them, carrying a tray of hot beverages.

"Bah," Hogan dismissed that. "As soon as you announce you've got something new, they'll come out of the woodwork. Tell me what it's about."

Colson had thought he'd need to look at his notes, but it was all there in his mind and it flowed off his lips.

"Okay. There's this little old lady—Millie Johnson. She actually exists and also lives on Willow—you know that big brownstone across the street from me? With the big wooden doors?"

"Yeah, I think so."

"I help her with groceries and fixing things around her house, so I know the layout. Her routine is pretty set. Grocery store, bookstore, the diner for lunch, and then home. Twice a week she goes to the bank. She keeps the door open because her arthritis makes it hard to manage the locks." It reminded him to check on her to make sure she was locking her door. Millie was way too trusting a soul. Only for her had he left his house to help with chores she needed or to carry packages if she couldn't get something delivered.

"So she never locks her door," Hogan filled in, "and this guy knows it."

"Yep. You got it. As I have it planned, she comes home from the bank, pushes open the door, and *bam.*" He pounded his fist on the table, rattling the napkin holder. *Crap.* Was he being too loud? It had been a long time since he was out in public. He'd forgotten how to behave and use his "indoor voice," as he'd heard Bea tell the kids.

Guilty, he glanced at the people nearby to see if anyone had heard him. No one sat by his right, but less than five feet away in front of him, the quartet of women had grown silent, drinking their coffee. His gaze slid away and came to a dead stop, caught by a man entering the coffee shop.

Colson almost swallowed his tongue. He was a little over six feet, with hair black as onyx curling at his nape. His neck was strong, his shoulders muscled. A broad back narrowed to slim hips, the crisp shirt tucked into charcoal gray slacks that were poured onto thick thighs and a butt he could write a dedication to. Colson tracked him as he waited on line, but the man never looked up. He studied his phone, a hank of that night-black hair falling forward, hiding his face.

Dammit. He wanted to see more.

"Colson, you there?" Hogan called into his ear.

"What? Yeah, sorry. Just got a little distracted." He gulped his iced coffee, and it went down the wrong pipe, causing a choking fit. His coughing up a lung drew everyone's attention, including the hottie's. Stubble shaded his jaw, but it did little to hide the man's sharp, chiseled features. Red-rimmed eyes swept over him, their color iridescent as a flawless diamond's, and Colson quickly shifted away but not before seeing the slash of dark brows rise high and a slight upward tilt of his lips.

Glad my imminent death from choking amused you, asshole.

"Anyway, I'm either going to bash her over the head, or stab her and cut up the body. I haven't decided yet. I need to do more research to see which is better."

Loud whispers floated over from the table of ladies. "Oh, my God! What do you suppose he's talking about?" Their faces reflected horror, and he grinned to himself. If they were going to eavesdrop, he was going to give them something to talk about. That was the price they paid for being nosy fuckers.

"So what's the premise?" Hogan asked. "It's not only killing the lady."

"I can't help it if I like killing," Colson said, raising his voice a bit so the ladies could hear. "There's something so soothing about it. Like squashing a bug."

The chatter grew frenzied.

"He's crazy."

"What should we do?"

"We need to call the police."

"Uh, Colson? Is there something you need to tell me?" Hogan's anxiety had him laughing.

"You know me. I'm a ruthless fucker. And Millie is rich. Very rich. Her brownstone is full of antiques. She's a little eccentric. Bakes cookies for everyone and wears her fabulous jewelry and Chanel suits to run her errands, that kind of thing."

"Got it."

"And it's not the first time. It's a pattern. Befriending wealthy older ladies, helping them, becoming indispensable to them."

"So he's a serial killer."

A curl of excitement lit his belly. "Yeah. I haven't done that yet."

"Well, it all sounds absolutely gruesome and perfectly you. Can't wait to read it."

"Thanks." The hottie had gotten his coffee and found a seat on the opposite side of the café from him. Still glued to his phone, he frowned. A flash of gold caught Colson's eye, and upon further inspection of his lower extremities, he caught sight of the shield clipped to the man's waist.

Detective, huh?

While researching, Colson had visited a few homicide divisions and spoken to many detectives. None resembled this man.

Maybe he could use him in his story. That would be a first. Normally his law enforcement personnel were older, rumpled, and grouchy. Hard-boiled and hard-living, with problems of their own that often spilled over into the investigations they handled. This man looked like he belonged on the cover of a fashion magazine, not poking around crime scenes. Having a hot-as-fuck detective might draw in more female readers.

The four women continued to shoot Colson terrified glances. He slipped his notebook into his bag, picked up his coffee, and walked past them.

"Have a lovely day, ladies. I hope you get home safely...and in one piece."

They all gasped, and he laughed and walked out. A side-eye at the large glass windows showed the detective still frowning, now in his direction. He'd done nothing wrong.

He decided to pay a visit to the real-life Millie Johnson to see if she needed his help with anything. Really, he was a pussycat.

He rang her bell and heard the tapping of her heels on the hardwood floor. When she opened the door, her smile beamed. "Colson. So good to see you."

"Millie. How many times have I told you not to open your door without asking who it is first? It's a dangerous world out there."

"Oh, phooey. Who'd bother an old lady like me? Come with me." She waved him in, and he made sure to lock the door behind him. "Would you like some tea? I was thinking of baking an apple pie."

She chattered as he followed her to the kitchen. A bag of flour, sugar, and several apples sat on a large wooden table.

"I hope you didn't carry this all yourself, Millie." He fixed her with a stern eye. "You know I'll help you whenever I can."

"You're a dear, but I need to get out. And no. A nice young man from the supermarket delivered it." She picked up a knife and set it down, rubbing her stiff fingers. "It's so humid and damp out today. My arthritis is acting up."

"Do you need me to help you?"

Her eyes brightened. "Would you mind? If you cut up the apples and measure the ingredients, I'll be able to do it."

"For your apple pie? Gladly."

"You're a very sweet man, Colson. I appreciate it."

"It's my pleasure." Millie needed protecting. She was one of those people who only saw good in others. He followed her directions, and as Millie was a big fan of his writing, he told her of his new book idea while peeling and chopping the apples. She laughed and clapped her hands when he told her he planned to use her in his new book.

"Oh, how exciting. You must let me read it when it's finished."

For a moment he felt a twinge of regret making her the victim. "I hope you don't mind me killing you off."

She brushed away his concern. "Not in the least. If it wasn't for me, there would be no book. I'm the star of the show."

He slid the pie into the oven for her, cleaned up the kitchen table, and loaded the dirty bowls and plates into the dishwasher. He rinsed off the knife and several spoons and put them into the dish drain. "Anything else I can do for you before I leave?" He wanted to get home and type out the chapter to upload to the cloud.

"No, I don't think so. Make sure you come by later for a piece of pie."

"I wouldn't miss it. And I'll bring vanilla ice cream."

Her laughter was as infectious as a young child's. "You know my weakness." Her eyes dimmed. "I'm so glad to see you happy again. You can't let a bad relationship keep you from enjoying life."

His throat closed up. Millie should only know it wasn't his first. It had all started with his parents, old-money Delacourts from Greenwich, Connecticut, who had no use for a gay son. And except for his grandparents, who'd unfortunately passed away, and Hogan, he'd yet to find anyone in his life who cared enough about him to stay.

"I'm fine. Now that I'm writing again." At the slight pattering sound, he glanced up at the skylight. "It's raining. I'd better go, but I'll check in with you later."

"I know." Her laugh was merry. "You don't want to miss out on your pie." She walked him out. "And don't forget the ice cream," she said cheerfully.

He kissed her cheek. "I won't. Make sure you lock the door after me." To be certain, he tested the knob afterward.

The rain had petered out, but a fine mist replaced it, cooling the sultry air, and after stopping at home to drop off his notebook, Colson decided to walk to

Brooklyn Bridge Park. The area—usually crowded with throngs of tourists during the summer—was now mostly deserted. The earlier shower, quick as it was, must've driven them away, for which Colson was grateful. A few hours in the coffee house and then time with Millie had left him peopled out.

Head down, shoulders hunched, he walked along the path that wound by the river. The benches were too wet to sit, and he didn't feel like standing at the railing, so he continued on, past the rocky inlet where ducks quacked and swam, and the barbecue grills, and the bobbing boats of Brooklyn Sail. Some parents braved the weather and stayed in the playground with their children, pushing them on swings or reading to them. He smiled at their innocence, wishing he could remember ever being that close to his mother or father.

Doubling back, he walked through to the other side, past the Time Out Market, which he noted was crowded with all the people who'd escaped the earlier rain. He headed over to the beach area, where he found a rock and sat, staring into the gray waters of the East River sloshing at the shoreline.

The disintegration of his relationship with Evan could be pinpointed to the beginning of his burnout. And Evan, who'd met him during the good times, hadn't been prepared for his slow slide from celebrated author to morose, introspective hermit. Later on, he'd realized that was when the cheating had started. Colson had been so lost in his own head and wrapped up in his inability to write, he hadn't even noticed that he and Evan hadn't had sex in months.

"You're supposed to stay and support your partner. Isn't that what being in love means?" He watched as *Evan packed his suitcases. "It'll get better once I start writing again. I know it will."*

Evan zipped up a rolling bag filled with his toiletries. "And if that never happens? What then, Cole? I have a life too." His black eyes darkened, and Colson searched their depths, but Evan had proved adept at hiding, and Colson was unable to read his intent. "I did support you. For almost two years, I sat and encouraged you, putting my life on hold. I've been waiting for you to wake up, and I can't sit around by myself anymore."

"And you haven't been?" He'd suspected Evan of cheating after he'd made excuse after excuse for late-night meetings keeping him at the office. Evan would come in after midnight, sometimes smelling like strange cologne and alcohol. Colson didn't have the energy to confront him, perhaps because he knew Evan would leave, and he'd be alone.

In the end, it didn't matter. Evan left him anyway.

Evan shrugged. "I didn't think you'd care. We've been more like roommates than lovers." He finished the last of his bags and reached out to put a hand on Colson's cheek, but he jerked away from the touch. "I guess I should've told you about the job offer, but I kept thinking you'd start writing again, and I hoped everything would be fine. Maybe you'd even want a change of scenery and you'd come with me. But it's not going to work," he hastened to add, likely to prevent Colson from agreeing. He lowered his gaze and sighed. "It's only for a year. Maybe we can see if we can work it out."

"You *guess* you should've told me." Colson pulled his phone from his pocket and found Evan's Instagram account. The pictures of him and another man hugging, having dinner with large groups of friends, and kissing while visiting famous Paris landmarks—Versailles, the Eiffel Tower, the winding steps of Montmartre—a trip the two of them had planned but never taken—shouldn't have hit him so hard. It shouldn't have hurt him to read the caption "Best day ever" because Evan had said that exact same thing to him when Colson had invited him to move into his town house. There had never been any intention to work it out—he hadn't heard from Evan since he left and didn't expect to.

With shocked sadness, he scanned Evan's photos, realizing he'd deleted all the pictures of the two of them. Their vacations, events attended together, anniversary dinners, and sweet sleepy moments of the two of them cuddled in bed.

Years wiped away. As if he'd never existed.

Maybe he hadn't. Maybe the reason he couldn't write was simple. Evan left and took with him Colson's soul and everything that had made life beautiful and worth living.

"Fucking hell." He pounded his fists on the rocks and brushed the tears off his face. He wouldn't—couldn't—live squirreled away any longer while the world marched on. This idea for the new book was nibbling at his brain, the characters and plot points unfolding before his eyes. He itched to write.

"You're back," he muttered like a mantra. "You are back. Let's do this."

He remembered to pick up the vanilla ice cream from the supermarket, not understanding why the clerk pushed the container toward him without meeting his eyes. Upon his return home, his reflection provided the answer—streaks of blood from his bruised hands covered his cheeks.

"Great. Now I really look like the killer I'm writing. Talk about getting into character." Laughing to himself, he put the ice cream in the freezer and went to take a shower, anticipating his piece of apple pie.

CHAPTER TWO

Detective Harper Rose was tired as fuck.

Eighteen hours straight on a case would do that, but when he'd slapped the cuffs on the latest bad guy—a rapist who'd broken into his ex-wife's apartment—it had driven away the brain fog. Nothing beat that adrenaline rush. Not even sex, although it had been so long, Harper could barely remember that kind of high.

Even sleeping for nine blessed hours hadn't helped—he'd need a week to play catch-up with his bed for all the OT he'd put in. So worth it, to tell Alma Rodriguez her slimeball of an ex was behind bars. Still, he'd had to wake up. He and his partner had to be fresh to report to their captain about the details of the arrest.

His brother, David, had woken up earlier than usual, and they'd shared breakfast at seven. Luis—David's live-in aide—came into the kitchen at eight, and Harper had decided to head in early and get started on paperwork, but coffee was a sly seductor and called to him as he passed by Perk Me Up, the neighborhood coffee shop.

Predictably, a line snaked through the store, but he sighed and waited, checking his messages. What he didn't anticipate was the sightseeing. As in the fucking hot guy in the corner. Tats up and down nicely muscled arms, a scruffy jaw, bedhead hair, and the glitter of a diamond earring.

Mmm-mmm. Damn.

Their eyes met briefly, and a sizzle of attraction crackled straight to his balls. The man swallowed his coffee the wrong way and choked. Harper thought about offering to give him the Heimlich maneuver and grinned, imagining all the filthy things he'd like to do to the hottie once he got his arms around him.

Ah well, nothing like some dirty thoughts about someone he'd never see again to make the morning more palatable. He ordered a quad espresso and wedged himself into a seat across the shop from his pervy fantasy, who was on the phone, talking and waving a hand about, his lips curved in wicked smile that did strange things to Harper's dick.

Jesus, he needed to get laid. Maybe this weekend, he'd head to one of the nearby bars and blow off some steam. He sipped his coffee, feeling it do its work as his eyes opened a bit more and he was able to read his messages.

Great. More red tape, meetings with the DA's office, and not to forget, Pride month was almost over, and the NYPD was holding special events. *Whoopie. Let's trot out the gays.* Leaving his phone on the table, he got up and ordered another coffee—a cold brew this time.

He still had a few extra minutes before heading to the precinct.

One PP could say whatever the hell they wanted about acceptance; there were a bunch of detectives in his squad who had no use for him once they knew he was gay. On patrol, Harper never hid his sexuality, and it was a sad truth that when he'd made detective two years earlier, the first thing his assigned partner—an old-timer named Vic Lombardi—had said to him was, "I heard you're into guys. Or are they into you?"

Lombardi had thought his joke was hysterically funny, but Harper had not. He'd reported him, which hadn't won him many friends, and Lombardi had then used his years and connections to request a new partner. Harper was put with Nolan Martinez. They'd clicked immediately, and Harper knew Nolan had his back and had no issues with him being gay. In fact, Harper had to tell Nolan's wife, Gina, whom he loved, that no, he wasn't interested in dating her hairdresser or the guy at Sephora who'd helped her pick out a new lipstick and was so cute.

Who had time for a relationship?

Between the demands of his job and taking care of his brother, Harper was stretched as tight and thin as a wire. After his father's death and his mother's suicide several years after, Harper became the sole caretaker for David, who'd been severely injured in a school bus accident as a child, leaving him a quadriplegic with profound brain injury. He had extremely limited ability to move his arms—therapy twenty years ago was different than today, and David had only learned to hold a fork or spoon in the past year.

Determined to keep his little brother at home with him, Harper had hired a full-time live-in aide, but he made sure almost all his free time was spent with his brother. No one else and nothing mattered to him more. The smile on David's face when he came home was enough happiness in his life.

Tears pricked his eyes, but he ignored them and gulped the rest of his coffee. Better get his ass moving. He slipped the phone into his pocket.

"Ex-excuse me?"

He glanced up to see a group of women in front of him, all with the same worried expressions. *Uh-oh.* His gut instinct, which rarely proved him wrong, buzzed.

"Can I help you?"

One of them, obviously the appointed spokesperson, looked to the woman next to her, who nodded.

"Go ahead, Marianne. We have to say something."

"You're a police officer? We saw your shield on your belt."

"Detective, ma'am. Is there a problem?" Harper had zero clue what they could be concerned about. He'd been sitting there for over twenty minutes and had noticed nothing awry.

"Oh, even better. See, we were sitting across from you over there." She pointed to the now empty table with four chairs. "A man was sitting behind us. He was very...different-looking. And acting very strangely."

Different-looking? For fuck's sake, what the hell did that mean? He tamped down his anger, hoping he wasn't listening to a bunch of nosy bigots. "Different how?" he asked, attempting to keep a neutral voice.

"He was covered in tattoos and...messy. But that wasn't the problem. It was what he said." She lowered her voice. "He was talking about murdering someone."

Harper blinked. "I'm sorry? What?" The hot guy he'd noticed when he walked in? Discussing murder?

Like bobbleheads, they nodded in unison. "It's true, Detective. He was talking about stabbing this old lady who lives on the same block as him." Her voice lowered. "He was even talking about dismembering her."

"It was horrible," one of the other ladies cried out. "And he was so blasé about it. He even threatened us as he left."

"Threatened you? What did he say?" Harper fixed her with a stare, but she didn't retreat.

"I think he knew we were listening—I mean, we couldn't help it—and as he walked by, he gave us a horrible grin and almost whispered to us, 'Make sure you get home safely. In one piece.' Or something like that. And then he laughed. Like it was a joke." She shuddered. "I still have goose bumps."

"He was definitely planning something. He talked about her house and how he knew what it looked like and what her routine was. But the worst was how he spoke about killing her. He joked that it was like squashing a bug." Marianne wrapped her arms around her waist. "When we saw you were a policeman—detective—we figured we'd report it."

Of all the gin joints...

Harper huffed out a sigh and asked them to repeat everything so he could take notes on his phone. They each gave the same story.

"You all said he mentioned an elderly lady...Mildred?"

"Millie," a woman name Jackie stated with assurance. "Millie Johnson. She lives in a big brownstone with wooden doors on Willow Street. That's only a few blocks from here." She pointed, and he gave her a thin smile.

"Yes, I know the area." He'd grown up near the Heights, across Atlantic Avenue, in the close-knit, mostly Italian neighborhood of Carroll Gardens. After

David's accident and insurance settlement, his parents had moved from the two-bedroom apartment they'd rented for years and bought a small house in the same area. It was immediate and necessary, as they'd lived on the second floor of a huge brownstone, and with David confined to a wheelchair, it had been impossible to get him up and down the steep stairs. Their new home had a walk-in front door and a backyard with a deck, where David could sit in the sunshine during good weather.

"Are you going to make sure everything's okay?"

"Can you arrest him?"

"He was so scary-looking."

Harper set his phone on the small round table. He had eight open cases and a stack of paperwork waiting to be filed. He should call it in and let the patrol officers swing by and check, but instead found himself saying, "Sure. I'll go by and see if, first of all, there is actually a house like that."

"Oh, there is," Marianne attested with a sharp nod. "I lived on that block. Millie's a fixture in the neighborhood. Everyone knows her."

"All right. Thank you very much." He put the phone into his pocket, indicating the conversation was over.

Unfortunately, they didn't seem to understand and didn't move. "Aren't you going to go now? What if he's there now, trying to kill her?"

"Yes, of course. I appreciate all of you being so diligent."

He stood. He'd been sitting there for almost forty-five minutes before the women came over to talk to him and needed to get moving anyway. He'd swing by Millie Johnson's and check on her, then head over to the precinct. When he'd made detective and requested a precinct closer to home because of David, he wasn't made any promises, but the department had come through for him in a big way and assigned him to a squad only a mile and a half from his house. On his walk over, he did an online search for a Millie Johnson on Willow Street and found her listed at number 728.

The earlier rain had subsided, and an anemic sun peeked through the clouds. Willow Street was one of the prettiest in the Heights with its grand brownstones and overarching tree canopies. He approached the house and whistled. It was huge—five stories and at least twenty feet wide—and boasted a well-tended garden and colorful flowerpots at the windows.

His senses started tingling a moment before he realized the large wooden door stood ajar. Harper drew his gun as he ascended the stairs. With his foot, he pushed the door open and crept inside.

"Ms. Millie Johnson, are you all right? This is NYPD Detective Harper Rose."

Gun at the ready, he soft-footed it along the long hallway, peering into the front parlor and dining room, all immaculately kept and filled with gorgeous antiques. Several drawers were pulled out, and the glass doors of the china cabinets were wide open. A slight noise—more like a groan—sounded from the rear of the house, and with gun still drawn, he approached.

"Shit," he swore at the sight of an elderly lady lying on the floor. Blood soaked through her dress, and an apple pie lay smashed on the floor around her. A knife, the blade streaked with blood, lay by her side. Harper holstered his gun and checked for a pulse. He breathed a sigh of relief when he found one—weak and thready but there nonetheless. He took a dish towel and put pressure on the wound, then pulled out his phone and called for backup, an ambulance, and CSU. Nolan was his next call.

"Listen, I caught one on my way to work. Meet me at 728 Willow Street. An old lady stabbed in her home. Still alive, but I don't know the extent of her injury." Harper gave him a quick rundown. "I'm waiting for the ambulance and CSU. See you soon." He ended the call. "Ms. Johnson, can you hear me? It's Detective Rose. You're going to be all right." No answer, only a whimper. His hand looked so large against her small, pale face.

"Millie. Millie, where are you?" Harper heard footsteps quickly approaching and stood, gun raised.

"Freeze, police! Hands where I can see them!"

A man stood frozen at the arched entrance to the kitchen. A canvas bag dangled at his side. "Wha-what's going on?" His bugged-out eyes found Millie Johnson on the floor. "Millie! Oh, my God." He took several steps toward her.

"Don't move," Harper ordered. *Well, damn.* It *was* the hottie from the coffee shop. Exactly like the women had said. He holstered his gun. "What're you doing here? What's your name?"

The man licked his lips. "I'm, uh, Millie's neighbor. I helped her make a pie, and she invited me to come back with some ice cream."

Harper's gaze swept over him. The man had cleaned up some from when Harper had first seen him, which only enhanced his heart-stopping good looks. "Name and address, please."

"Colson Delacourt. I...I live across the street. 733 Willow."

Sirens sounded, and footsteps pounded. Two uniforms appeared. "Detective?" one of them asked, his brows rising as he observed the crime scene.

"Yeah. Secure the scene and begin canvassing for anyone who saw or heard anything."

Two EMTs ran inside, and Harper pointed a finger at Colson. "Don't go anywhere. I'm not finished with you." He directed his next words to the medics. "She's been stabbed in the side. I put pressure on it, but I have no idea how long she could've been lying here."

"Less than an hour and a half," Delacourt called out. "I left her here then. Unharmed," he added hastily at Harper's scowl.

They loaded the woman onto the stretcher and took her out. CSU had arrived, and he called over Bruce Stoger, whom he'd worked with often.

"Elderly lady. Dust the whole place for fingerprints—I haven't even made it upstairs. And get the knife to forensics." With his toe, he pointed to the bloody piece of evidence.

"You got it, Harper. Man…" Stoger grimaced in disgust. "What kind of fuckin' sicko hurts a little old lady? What the hell's the matter with people?" Still shaking his head, Stoger pulled out an evidence bag and secured the knife.

"When you find out, let me know," he responded and returned to Delacourt. "So, Mr. Delacourt, let's start over. You just happened to be making apple pies with Ms. Johnson. A very domestic scene. You don't work?"

A flush rose over his face. "I work from home. And yes, I help Millie out with groceries, things that need fixing at the house. It was raining earlier, and her arthritis was bothering her, so I offered to cut the apples and measure the ingredients."

"A regular Boy Scout." He smirked, and Delacourt turned a brighter red.

"Millie was a nice lady."

"Was?" Harper frowned. "She's still alive."

"Oh, yeah, I know. I mean is." Flustered, he ran his hands through his hair.

"You're very nervous, Mr. Delacourt. Are you all right?"

"No," he snapped at Harper. "I just saw someone I care about lying bloody on the floor. How am I supposed to feel?"

That gave Harper a nice segue to ask his questions. "I don't know. Let's talk about that. You were at Perk Me Up this morning, weren't you?"

Surprise widened Delacourt's big blue eyes. "Y-yes." He blushed, and Harper knew Delacourt remembered seeing him.

Harper checked the notes he took from the coffee klatch. "You were overheard describing in extremely graphic detail the murder of a Millie Johnson by either striking her over the head or stabbing and dismembering her." He leveled a stare at Delacourt. Bile rose in Harper's throat at the thought of someone doing that to someone as helpless as the frail eighty-year-old he found on the floor. It reminded him why he was so wildly protective of his brother, who was as powerless as Ms. Johnson.

"Wait, no. I can explain that," Delacourt insisted.

"I'm all ears. It's got to be a good one, seeing how everything you predicted a couple of hours earlier came gruesomely true." He pushed his face close to Delacourt, who flinched. "There's nothing I like better than putting away scumbags like you."

"I didn't do it. I swear." Sweat poured down his face, and he blinked rapidly.

"They all say that. But I'm going to bet your fingerprints are the only ones on the knife. What's the matter, Delacourt? You run out of money for your drug habit? Owe the bookies? What would make a big, tough guy like you push a knife into a sweet little old lady?"

"I didn't. I swear," Delacourt cried out. "It wasn't me."

"Harper?" Nolan called out.

"In the kitchen. The back of the house." He waited until his partner arrived. "The vic is on route to the hospital. Meet Mr. Colson Delacourt. Neighbor, apple-pie maker, and potential murderer."

"I didn't do it," Delacourt yelled, desperate and pleading.

Nolan's brows drew together. "Colson Delacourt, the author?"

"Yes, yes that's me," he nodded, relief evident in his voice.

"Harper, this is Colson—"

"Yeah, I heard. An author. So?"

Nolan frowned. "You've never read his crime thrillers? *The Killer Behind the Stairs* or *One Step to Death*?" He tilted his head, and Harper sighed and pointed to Delacourt.

"Sit and don't go anywhere." He followed Nolan to the hallway. "What?"

"Are you seriously thinking that guy stabbed an old lady? He writes murders; he doesn't commit them."

"I'm not talking out of my ass. There's a reason I was here to begin with." As he relayed what he was told earlier, Nolan cut his glance to where Delacourt waited.

"It's got to be a mistake. I can't believe it. The guy has two *New York Times* bestsellers."

"So? That doesn't mean he can't kill someone. Let's talk to him again, and you can judge."

They reentered the kitchen and approached Delacourt, who sat scrolling through his phone. Nolan nudged his arm. "Hold up."

"What?"

"His hands. Look."

Harper squinted at the hand holding the phone. The knuckles were bruised and swollen.

"Maybe you weren't wrong after all."

CHAPTER THREE

This was a nightmare. How could he be on his way to a police station? Colson knew they were only following procedure, but he'd thought after explaining who he was, they'd understand and realize it was all a mistake and let him go. That bastard detective hadn't even wanted to listen to his explanation. Once they'd returned from their huddle, neither of them had been willing to take his statement at the scene. They'd told him to either come in voluntarily to talk to them, or they'd arrest him right there and ask questions later.

It was one thing to write a crime drama, but a hell of a difference to live through it, Colson was learning. This wasn't exciting or fun. At all.

At the station, they walked him through a maze of desks and past offices, where people wearing handcuffs were being processed—a far cry from the last time he'd been inside a precinct. Back then, he'd been treated like a guest and mini celebrity, as many of the law enforcement people he'd met had read his books. He'd always treated the police well in his writing, but maybe after this experience, he'd have to change his view.

"Have a seat, Mr. Delacourt." Detective Martinez indicated a chair. "Can I bring you some coffee or water?"

"He's already had coffee this morning." Detective Rose smirked, and Colson glared.

Bastard. How could he have ever thought this man was attractive? He'd like to punch him in that perfect face.

"I'm fine, thanks. Has anyone checked to see how Millie is doing?"

Rose glowered. "She's still unconscious. They're prepping her for surgery."

He rubbed his face. "I can't believe anyone would do something like that to her."

"Why don't we start by you telling us about your conversation in the coffee shop?"

Colson rolled his eyes. "I was planning my next book and talking about it with my friend Hogan. I knew people were listening in—this group of women kept staring and making comments."

"Your next book?" Martinez questioned. "You haven't had a release in almost three years."

"And?" he challenged. "Burnout is real. But I had an idea, and I wanted to share it with my best friend."

"That's sweet," Rose sniped. "What's this best friend's full name?"

"Hogan Carmichael. He works at Pomerantz and Co., a CPA firm in the city."

"We'll check him out." Unsmiling, Rose met his eyes. "Go on."

"Uh, well, part of how I write is I immerse myself in my stories by becoming the character I'm writing about."

"Murderers," Rose interrupted. "You're telling us you pretend you're a murderer to write murder."

"Yeah." He raised his chin. "Maybe it's unconventional, but—"

"Maybe?" Rose's disbelieving laughter filled the air. "You've got to be kidding me."

He glared daggers across the worn metal table. "You're obviously not a reader of crime fiction. Or anything at all," Colson mumbled, and saw he scored a direct hit from the flush of anger on the detective's face.

"I don't have the time."

"I've read your books, Mr. Delacourt. And I've seen your interviews where you've stated what you've just told us. But please, continue." He guessed Martinez was the good cop in this scenario.

"I was working through a new idea for a serial killer, and I was explaining it to Hogan, going through the type of murder my killer might commit—striking her over the head or stabbing and dismembering."

Rose winced.

Colson pressed on. "I knew the ladies were listening, so I might've hyped it up a little for their benefit. Made it a bit more gruesome than necessary. And when I left, I said something snarky to them."

Rose's face remained unreadable.

"What did you do after you left?" Martinez took notes as he spoke.

He gulped. "I, uh, went to Millie's, to see if she needed anything, but she'd just had a delivery from the store. She was baking, and since her hands hurt from her arthritis, I offered to cut the apples and measure the flour. Helped with the oven." He found Rose's eyes on him. "I told you all this already."

"Humor us." Rose's lips thinned.

"I told her I was putting her in the book, and even though she was the victim, she was excited." Despite his bleak surroundings and being questioned for attempted murder, he smiled. "She said she was the star of the show. She invited me to come back later for a piece of pie, and I told her I'd bring the ice cream."

"And you went home after that?" Martinez asked.

"No." His gaze dropped to the ugly, scarred table. "I- I went for a walk through the park and then to the water in Dumbo."

"How did you hurt your hands, Mr. Delacourt?" Rose didn't sound quite as angry as before.

His face grew warm. "Uh. It's personal."

Rose's brows arched high. "You're in a police station being questioned for attempted murder. I think we're past the point of questions being too personal."

Colson clasped his hands over the table. "Uh...a few months ago my boyfriend of three years left me to take a job in Paris, and I was looking at his social media." His gut twisted, and to his horror, those damn tears burned in his eyes. He blinked rapidly. "I saw he'd deleted all our pictures together, and he'd met someone new. I got upset and pounded the rock I was sitting on with my hands."

To his shock, Rose had no obnoxious, cutting comeback. Instead, he dipped his head. "I'm sorry. That must've been rough."

He blinked. "Y-yeah. It was. Anyway, I went to the store to buy the ice cream, went home to take a shower, and came to Millie's. That's it."

"Can anyone corroborate what you told us?"

His heart sank. "I don't know...it was pretty empty because of the rain. I was happy because I hate how crowded the park gets."

"Yeah. Full of tourists," Rose agreed, surprising Colson yet again. Was he being nice to him, preparing for the kill? All this put him on edge and made him jumpy. He should never have left the house today. His bed never hurt him. His bed was his friend.

"But I did buy ice cream at the deli. I can give you the name. They'd remember me."

"Why? What made you so memorable?" Rose asked.

Oh, good. There was the rude SOB he'd hidden for all of five minutes.

"When I came home, I saw blood on my face. They must've thought–"

"You were a killer?" Rose finished for him with a quick twist of his lips.

"For fuck's sake, I didn't try and kill Millie. I care about her," he yelled. "There's a real criminal out there. You should be looking for them instead of concentrating on me."

Martinez and Rose stared at him.

"We'll be right back," Rose said, and he and Martinez left him alone.

From his research, Colson knew they could see and hear everything he did. He sighed, stretched out his legs, and closed his eyes. How did this all happen? Poor Millie. She'd looked so white...so frail.

"Please let her be okay," he whispered. He felt so terrified. So alone. He knew Detective Rose didn't believe him, but Martinez seemed to understand. At least he hoped.

Close to an hour passed before the door opened and Martinez walked in, carrying a bottle of water, a packet of peanut butter crackers, and a bag of M&M's.

He raised a brow. "Health food diet?" He peered over the detective's shoulder. "Where's your charming partner? Did he find some raw meat to chew?"

Cackling, Martinez slid the snacks to him. "Good one. He's making some calls based on the information you gave us."

"If he speaks to Hogan, he'll repeat everything I said. I'm telling the truth."

"What's your ex's name?" At his startled expression, Martinez explained. "I want to check out his social media to verify what you told us."

"Oh. It's Evan Perez." He gave Martinez the Instagram handle and watched as he found Evan's account and started scrolling.

"What you stated checks out here."

The door flew open, and Rose strolled in. "I just got off the phone with your friend Mr. Carmichael." Those moonlight-pale eyes Colson had lusted over earlier locked on his through a thick sweep of dark lashes.

For some inexplicable reason, his heart pounded and adrenaline rushed through him. "Yeah? And?"

"He basically stated word-for-word what you did. By the way, he thinks it's creepy as shit too."

Relief tore through him. "I-I told you he would." Somehow he managed a weak laugh. "And yeah, I know. He tells me all the time."

"Since we have your prints in the system from one of your book-research visits, forensics identified a print on the knife handle as yours," Rose added.

The dread returned. "I told you why."

"Yes, sir. That's why we're going to release you." Rose paused. "For now. But stay close to home." His lips pressed into a thin line. "In case we need to contact you further. Have a good day."

He couldn't wait to escape but hesitated at the door. "Is Millie—will she be okay?"

"She's still not awake."

"I'm gonna go there to see. Millie has no family. I think when she wakes up, she should see a face she knows."

"Boy Scout," Rose murmured as he passed by.

"Jerk," he muttered, and Rose snickered as he walked away.

He couldn't leave the police station quickly enough, and he called a car to the hospital. When he arrived, they directed him to the emergency room, where he sat waiting. With regret, he realized he should've taken the food Detective Martinez had brought him. He was starving.

A doctor entered the room. "Mr. Delacourt?"

He jumped to his feet. "Yes. How is she? How's Millie?"

"Are you family?"

His heart sank. "No, but—"

"I'm sorry. I can't tell you anything."

"Maybe you can tell me, then." The deep, smooth voice of Detective Harper Rose startled him. "I'm a detective with the NYPD investigating this case. Is Ms. Johnson awake? Can she answer any questions?"

The doctor stared at Rose. "This is an eighty-four-year-old woman with a knife wound."

"I'm aware, Doctor," Rose responded, not backing down in the least. "And I'm trying to catch the person who did that to her. So I'm going to ask you again if I can speak to her for a few minutes."

The doctor blinked. "She should be awake soon. Lucky for her, it wasn't as bad as it looked. The knife didn't penetrate enough to damage vital organs, so we stitched her up, but because of her age, we're concerned. Don't stay long. I'll make sure the nurses keep an eye on her."

"Not a problem."

The doctor walked out, and Rose cast a glance his way, said nothing, and left.

"Jesus, what a jerk." Colson sighed, and realizing there was nothing left for him to do, decided to leave. He could come visit Millie tomorrow.

Once home, he took another shower, feeling dirty after sitting in a police car, at the precinct, and at the hospital. Checking his phone, he saw three missed calls from Hogan.

"What the hell, Colson? Are you all right? Where are you?"

Weary, he lay on the couch, facing Willow Street and Millie's house. "I'm home. They said talking to you made them realize I was telling the truth, but that I'm still not ruled out as a suspect. It's crazy. I didn't try and hurt her. I couldn't."

"Of course not. That's what I told that detective. I trust you with my kids, for God's sake."

"Thanks. I'm just going to sit in my house from now on. It's safer in here."

"That's not the answer," Hogan protested.

"It is for me," he muttered, and watched out the window as a delivery truck pulled up. Something bothered him, and he needed to think. "I gotta go. I'll call you later."

"If you don't, I will," Hogan warned.

He remembered Millie saying she'd had a delivery earlier in the day–"a nice young man" she'd called him. The neighborhood watch had reported that because of the increase in home invasions lately, they were installing cameras up and down the area. Colson dug out the card Martinez gave him and called. He wasn't there, but Colson gave a detailed message to the person who answered.

He ate a peanut butter sandwich and decided to type his handwritten chapter, but gave up halfway through. It was eerily close to what happened to Millie, and Colson couldn't bring himself to finish. He called the hospital but was told they couldn't give him any information.

"Dammit."

How could it be only afternoon? It felt as though he'd lived a year this day alone. To keep from thinking about Millie or that annoying detective, he flipped on the television to some nature show. He'd always found them fascinating, but even that didn't hold his interest, and he awoke with a start to his doorbell ringing. The sky outside had dimmed to blue-violet, and he rubbed his eyes as he peered at the video screen to see Detective Rose on his doorstep.

His stomach tumbled with a mix of fear and, for whatever reason, anticipation. He opened the door. As irritated as the man made him, Colson couldn't help admiring his gorgeous face.

"Detective. Is Millie okay?"

"She's in the hospital, so I doubt she's okay." He crossed his arms, so nonchalant that Colson's ire rose. He should've known better than to think the detective was human.

"You know, I could do without the wiseass comments. I've been accused of attempted murder. I've had kind of a rough day."

"Well, I'm here to make your night a whole lot better." A wicked grin curved his lips, and Colson stared at him as his mouth dried, his heart accelerated, and a curl of desire tugged in his belly. Yeah, he was a jerk and a sarcastic son of a bitch who thought Colson could stab an old lady, but damn...he was gorgeous.

"Wh-what're you talking about?" He licked his lips.

"I had a chance to speak to Millie." Rose paused as several people walked past. "Can we take this inside? Unless you want your neighbors to hear."

"Yeah, sure." Colson stepped aside. Rose passed by him, and instead of waiting, walked right into his living room.

"Nice house." His measured, assessing gaze swept over the room, then returned to him. "How'd you end up in Brooklyn from Greenwich, Connecticut?"

"You looked me up?" He shouldn't be surprised, but it still felt like an invasion of privacy.

Unrepentant, Rose shrugged. "SOP—that's standard operating—"

"Procedure. I know. I do research for my stories." Colson glared at the detective and decided to ignore his question. "What's the purpose of your visit? You said you spoke to Millie?"

"Yes." He should've known Rose wouldn't let go of his question. "Your family is one of the oldest in New England. Practically Mayflower. Fancy boarding schools and all that, yet you left to live in Brooklyn." Those penetrating eyes traveled over his arms, leaving Colson breathless and trembling. "How'd they feel about those tattoos and your earring? Were you one of those rebellious youths?"

"Not that any of this is your damn business." Colson gathered his wits. "I left home because my parents didn't want to deal with a gay son. Does that satisfy you?"

Rose blinked, and for a second, Colson thought he spied sympathy in his eyes. "Millie exonerated you. I had a chance to ask her if she saw who did it, and she said it was the delivery boy. We're searching for him now. I wanted to let you know." His lips twitched. "She was very adamant it wasn't you. Said you were too sweet and couldn't hurt a fly."

He glowered at Rose. "You think this is funny, don't you?" When he remained silent, Colson sighed. "I actually called your partner because I remembered that the block association put up cameras because of the home invasions." It was his turn to smirk. "Maybe now you could concentrate on those and find the real criminal, instead of harassing innocent citizens."

Rose's expression darkened. "You're cleared. Have a nice night, Mr. Delacourt." Rose walked to the front door, and Colson unlocked it and waited for him to leave. "And a word of advice? Keep your conversations about your books within the walls of your house. Safer for you that way and saves the NYPD valuable time."

Detective Rose was annoying as hell, but Colson could concede he had a point. "Thanks for letting me know. Good night."

"Good night...Boy Scout." Rose took off down the street, and Colson slammed the door.

"Jerk."

CHAPTER FOUR

Harper sat in his sun-filled kitchen with his brother and fed him the last of his breakfast. David smiled, and his gaze latched on to the cup of orange juice. Harper immediately picked it up and put the straw to his mouth.

"Good, huh? You like OJ, don't you?"

David blinked and licked his lips, and Harper blotted the drops that had spilled onto his chin.

"Good morning." Luis entered the kitchen. David grunted, and his smile grew wider. "Hey, big guy. How are you? Enjoying breakfast with your big bro?"

David's head jerked, and Harper's heart squeezed so tight, it hurt to breathe. "We just finished cereal, and he's had some juice." Harper checked outside. "Looks like a nice day. Maybe you can go to the park."

"I was thinking that. David likes to see the kids playing, and we get ice cream from the truck." He sat across from David and made eye contact. "How about it? The park and ice cream? We can do that this morning before your therapy later on."

"Thanks, Luis. I've renewed the membership for the zoo and aquarium, so you can go anytime." He'd bought a special van for David to travel to therapy, and Luis loved taking him for drives. They drove all over the city, and Luis made sure to send him pictures so Harper could see David enjoying himself.

"Perfect. With the nice weather, it's good to get him out of the house more. It keeps him stimulated, and he loves the animals."

Harper remembered their dog, Astro, who'd waited by the front door every day for David to come home from school. His mother had told him it was Astro's frantic barking that had alerted her to the accident that had killed several students and injured David. A truck had blown through a yellow light and T-boned the school bus. David had been out of his seat on the steps, ready to get off, when the truck hit. He'd flown out of the bus and hit the ground several yards away. He'd suffered massive head trauma and spinal injuries, and the doctors hadn't thought he'd survive, but he was a fighter.

Harper pinched his eyes shut against the brutal memories of that day. "I've got a full schedule, but as always, if you need me, I'll have my cell phone."

"Don't worry," Luis reassured him as he did every morning. "We're fine." He poured some coffee. "I heard you finally got that bastard who cut that old lady. Good for you."

"Yeah. Finally." The kid had gone underground, and it had taken a week for Harper and Nolan to find him holed up in some friend of a friend's apartment in the Bronx. "He confessed and cried like a baby, hoping to make a deal. Seems he made an earlier delivery to Ms. Johnson, saw she lived alone, and decided to return and help himself to some of her things. When she confronted him, he grabbed a knife. Lucky for her, it didn't penetrate far through her clothes, but she lost blood."

"Jesus." Luis grimaced in disgust. "You gotta be a cold-hearted SOB to do that to an old person."

"Or anyone helpless." A shiver ran through him, and he automatically looked to David. It was Harper's greatest fear and why he relentlessly—obsessively, some people had said—did everything he could to protect his brother.

"Agreed." Luis took David's dishes and brought over a wet washcloth to clean his face and hands. The man had been David's caretaker for over fifteen years—he'd helped not only David but Harper too through the trauma of losing their parents, and Harper considered him part of the family, somewhere between a surrogate father and older brother. They might not have had much good fortune in their lives, but the home health care agency matching Luis with their family was the luckiest day of both David's and Harper's lives. They couldn't have made it without his dedication and strength of not only his body but his soul. "What was it like meeting Colson Delacourt? He's cool?"

Harper stifled a groan. "Not you too...am I the only one who hasn't read his books?"

Luis's brown eyes crinkled shut with laughter. "You haven't? Man, you're missing out. I gotta keep the lights on when I read his stuff."

"I think I see enough death and destruction on the daily. I don't need to bring it home with me."

Ignoring him, Luis continued. "He really gets into the mind of a killer. Like it's twisted, you know?"

"Trust me, I know." Harper finished his coffee.

"I can't believe you had him pegged as your perp." Luis's laughter rang out, and David, who loved seeing people happy, smiled. "Right, David? Your brother's a silly guy."

Harper let them have their fun. "There was circumstantial evidence, so he was brought in for questioning. When it was apparent he wasn't the perp, I let him know he was no longer a suspect."

Luis side-eyed him. "He's a good-looking dude too, right? I've seen his bio picture. Is he single?"

Harper sighed. Luis was another one who was forever pushing him to have a social life. "Yes."

"Yes to what?" Luis persisted.

"To both. He's good-looking and single. But a most definite no to whatever else is going on in your head."

"Why? It's been a long, *long* time since you put yourself out there. It wouldn't hurt to try."

"Never." His response was swift, sure, and deadly serious. "No way in hell. Once was enough to show me people's true colors. Not that I didn't already know. But I'm not interested in going through that mess again."

"I know it's hard. When I lost Maria, I gave up. Now I regret it." Luis's girlfriend, an EMT officer, had been killed on the job eleven years earlier. It was before he'd moved in with Harper and David full-time. Her parents were in the Dominican Republic, and Harper's family would have her to the house for Thanksgiving and Christmas. David had adored her.

He could turn the tables on his friend. "You could start dating, you know. You're a good-looking dude too."

"I go out. There's the difference between us. I at least try and have some fun."

"I have fun," Harper grumbled.

"Bullshit," Luis shot back. "When was the last time you were with someone?"

He shifted in his seat. He didn't like discussing his personal life in front of David. The doctors had told him that though his brain damage was irreparable, he still had some cognitive function. It was a murky area, as much about the brain was still unknown, and the doctors urged him to treat David as if he understood the world around him. Over the years, he'd witnessed David expressing emotions, and Harper's focus was to make sure David never felt like a burden or that Harper was sacrificing himself for his care.

"I dunno. It's not like I keep a calendar. I'm busy, you know? Crime doesn't take a vacation." To escape Luis's eyes, he left the table to rinse his cup. "The bad guys don't give me a chance to hang out at the club."

"Make the time. You know I'm here if David needs me. You gotta fill the well sometimes, my man. Otherwise you're gonna dry up and shrivel away. Don't think I haven't noticed how you've changed."

His hand tightened on the dishcloth. "No I haven't," he responded woodenly. "I'm the same miserable person I always was." He forced a smile, but Luis, the canny bastard, wasn't buying it.

"Not when you were with Ronnie. You were happy."

The mention of his former lover—his first and only—sent both a chill and a hot burst of anger through him, and he tossed the dishcloth aside.

"Yeah. I was. The happiest. But he turned out to be a miserable fu—" He stopped before letting loose with a torrent of curse words. One thing he'd promised himself was to try and not get angry in front of David.

Only calm, happy faces. "Person." He blew out a frustrated breath. "I was completely wrong about him. Which means my judgment in that particular area sucks. So it's better to keep it light. I have to get going, or I'll be late." He kissed the top of David's head. "Gotta go to work, buddy. See you tonight." David made kissing noises, and Harper put his cheek to his lips. "Love you."

David made a sound, his mouth moving, and Harper knew it was an attempt to say "I love you" back. "Have a great day, and don't eat too much ice cream." He left the house and locked the door behind him.

"That was a nice, clean collar." Nolan clicked his mouse. "Just the way I like 'em. Last form filed."

"Same," Harper answered. "The old lady's making a nice recovery too. The asshole is pleading guilty and crying for his momma. Hope they deep-six him." He grimaced.

"I wonder if he's behind all these home invasions in the Heights in the past week. Captain says he wants us to review the tapes and recanvass the neighborhood."

"Somehow, I doubt it. I think it was a crime of opportunity. A rich old lady who lives alone." He sipped his coffee.

"Speaking of said little old lady, how do you know about Millie Johnson's recovery?" Nolan gave him the side-eye. "You pay her a visit? Maybe hoping to bump into Colson Delacourt?" A sly grin played on his lips.

Good thing he'd perfected a poker face over the years. It took a lot more than teasing to make him crack. "You're delusional."

"And you're gay and unattached, and so is he."

Harper crumpled the empty coffee cup and tossed it into the trash. "Well, that settles it. We're two gay men in New York City, which means we must want to hook up." He scowled. "Are you fucking serious?"

"I saw a look." Nolan sounded amused, and that annoyed him more than anything. "Don't matter if you're straight or gay. You're interested. And it was reciprocal. In case you were wondering."

It *was*? That was news to him.

"I wasn't. The only thing I was interested in concerning Colson Delacourt was figuring out if he was our perp. Now that I know he's not, he's forgotten." Maybe if he said it often enough, he'd believe it himself. But he'd be damned if he'd say that out loud. "And, since you seem so interested in my comings and goings, I thought it would be nice to check in on the victim, since she's an old lady who lives by herself and is recovering from a crime, so I called the hospital. You know the brass always wants us to be compassionate." He smirked. "This is me showing I care."

Nolan didn't return his banter. "I know you're compassionate and caring. I see how you are with David. You've put your life on hold to make sure he's taken care of. Not many people would do that."

Fuck. First Luis and now Nolan. He did not want to talk about this shit in the middle of the squad room. "So listen, about the Hamilton assault—"

"Harper."

"I met the ADA outside. She was here for another case, and we stopped to talk."

"Good for her." Nolan was determined to pick a fight with him, obviously, as he steamrolled ahead. "You can have both, you know. A personal life and still make sure your brother is looked after."

Desperate to avoid further conversation concerning his brother, Harper ignored Nolan and continued to talk about the other case. "The vic positively ID'd the suspect. The ADA said he's part of a punch-down gang going around the area–"

"Enough," Nolan snapped, loud enough that several heads popped up over their cubicle walls, but retreated when Nolan glared at them.

Harper's hands clenched. "I do *not* want to talk about this."

"Good. Because I've heard all your bullshit excuses, and now you can listen." Nolan rolled his chair over so they were side by side.

Harper tried to lighten the tension. "Gee, Nolan. Any closer and you'll be in my lap," he joked. "Does Gina know you have a crush on me?"

A muscle ticked in Nolan's clean-shaven jaw. "Damn fool. I know what you're trying to do. And why. But it's wrong. You're wrong."

"I said I don't want to discuss this," he gritted out through clenched teeth. "I mean it, Nolan. There are some things that are off-limits, and David is one of them. Even with you."

"This isn't about David. It's about you and your absolute refusal to think you can have a personal *and* a professional life."

"To me, they're one and the same. So if you want to keep working with me, knock it off. Please."

Nose to nose, he gazed into Nolan's brown eyes and winced at the compassion. He despised it. He wasn't doing anything extraordinary by being his brother's caretaker. All he wanted was for people to stop telling him what a good person he was for simply doing the right thing.

"Fine." Nolan gave a sharp jerk of his head and rolled his chair away to his desk. "And I think it's a good idea for us to pay Ms. Johnson a visit."

"Let's do it." He clicked out of his reports. "I have a call in to the block association, and they said they'll have a copy of all the videos of the past three weeks—from when the break-ins began."

"Look at you, being all organized and stuff," Nolan teased.

"That's because I'm not wasting my time playing matchmaker."

They drove to Pierrepont Street, where the block association had their headquarters, and were given a room and a computer. For several hours they viewed the tape, stopping only for a quick lunch run for some wonton soup, egg rolls, and chicken fried rice.

Nolan pointed his chopsticks at the monitor. "See that? White hoodie? He's the leader, I'm thinking. He goes in, leaves his buddy at the front door as a lookout. If he sees someone coming, *tap-tap-tap* on the door, to alert homeboy inside to hurry up."

"Uh-huh." Harper chewed his egg roll. "Not our delivery boy. These guys are older, and they definitely knew what houses they were after. They wait until after the owners leave, then make their move." A chilling thought hit him. "That means Millie Johnson is still a mark." He met Nolan's eyes. "She's not safe. We should go over there and make sure she's okay."

"Yeah. I'll let Poole know they should start a sweep of the area with unis. 'Cause soon they're gonna run out of houses without people and move on to ones where people are home, which is moving into way more dangerous territory. And they might expand to more neighborhoods. We need to nip it in the bud."

Harper tossed his trash into the bin. "We will."

By five thirty, they'd reviewed all the tapes and sent copies to the lab for facial recognition and enhancement. They walked the three blocks to Millie Johnson's house and after two pushes on the doorbell, she answered.

"Detectives. So nice to see you again. Come in, come in. I just made some fresh coffee."

Harper frowned. "Ms. Johnson, you really need to stop opening the door without checking to see who it is. You should think about getting a camera installed."

They followed her down the long hallway, and Harper was glad to see that although her gait was a bit stiff and stilted and she used a walker, she seemed to not be suffering any long-term ill effects.

"I didn't have a chance to tell you, Ms. Johnson, but you have a beautiful ho—" Harper stopped short.

Fuck.

Colson Delacourt sat at the kitchen island, a piece of pie in front of him, a scoop of vanilla ice cream perched precariously on top. He looked up and when their eyes met, the easygoing expression on his face fled, replaced by a flat wariness that dimmed the brightness of those sky-blue eyes.

"Look who stopped by, Colson. The two detectives who helped me. Isn't that nice?"

"I should get going, Millie." Frowning, Colson rose to his feet.

Obviously, Colson Delacourt did not think it was nice.

"Nonsense. You haven't even begun eating the piece you cut. Sit, please." She turned to Nolan and him. "Detectives. Would you like some pie with your coffee?"

"One moment. I have to check this message." Nolan reached into his pocket. "Wouldn't you know it? My wife called. I need to get home to help with the baby. So fussy. Thanks so much for the invitation, Ms. Johnson, but Detective Rose will be happy to stay and have some."

"Nolan," he warned. He hadn't heard the phone buzz, but more importantly, Nolan and Gina had no children. He was so going to kill his partner.

"See you tomorrow," Nolan called as he raced out of the house. The door slammed.

"Please stay, Detective. Colson, dear, you remember Detective Rose?"

"Yes," he clipped out.

"You will have some pie with us, won't you, Detective? Colson helped me make it, since the other one was ruined."

"Did he, now? How very domestic of him." Harper gave his most sunny smile.

Delacourt's icy-blue eyes flashed murder, and damned if that fire didn't kick-start his desire. Harper might lie to everyone else, but he could admit to himself that Colson Delacourt was sexy as hell and that he wanted him.

"I'm sure an important man like the detective is way too busy."

Harper had planned to refuse—if he left, he'd be home early for David, but he could take the extra half an hour here and still have plenty of time with his brother. And this was too tempting an offer to turn down.

"Thanks, Millie. I'd love to have some pie, especially if Mr. Delacourt helped make it."

He grinned at Colson's death glare across the island.

CHAPTER FIVE

Colson knew he should've left earlier.

It had been a productive day. He was deep into the character building of not only his killer but the detective on the hunt.

A character's backstory had never come so easily to him as this detective's. Maybe because he'd had the perfect man to model him after. Detective Harrison Rosa was in his late thirties, tall, dark-haired, with ice-gray eyes and a bad attitude that was always getting him in trouble with higher-ups...but they kept him because he got his killers.

Colson's realization that he'd based his new character on the real-life Detective Harper Rose gave him a moment of hesitation, and he'd considered revising but had decided against it. Rose himself had stated he'd never read Colson's books. He'd never see the man again anyway, which was probably for the best, as each time they'd faced off, Colson was left pissed off—and even more aggravatingly, turned-on. He'd never met anyone who'd gotten under his skin so fast.

Earlier, Colson had brought Millie some things from the store, and when she'd asked him to stay, he hadn't been able to refuse. He'd even brought over his notebook and read her some of the chapters he'd written. Now, seeing Detective Harper Rose perched so casually on the barstool, making nice with Millie, he wished he'd never come.

"Colson was sweet enough to pick up my groceries from the supermarket," Millie gushed to Rose, who wore the sightly amused but patronizing expression that annoyed the shit out of Colson. Millie, of course, remained unaware and chattered on. "He's been a tremendous help all week, in fact, stopping by to check on me, taking me to the doctor for my checkup." She gazed at him fondly, and he smiled at her.

"It's no problem. I'm home, and I'm happy to help."

"You're lucky, Ms. Johnson, to have such an accommodating neighbor. That's unusual these days."

Colson shot Rose a glance to see if he was being a smartass, but there was no smirk on that handsome face. They each ate their pie, and after taking several bites, Rose glanced up at him.

"You really helped make this?"

"Yes. But it's Millie's recipe."

"Still," Rose mused. "I've tried to make cookies from a recipe and...well, it wasn't pretty."

Colson's lips twitched at the thought of Detective Harper Rose making cookies.

"I'll give you my recipe, Detective. Foolproof chocolate-butterscotch cookies." Millie went to the cabinet and pulled out a box of recipe cards.

"Thank you. I'd love it."

Colson watched as Rose finished his pie. He wasn't joking. He cleaned every crumb off the plate and licked his lips. "Aren't you eating yours?"

Colson blinked and roused himself from obsessing over Rose's tongue. "Uh, yeah." He shoveled in the last few pieces.

"Don't eat so fast, Boy Scout. You might choke...again." Rose's teasing grin brought furious heat to Colson's cheeks. Evidently, Rose was recalling the time in the coffee shop when he'd coughed up a lung.

"I don't know what you mean."

Rose chuckled. "Didn't anyone ever tell you not to lie to the police?"

Millie returned with the card, and Rose took a snapshot of it on his phone. "Thank you. This was delicious, whoever made it. I'm glad you have help, Ms. Johnson, but I will warn you that there are still push-in robberies happening. And the fact that you opened the door without asking for identification or looking through the peephole is troubling."

"Millie, no." Exasperated, Colson swung around to face her. "I've told you a hundred times not to open the door without checking first. You need a video camera like the one I have."

She sighed. "Please don't be mad. I knew you were coming. But I promise to get one soon."

Colson met Rose's eyes over the table and read his expression: if you can bring over groceries, bring her a damn alarm system.

God, he hated that the man was right.

"I'm going to order it right now and it'll be delivered tomorrow." He took out his phone and made the purchase.

"Good." Watching him, Rose nodded with approval. "I'll stop by and check to make sure. We're in the neighborhood because of all the break-ins." He picked up his plate. "Would you like me to put this in the dishwasher?"

"Thank you. That's very nice of you."

To Colson's shock, Rose stopped by his side and reached out to take his plate, close enough to brush their arms together and for him to fixate on the swirl of dark hair from under the cuff of his white button-down.

"The NYPD aims to please," Rose murmured in a husky voice that went straight to Colson's dick, and he shivered at the thought of pleasing a man like Rose.

Whoa. Who said he was gay?

Through lowered lashes, he watched Rose put the plates in the dishwasher and admired the perfect curve of his ass. Time to roll his tongue up in his mouth and leave.

"Millie, I have to get going and finish rereading what I wrote, but I'll be back tomorrow with the video camera."

She made a face. "Such a terrible world we have to live in."

"I'd better go home as well."

"Does your wife work, Detective?" Millie asked as she walked them to the door.

"I'm not married, Ms. Johnson. My partner and I will be around to check on you and the rest of the neighborhood. Again, please do not answer the door without asking who it is first or looking through the peephole."

As much as Rose's arrogance and teasing annoyed him, Colson believed he was concerned about Millie and the other people in the neighborhood.

"Detective Rose and I are in agreement on this. And I'll be here tomorrow before noon with your new door cam."

She opened the door. "Good night, both of you. Thank you for caring about me. I just hate all the fuss."

"Lock the door," he and Rose said in unison and gazed at each other in surprise.

They waited to hear the lock turn, and side by side, they descended the stairs. Once they reached the sidewalk, instead of saying good night, Rose matched his steps. Colson stopped.

"You don't have to walk me home. I'm a big boy." Rose lifted a brow, and Colson's hands fisted. "Good night, Detective Rose." Furious with himself for allowing Rose to rattle him, he strode across the street, resisting the urge to see if Rose was watching him or walking away.

He hurried up his steps and took out his key, but he stopped at the sight of his door ajar. Adrenaline surged through him, and he stood waiting, then glanced across the street where Rose had turned and begun to walk away.

"Detective," he called out, alarm raising his voice several octaves higher and louder than usual. "Detective Rose," he shouted.

Rose stopped and ran to him. "What is it?" he asked, and without waiting for an answer, peered at the door. "You obviously didn't leave it open like this."

Shaken, he wrapped his arms around his waist. "N-no. I always lock up when I leave the house."

"Stay back," Rose warned and pulled out his gun. Colson's eyes widened, but he did as requested. Rose took out his phone and called for backup, then pushed the door with his foot. It swung open on silent hinges. He crept inside, and Colson strained to see but was blocked. It seemed like hours, but within three to four minutes Rose walked out, his face taut and grim.

"It's all clear." Rose stood in front of him, disarmingly close. "Can I assume you don't normally leave your apartment in a mess?"

He shook his head, still in shock that this had happened to him. "No. My ex used to complain I was a neat freak." A shudder ran through him.

"Come on. Let's go sit and wait for CSU."

He stared mutely at Rose, whose pale eyes glittered with a fiery anger.

A heavy hand settled on his shoulder. "Don't worry. I'm not going anywhere. You're safe."

Those words, coming from a man who only minutes earlier he couldn't wait to escape, were strangely comforting, and he allowed Rose to steer him into his house. He gasped at the destruction.

"Bastards," he hissed. Every drawer was open and rifled through, and papers were scattered on the floor. Books had been pulled off the shelves and the couch cushions tossed.

Unlike Millie's grand brownstone, his was a smaller brick town house he'd renovated so the first floor would be one wide-open room. He liked the loftlike feeling of the space, but he'd kept the old-world charm, such as fireplaces, crown molding, and the original wooden floors. His pride was the early twentieth century stained-glass windows in the living room.

"First, do you see anything missing?" Rose asked as he stalked through the room, his intense gaze scanning the space.

"My computer." He ran to his desk and frantically pushed aside the mess of books and papers, searching for his MacBook. "Fuck. They stole my computer. It has everything on it. All my writing." His heart pounded, and he smacked his hand on the desk. "Those *bastards*."

"Calm down, Colson." Rose's calmness irritated the fuck out of him. "Doesn't it have tracking on it? Pull up the signal, and we should be able to find it."

"Yeah, of course, of course." He pulled out his phone, and while he was getting to the app, a bunch of uniforms and people with NYPD jackets emblazoned with CSU trooped through his front door.

"You do that while I speak to the officers."

Again, Rose squeezed his shoulder, then walked away. Colson ignored the instant regret of losing the warmth of Rose's hand and concentrated on getting the tracking signal on the computer and looking for other missing items.

"Detective Rose?" he called out, and footsteps approached.

"What do you have?"

Colson pointed at the screen. "Here. It says it's in the vicinity of the park."

Cadman Plaza Park was less than five blocks away.

"You sit tight while we handle this." He glanced around the room filled with police personnel. "You're not going to be able to get any sleep here tonight." For one crazy second, he thought Rose was going to ask him to come stay with him. "Do you have a friend you can call to stay with?"

"I-I can call Hogan. He doesn't live far."

"Do that. Give me your number, and I'll let you know what happens. Meanwhile, try and take an inventory of anything else you find missing."

"Shit. My wallet. I left it here, in the desk drawer. I figured I wouldn't need it just walking across the street to Millie's." Of course, when he searched the drawer, it was gone. "What a nightmare. All my credit cards, driver's license..."

"Do you need me to get you a car? I can give you some cash..."

"No, it's fine. Hogan and his wife live in Cobble Hill. It's only—"

"I know Cobble Hill." Rose's smile came and went like the wind. "I'll let you know what we find." And he walked away, leaving him standing there like a fool.

Okay. Forget about Detective Rose. He was doing his job, and Colson had to get his head out of his ass, thinking Rose was giving him signals. He wove his way past the CSU people dusting for fingerprints and searching for whatever they were hoping to find, and ran upstairs. Like the first floor, the rooms were ransacked, but there hadn't been anything to take.

Entering his bedroom, he made a beeline for the nightstand and the only thing of value to him—the picture of his grandparents and him, framed in heavy sterling silver. Growing up as a closeted teen, in an uptight inner circle where you followed centuries-old traditions without stepping out of line, Grandpa Alex and Grandma Betty were the only ones he'd felt safe with, and he'd confided in them about his sexuality— coming out in the middle of the assisted-living facility where they resided. He hadn't been able to hold it inside him any longer. They'd hugged him and told him everything would be okay. That they loved him no matter what. The opposite of his parents' reactions when he'd come out to them. The contempt and disgust on their faces would be forever etched in his memory.

"We are so very disappointed in you, Colson. This is something we can't accept." Those were the last words his father had said to him, standing in the living room,

a frown on his stern, arrogant face. The face of a man who'd never been denied anything in his life. A man who'd never known hardship and had contempt for those who did. "*It would be better if you left now.*"

"Mom?" *He couldn't believe she'd allow this to happen. She loved him.*

But she shook her head. "It's not normal. What are we supposed to tell everyone? It's such an embarrassment to us."

A knife through his heart couldn't have given him greater pain than her icy contempt. Shoulders back and head up, he'd marched to his room, packed a bag with some clothes and the only family memento that held any meaning—the picture with his grandparents—and left without another word. Close to fifteen years had passed since he'd last seen them, and he had no regrets in leaving. The greatest loss in his life was the death of his grandparents.

But Grandma and Grandpa had taken care of him, leaving him all their assets—cash, stocks, and bonds, plus their house in Connecticut. Their generosity had enabled him to buy the house he lived in now and become a writer, something he'd always dreamed of. He'd taken courses and studied the craft, written short stories for crime fiction and mystery magazines. He hadn't needed the money, only the validation that he had the ability and could get published. Once he'd felt confident enough in his storytelling, he'd found his agent.

Now, instead of their sweet, smiling faces, all that was left was empty space where the frame had sat for years. Tears sprang to his eyes and he sank to the bed, crying like a baby.

"It will only be a day or two. Thanks for putting me up."

The following morning, he sat on Hogan and Bea's sectional couch in their living room, a cup of coffee on the table.

Hogan approached with his own cup and sat next to him. "What the hell is going on? First I'm talking to a detective about whether or not you're a murderer, and now your house gets robbed? Are you living inside one of your books or what?"

He barked out a weak excuse of a laugh. "Hell if I know."

"This is an anomaly," Hogan insisted. "They'll catch the bastards who did this, and it'll go back to normal."

He sighed. "What's even normal anymore? They took the picture of my grandparents, Hogan. The only thing that mattered to me."

"I know." Hogan put an arm around his shoulders. "It's Saturday. Bea has a spa day with her sisters. Hang out with me and the kids. If anything will take your mind off your problems, it'll be mindless hours on the swings."

He needed to go home and take care of the aftermath of the break-in, but that thought sent a rush of bile to his throat. Not yet. He checked his phone to see if he'd received any messages from Detective Rose, but it was frustratingly silent.

"Yeah, sure. Why not? I just have to do something first. I'll meet you there." He couldn't forget the door cam he'd promised Millie. Good thing he'd placed the order when he did, as he'd had to cancel his credit cards.

The package sat on his stoop and installation had proved easy. With a stern warning to Millie that she actually use it, he left for the park. Now he stood next to Hogan, who was pushing Jamie on one swing, while he had Mikey on the other. They'd brought peanut butter and jelly sandwiches for lunch, along with grapes and goldfish crackers. A beautiful sunny afternoon found the park crowded with joggers, families, and couples walking hand in hand.

"Okay, kids. Time to give Uncle Colson a break. Let's have some ice cream." Hogan stopped the swing.

"Is the break for Uncle Colson or Daddy?" Colson laughed. "Come on, Mikey. What's your favorite flavor?"

"Strawberry," the little boy yelled and ran ahead of them to the truck, where a crowd waited.

Not to be outdone, Jamie ran after him, shouting, "I want chocolate."

"Now there's a business," Hogan remarked as they waited on line.

"You'd eat yourself out of the profits in a day."

Laughter sounded behind him. "I'd be the same."

He turned around to see a man in his fifties with a younger man in a wheelchair. Colson could tell he was a quadriplegic, and his heart went out to both of them. The young man couldn't have been more than twenty-five or so. He wore a Superman shirt and a Mets cap. Colson smiled at him and received the same in return.

"This is David. He loves ice cream. Vanilla is his favorite flavor."

"Mine too, David. My name is Colson, and this is my friend Hogan. Mikey loves strawberry, and Jamie likes chocolate."

The man's eyes lit up. "Colson? As in the writer, Colson Delacourt?"

"Yes. That's me."

"I love your books. I even have them in paperback." The man chuckled. "Although I gotta say, I might sleep with the light on afterward."

"That's great to hear, thank you." At least someone hadn't forgotten him. "Not about the lights on, but I guess that means I'm doing my job."

"You sure are. Super creepy but addicting. My name's Luis. I take care of David."

"Oh, you're not his father? You seem very close."

Hogan busied himself ordering the ice cream. "Luis, what would you like? Our treat."

"You don't have to."

Hogan dipped his head. "Yeah, I know. But I want to."

"Just a cup of vanilla for David." Luis brushed a hank of dark hair off David's brow. "Yeah. We're very close. I've been with him for fifteen years. David was hurt in a school bus accident when he was five."

Mikey and Jamie stood next to him, licking their cones. "Why can't he walk?" Jamie asked.

Colson winced, but Luis's face was kind. "It's okay. I'd rather they ask questions than whisper and point." He crouched to their level. "David used to be able to do everything you can, but one day he was hurt very badly. He can't use his arms much or his legs anymore or really speak, but he tries to understand some of what you say. He loves superheroes and coming to the park or going to the zoo."

"I love superheroes too," Colson said to David, and he could see the intelligence in his light blue eyes. "When I was little, I wished I could fly like Superman."

David moved his head and grunted, his mouth opening and closing.

"He's David's favorite too," Luis explained.

"Mommy takes us to see the seals at the park." Mikey licked around his cone. "They're my favorite."

David made some more noises, and the kids laughed. "That sounds like the seals." David moved his head.

Luis smoothed David's hair. "David loves them and the petting zoo. We try to go at feeding time."

Colson's heart broke, and maybe his face reflected his sadness because Luis touched David's shoulder. "Don't feel sorry for him. David has a wonderful life. He has me, and more importantly, a brother who loves him and has devoted his life to taking care of him and making sure he has whatever he needs. He's very lucky." Luis held out a hand. "It was great to meet you. I hope you're writing something new?"

"I'm trying. Unfortunately, my home was broken into, so unless the police find my computer, after I leave here, I'll have to go buy a new one, then contend with insurance claims and all that."

"That's awful, I'm sorry. But I'm sure the police are doing whatever they can to find it." His eyes twinkled. "Especially since they thought you were a murderer. I read the story in the local paper. They need to redeem themselves."

His heart sank. "I'm never going to live that down, am I?"

"Sorry." Luis laughed. "I thought it was pretty funny. Maybe you can use it in your next book. I'd better go before the ice cream melts. I hope we'll see you again."

"See?" Hogan nudged him as Luis wheeled David to a bench and sat beside him. "You still have fans. Now what you need is distraction."

With the kids tagging along, they returned to the playground, and stood surveying as the kids ran all over the place. "You mean this isn't enough of one?"

Hogan snorted. "I mean a distraction of another kind. Go out and meet someone. I saw there was a new gay bar that opened near here. The O?" He shrugged. "Maybe you'll meet a guy. Or you could join a dating app." They took a seat on a bench not far from Luis and David.

"Since when are you into hookups? You were always about falling in love." His mouth drooped. "And you saw how well that worked out for me."

"Because he was the wrong guy. Evan was the kind who only wanted to be with you when things were going well. Look at that kid David." He tipped his head toward Luis and the young man. Luis smiled at him and waved, and Colson waved back.

Hogan dropped his voice an octave. "God forbid anything like that had happened to you, Evan would've bailed. Luis said David's brother has devoted himself to taking care of him. Find yourself a man like that."

Colson snorted. "Trust me, they don't exist. His brother must be a unicorn."

CHAPTER SIX

"God bless the freaking weekend. Or at least what's left of it." Harper walked into his house and called out, "I'm home."

"We're in here," Luis answered.

In the kitchen, Luis and David were finishing dinner. "Hey, you two. How was your day?" He kissed David's cheek, pleased to see an almost empty plate in front of him.

"We had a great time. First we went to the library, then the park and had ice cream. Aqua therapy in the afternoon, and David did great. Theo said his muscles are holding up nicely."

"Better than my day." He stretched. "Let me go lock up my gun."

"You want some meatloaf? There's plenty left. I wasn't sure when you'd be home. I know Saturday overtime is a bitch."

"Sure. I'm starving." He ran upstairs, put away the gun, took off his shield, and returned to the kitchen. "You don't have to serve me."

"It's no biggie."

He sat and dove into the meal, not stopping until his plate was cleaned and he took another piece. "Delicious as usual. Beats the hell out of the crap I had for lunch." He took another bite, feeling the weight of Luis's stare. "Okay, what?"

"David and I went to the park today. We had ice cream."

His brow furrowed. "Yeah, you said. That sounds nice. David loves ice cream." He cast a fond glance to David, who licked his lips and smiled at him.

"We met a friend of yours."

Harper swallowed a sip of water and set the glass on the table. "A friend? Who? I don't have friends."

Lips twitching with suppressed laughter, Luis crossed his arms. "Colson Delacourt." Knowing brown eyes met his.

Harper forked another piece of meatloaf into his mouth. "He's not my friend. He's a victim of a crime."

"He mentioned his house had been broken into. Are you handling the case?"

Harper shrugged. "I was there when he walked in on the wreckage." At Luis's grin, he rushed to explain. "I was paying a visit to the lady across the street, and he was there. We walked out together."

"He's very nice."

"What was he doing at the park?"

"He was with his friend and two little kids. They were all getting ice cream, and we were behind them."

"David?" Harper reached over to touch his brother's shoulder.

"They were very kind."

He sighed. "Good to hear." You never knew with people. His job and past relationship had made him cynical in the worst way.

"He's very good-looking. I could see you two together."

"You need to up your fantasy life if you're thinking about me and other guys."

"I'm thinking about your life, period. Colson Delacourt is exactly the right kind of guy for you."

"Why?" he shot back. "Because he was nice to David while standing on line for ice cream? Please."

"No, because he engaged us in conversation and didn't treat David like he was invisible. So many people look right past him, or treat him like he doesn't exist, or as if he can't understand anything."

Harper's heart squeezed tight. "It's not right."

Luis's expression softened. "Of course it's not. But Colson Delacourt wasn't like that."

"And you can tell from one conversation, huh? From vanilla or chocolate?" Harper laughed. "Luis is funny, isn't he, buddy?"

David's head jerked in a nod.

"David liked him, didn't you?" Persistent bastard that he was, Luis pressed David. "The man with all the tattoos on his arms? He was nice."

David made a kissing sound.

"You're pushing, Luis," he warned.

"Nope. Just stating facts." Luis rose. "Now it's time to give David his bath and get ready for bed. He had a big day today."

Harper could see David was sleepy, and he leaned over to rub their cheeks together. "I'll be by to give you your good-night kiss in bed."

Luis bent to whisper as he walked by. "Colson's friend was trying to get him to go out tonight. Loosen up and meet someone. He might be at the O. In case you were thinking of going out to have a drink and relax."

"I wasn't."

"I'll be reading in my room after I put David to bed."

Harper drank some more water. "I have to shower."

Under the hot spray, he groaned, tense muscles releasing after a day at his desk, tracking down leads, then walking the streets talking to people. He was looking forward to his day off tomorrow and had no desire to do anything except lie in the backyard with a cold drink. He never touched alcohol when he was alone with David. In case of an emergency, he'd need all his wits.

But tonight...he hadn't planned to go out. He was tired and should use the time to catch up on sleep. He dried off and entered his bedroom. He could taste the burn of Scotch on his tongue, and maybe he could use a little mind-numbing conversation for an evening.

"Just one drink," he decided as he put on a blue shirt and black jeans.

David was in bed, and Luis was reading him a story. Harper waited until he finished and approached. He could tell David noticed his change of clothes. "I'll be back soon. Love you, kiddo."

After turning off the light, Luis followed him out. "Looking hot, Harper. Good for you. Go have some fun and get lucky."

"Yeah, sure. See you later." He knew his luck had run out years ago.

The night was balmy and sweet with the scent of all the flowers in bloom. He walked slowly, scanning the street and the people walking past him, unable to turn off his internal cop antennae. It worked in his favor as he walked into the O and spotted Colson Delacourt in a corner seat at the bar.

The bartender strolled over. "Hello. You're new and delicious."

Harper's smile was thin. "Johnnie Walker Black on ice."

"You got it."

He took his drink. "Start a tab, please." Harper made a beeline for Colson, who sat with head bowed over his bottle of beer. "I thought Boy Scouts don't drink."

Colson jumped and met his eyes. "What're you doing here?"

He put the glass to his lips. "Having a drink."

"But this place—"

"Is a gay bar. I'm aware." He slid into the seat next to Colson, who gazed at him.

"Oh. I—"

"Didn't know? Why would you?" Harper took another sip.

"I guess you're right. I like to think because I'm a writer, I'm observant and I can see things others can't." Colson finished his beer and signaled the bartender for another.

"Here you go, sweetie."

Now that he could stare, Harper took notice of the tattoos—all different kinds of birds and butterflies. He set his glass on the bar. "Any significance?"

Colson swallowed his beer. "To what?"

Harper reached out and traced one of the tats—a swallowtail butterfly. The bar was almost filled to capacity, yet he heard the sharp intake of Colson's breath. He liked that sound. He'd like to hear it with the man naked and under him.

Whoa. Slow your roll.

"The birds and butterflies. Why only them?" He continued to trace the edges of the tattoo on Colson's strong forearm, taking notice of the goose bumps.

"Because they're so free. They can simply fly away from any and all of their problems. Find a new home." His blue eyes were far, far away.

"Is that what you did?" At Colson's startled expression, he shrugged. "You mentioned your parents didn't approve of you. Did you up and leave everything behind?"

Colson's jaw hardened. "I'd rather not talk about it."

"You know, changing venues never makes your problems disappear. Life with all its miseries follows you wherever you go."

"How extremely deep and utterly depressing, Detective Rose. But coming from you, not surprising." An unexpected and totally charming smile curved Colson's lips, and lust punched Harper in the gut, leaving him trembling. He struggled to regain his balance.

"I can be funny," he grumbled. "I have a sense of humor. If I didn't in my job, I'd lose my mind." He finished his drink and raised his glass. "Another, please."

Sympathy creased Colson's brow. "You must've seen a lot of the ugly side of life."

"You don't know the half of it," he muttered, took the refilled glass, and drank most of it.

"Detective—"

"Harper. We're sitting in a bar, drinking together. I think you can call me by my first name."

"Harper. Are you okay?"

He laughed. "Are you concerned about me, Boy Scout? Don't be. I'm fine."

Colson's lips tightened. "I should've known not to feel sorry for you."

"I didn't ask for sympathy. I came here to get a drink after a busy day trying to hunt down some of your stolen goods along with other victims' property." And not having much luck. That was what had put him in a pissy mood. He hated thinking criminals had gotten the better of him.

"I already replaced my computer, and they're sending me new credit cards and my license." Harper noticed his white-knuckled grip on the bottle of beer. "All I care about is the picture of my grandparents. They can have the damn frame—I don't care. I just want the picture back." Tears rested on those thick, dark lashes, and Colson tossed out a few bills. "I gotta leave. Good-bye."

He took off, disappearing into the sea of men, and Harper waved to get the attention of the bartender to close out his tab. He added a tip and signed the receipt, then took off after Colson. When he finally made it outside, he spied him a block away. Harper easily caught up with him, but Colson stopped in his tracks, his face anything but friendly.

"What do you want?"

Harper gazed at him. "I don't know. You were upset and ran off. I didn't mean to hurt your feelings."

Colson hunched his shoulders. "It's not you." He began to walk again, and Harper followed, relieved that Colson didn't ask him to leave. "It's the picture."

"You said it's of your grandparents. You were close?"

"Yeah. Very."

They didn't speak again until they approached Willow Street.

"You're staying at your house? Not with your friends?"

Colson's smile was wry. "I love my friends, but they have two little kids, and one night was enough. They don't need me underfoot, and I'd prefer not to be."

Harper's stomach twisted in a knot. "You don't like children?" David might be an adult in years, but the responsibility was as all-encompassing as caring for a baby. He'd thought Colson Delacourt was different, especially after what Luis had said earlier.

"Funny enough, I love their innocent way of looking at things and the way they have no filter. They say the truth about what's on their mind. But they live in a two-bedroom, and I'd be on the couch. Seems silly when I have the big house."

"Makes sense."

They passed Millie Johnson's brownstone. "I got her the video camera this morning and set it up."

"Now she just has to remember to use it."

Colson laughed. "Exactly. I also put a new lock system on my door." At the foot of the stairs, they stopped. "I appreciate the walk home, but it wasn't necessary."

"Are you sure?" He raised a brow and met Colson's eyes. Desire, as dangerous as a live electrical wire, sparked between them, and when Colson didn't answer but mounted the steps, Harper decided to follow. Once inside, Colson dropped his keys on the table by the door.

"What—"

Harper dipped his head and settled his mouth over Colson's, cutting off his words. Every nerve ending sprang to life, and he wrapped an arm around Colson's waist, hauling him closer.

Colson shoved him to the wall and thrust his tongue past Harper's lips. Surprised but excited by the passionate response, he grunted as their teeth clashed and tongues battled. Though they were of similar height and weight, Colson had given him the impression of being much more passive.

Damn, was he wrong. And glad of it.

Colson's weight pressed him harder, while his mouth ravaged Harper's in a kiss that sucked all coherence from his brain, leaving him unable to think. Only feel.

And what he felt was the thick, heavy prod of Colson's dick against his, and he ground his hips into Colson's, all while hungrily sucking his tongue and biting his lips.

Colson flung his head back. "Fuck," he muttered, blue eyes glittering as Harper scraped his teeth along the strong cords of his neck.

"Oh God, yeah, that's gonna happen," Harper rasped before crushing their lips together again. Jesus Christ, he was an animal for this man.

Colson groaned, and they bucked and humped each other. Colson's tongue, slick and wet in his mouth, blew Harper's self-control apart, and his toes curled. This wasn't what he'd expected from the paradox known as Colson Delacourt. Tattooed, gruesome-murder author. Apple-pie baker, helper of sweet old ladies. Greedy tongue sucker, whose kisses stole the breath from Harper's lungs. For fuck's sake, he didn't even like kissing all that much, but he couldn't keep his lips from mauling Colson's.

They stood together, foreheads touching, chests heaving, Harper a hair trigger away from exploding. He gathered what was left of his brain.

"Aren't you a surprise?" Harper murmured, trailing kisses along Colson's jaw and sucking his earlobe. Colson shivered, and Harper tightened his hold on him. "Cold?"

Colson stepped away from him, ignoring the question. "You think *I'm* a surprise? Seriously?" He folded his arms, and Harper wanted to know how much more ink covered his body. And where. "First you treat me like a criminal—"

"Justifiably, I might add." He smirked. "If you're going to talk in a public place about murdering your neighbor, you better expect the consequences. Plus, you were ruled out pretty quickly."

"Only to become a victim." Colson touched his lips, and Harper's tongue moistened his own. They felt swollen and puffy, and if they looked anything like Colson's, he'd need to fix that. Fast. Luis would never let him live it down. Hopefully he'd be asleep by the time Harper returned home.

Colson had a funny expression on his face.

"What?" Harper asked.

"Is this something you do often?"

"What? Kiss men? News flash. I'm gay. I've kissed men before."

Colson's blue eyes darkened to stormy midnight, and Harper grinned to himself. He enjoyed riling the man up. "Yeah, I'm sure you're hot stuff. I mean, have you done this with other gay male victims?"

Disbelief trickled through Harper. "Excuse me?" He took a step toward Colson. "Are you accusing me of using my position to have sex with crime victims?"

Colson's eyes bore into his. "Have you?"

Harper turned around, opened the door, and walked away. It was the best thing to do, otherwise he might've punched Colson in that pretty face of his. By the time he arrived home, he'd cooled off, and after washing his face and putting on a pair of athletic shorts, he peeked into David's room.

Luis was wrong. So was Nolan. This was all he needed.

CHAPTER SEVEN

Another chapter finished. Colson saved it and sat back with a sigh. While the words still flowed—and his agent was texting him every day with encouragement and not so subtle hints that if he finished by the end of the summer, he could arrange for foreign rights to be secured by year's end—all the initial excitement and joy had diminished after the break-in.

He knew it was silly to be so wrapped up in a picture, but its loss left a gaping hole inside him. Each morning when he awoke, he looked where their picture should've been and felt their absence. His grandparents, even in spirit, had always given him the strength to keep going.

His phone rang with an unfamiliar number. "Hello?"

"Mr. Delacourt, this is Detective Martinez."

"Oh, hi." Immediately, his mind went to that night a week ago with Harper Rose. God, the filthy dreams he'd had of that man. He'd spent every night since then thinking what it would've been like had they taken it to the next step. But then he'd accused Harper of unprofessional behavior.

He'd instantly regretted the accusation because it had been made out of fear. With Evan gone—and if he were honest, even before Evan had dumped him—he'd lost the part of himself that had found pleasure in writing, in life...in love. Sparring with Harper had been more than fun. It had awakened his long-lost passion and the lust he'd thought gone forever. As much as it shocked him, it scared the hell out of him as well.

But why him—why Harper? For God's sake, he didn't even like the man. Harper Rose was arrogant, annoying, overly confident...and the best damn kisser who'd ever put his mouth on him.

Colson sighed. Nothing he could do about it now.

He'd plotted a romantic side angle in the book for Harrison Rosa, where he'd fallen for someone he worked with. In his writing, he could explore what might've happened between Harper and him if he hadn't said something stupid.

He rubbed his face as if to wipe away the memory.

"If possible," Martinez said, "could you come down to the precinct?"

Alarmed, he gripped the phone tighter. "Why? Is everything okay?"

"I'm sorry. It's nothing we can discuss over the phone."

Martinez's terse voice didn't bode well.

"I can be there in about thirty minutes."

"That works. See you then."

Before he had a chance to say anything further, the call ended. He quickly showered and dressed and walked to the precinct, about a mile away. He was ushered into a room where he waited for almost ten minutes, tapping his fingers and scrolling through his phone, growing more agitated by the minute.

The door opened and Martinez walked in, carrying a file. Colson peered over his shoulder, expecting to see Harper. Martinez's lips quirked.

"My partner is in court this morning."

He hoped his cheeks weren't red. "I—uh, wasn't...what did you need me for, Detective?"

Martinez sat across from him. "We've found some items from the break-ins, and we wanted to see if you could identify them."

"Oh. The picture of my grandparents?"

"I'll show you what we have." He set the file on the table, pulled out a sheaf of printed photographs, and set them out on the table one by one. "If you recognize anything, please let me know."

Colson scanned the photos, recognized his wallet and a laptop that could be his, and pointed them out to Martinez. Spying the picture frame, his heart sank. With a trembling hand, he reached out and picked up the photo.

"Dammit."

The frame was disappointingly, heartbreakingly empty. Colson ran his fingertips over the blank space. "No sign of the photograph?"

"No, I'm sorry." Martinez met his gaze. "I heard it was a sentimental picture."

"My grandparents. My favorite one I had of the three of us."

The detective's brow creased, and his eyes reflected sympathy. "We're still looking, Mr. Delacourt. If we find it, we'll be sure to return it. I can't give you the items just yet as they're in evidence, but we believe we're closing in on the gang. So hopefully soon."

"I hope so too. You think you know who these bastards are?"

"We have an idea, but we want to make it as tight a case as possible."

"I understand. It's just so...creepy, knowing someone's been in your home, touching your things." He shivered. "Have you ever been robbed?"

"No, but I understand what you're saying. It's a violation of your personal space. But you're home now, correct?"

"Yes," Colson answered with more confidence than he felt. "I refuse to let these fuckers drive me out of my own space."

Martinez nodded with approval. "Good. That's the right attitude. We'll get them, and things should return to normal for you soon."

"Thanks."

But on the walk home, Colson realized he wasn't sure it would ever be normal again. Even now, in the early afternoon, he was hesitant to be there alone. Was it only a few weeks earlier he'd considered his house a sanctuary? His safe space? He hesitated at the foot of the stairs, then decided to head to the park and sit in the sun. He'd written his words for the day and deserved a break.

He sat on a bench by the water and stared out at the skyline across the river. Seagulls skimmed the surface, and boats sailed past. When he'd turned four, his father had started taking him out on their boat, and they'd spend the day together on the Long Island Sound. But after a few years, after he'd shown no signs of sailing aptitude and preferred reading a book rather than learning about masts and flaps, his father had stopped bringing him. He left for college, with his father's words ringing in his ears.

College will make a man out of you.

And when he lost his virginity to a man he barely knew, he heard that taunt in his head. With each and every man he let touch him and whom he touched and kissed and fucked, he'd think, *Am I enough of a man for you now, Dad?* Knowing all along, he'd never measure up to who his father wanted him to be.

Futile as it was, he'd tried to keep communication open between him and his parents, but they'd never reciprocated. It had always been him reaching out. Even Evan had dismissed it, but Colson understood. Evan had kept his sexuality a secret until he'd graduated business school. The day he came out, his parents refused to accept it and cut him off, so Evan had little desire to have Colson and his parents make peace.

But now, after the break-in, the desire grew stronger, and without thinking about what he'd say, he placed the call. It rang several times.

"Hello? Colson? Is it you?"

"Mom, yeah. How are you?"

"Is everything all right?"

Not exactly a warm and loving response after not speaking for so long. But Colson wasn't surprised. That was the way they were.

"Yes. I'm okay. I was just thinking...maybe it would be nice to talk."

"About what?"

He blinked and huffed. "I don't know...what we've both been doing all these past years. Come on, Mom."

"I don't understand what you think I should say. You told us the distressing news and didn't even ask us how we felt."

As usual, his mother was making it all about her and her feelings, completely negating his. Not to mention calling his coming out "distressing news."

"Out of curiosity, what would be the purpose of asking how you felt about my being gay? It's not going to change anything."

"Really, Colson. I know you like to think of yourself as rebellious, but couldn't you have—"

"What, Mom? Not been gay?"

"I've heard that sometimes men think they are...that way...but later they realize it was only curiosity and they return to normal."

Tears burned his eyes. "I am normal, Mom. This was a mistake."

He ended the call and wiped at his eyes, furious that he'd allowed her to get to him. What he needed was to walk it off, then bury himself in something mindless. He put his earbuds in, and head down, walked until he reached the children's park. Remembering his sweet conversation with Luis and David, Colson scanned the crowd, his gaze alighting on the two men sitting and watching the children on the swings.

He settled next to Luis on the bench and removed the earbuds. "Hi. Remember me?"

Luis laughed. "I sure do. And look." He showed Colson the e-reader with his first book: *The Killer Behind the Stairs*. "I'm rereading because I can't find anything else to hold my interest."

"Wow, that's great. Thanks for showing me. It's always nice to see."

"How is your day so far?" Luis gave David some juice.

"I was writing all morning, and then I had to go to the police station to identify some items they found from the break-in at my house."

"They caught the guys? It's definitely a ring going around the neighborhood."

He frowned. "Not yet, but the detective assured me they have leads and they're close." He sighed and propped his chin in his hand. "It's not going to bring back the picture of my grandparents. They found the frame, but it was empty. I'm afraid that's gone forever. Everything else is replaceable but that."

Luis's smile faded. "I'm sorry. That's rough. But I'm sure the detectives working on the case are trying their best."

"I hope so." He thought for a moment. He used to have Hogan preread his books, but with the two kids and a full-time job, his friend was stretched pretty thin. "Anyway, I've been working on this new book and was wondering...would you like to read the rough copy? I'd love to hear your thoughts on how it's going and any problems you come across. No pressure, of course."

Luis's jaw dropped. "Are you serious? Man, that would be so cool. I'd love to do it."

"Are you sure? I know you have a full plate taking care of David."

Luis brushed him off. "No worries about that. My boss is cool, and I have plenty of free time once he gets home from work. He's super devoted to David."

"Must be a nice guy," Colson mused.

"He's great, except I wish he'd make more of an effort to have a social life."

"I guess if he wants to, he will. Anyway, give me your email, and I'll send you the file later."

"Can you tell me a little about the book?"

Colson explained the plot, and then, curious to see Luis's reaction, revealed the romantic angle.

"First book where you'd have a detective with a girlfriend."

"Or a boyfriend," Colson said. "I haven't decided yet."

"Huh. Interesting. I'll let you know what I think."

David made a noise and turned his head. Colson spotted the ice cream truck pulling up. "How about if I seal the deal with a chocolate cone for you and a vanilla cup for David?"

"You don't have to," Luis protested.

"I know, but trust me, you've made a lousy day much better." He joined the line at the truck, and when he returned, handed Luis the cone. "Would you...if you want to eat your ice cream, I could help with David, if it's okay with you."

David gave him that sweet smile, and Luis stared at him. "You want to help with David?"

Colson worried he'd overstepped, but he felt such a pull toward these people he barely knew.

"Yes. Before my grandparents passed away, they were in an assisted-living facility, and I would visit them and help feed my grandfather after his second stroke and then my grandmother when her Alzheimer's became too advanced. They had full-time help, but I was determined to be there for them, just as they were always there for me when I was young—and in fact, without them, I wouldn't have been able to live here right out of college."

"That's very kind of you."

"Believe me, it takes my mind off...stuff." Colson put the spoon to David's lips, and he licked at the ice cream. It was impossible to be with David and not fall for his gentle sweetness.

"Care to share? I'm a good listener." Luis took a lick of his cone, but his eyes were focused on Colson.

He lifted a shoulder, trying not to allow his mother's cool indifference to hurt him any longer.

"It's pretty simple. I was feeling a little down, and I-I haven't spoken to my mother in a long while, so I thought I'd call."

"Uh-oh. Doesn't sound like it turned out well."

"I'm gay. I don't know if you were aware."

Luis shrugged. "I might've read it somewhere, but it doesn't matter to me."

"Well, it mattered to her and my father. And I just thought maybe after fifteen years, their feelings might've changed." He fed David another spoonful and wiped his lips. "Turns out, nothing's changed. So I started feeling a little sorry for myself, and here I am."

"I'm sorry. But it's their loss. As I see it, you're a great guy."

Colson laughed, and David laughed with him. "Luis is funny, huh? He doesn't know me, but he thinks I'm a great guy."

Luis didn't join in their hilarity. In fact, he was frowning.

"Colson, look at you. Here you are, sitting with practically two strangers, feeding ice cream to a man in a wheelchair. You may say that's not being a great guy, but from my perspective, it's pretty amazing."

"Well, thanks, but it's just being a decent human being as I see it."

"Trust me, there are way too few of those types of people as I see it. Do you know, in all the years we've been coming to the park, no one has ever come up and spoken to us? They give David a wide berth, like he's got a communicable disease. You and your friend and his children were the first to show him kindness. So thank you for seeing him."

"We all need to be seen."

He wished them a great rest of the day, and still feeling blue, texted Hogan, telling him about the conversation with his mother.

She's the loser. One day maybe she'll wake up and figure out you're the best.

Thanks, but after all this time, I doubt it.

Want to come by for dinner?

Much as he loved Hogan, Bea, and the kids, he wanted to be alone.

Rain check? I'm going to work on the book.

On his way home from the park, he received a text from Harper, and all thoughts of his book flew out the window.

We're close to an arrest.

Colson reached his house and entered.

Determined to keep it as informal and brief as possible, he replied: *So your partner said. Still mad at me?*

No.

He wondered what Harper was up to and why he was texting. It wasn't necessary. Did he want to come over? Finish what they'd started? It would give him a chance to apologize. A thrill ran through him, while at the same time, he was annoyed with himself at how badly he wanted to see Harper.

But Harper didn't text him back, and that only added to his frustration. Had Harper only used him that night? If so, Colson sure as hell wasn't going to allow that to happen again.

CHAPTER EIGHT

"Another hell of a goddamn week." Nolan stretched his arms above his head. "But we finally got our bad guys."

"We did." Harper studied the array of evidence they'd found. Loads of computers, phones, jewelry, and other expensive items. But not Colson's photograph. After they'd arrested the band of thieves, Harper had spent an extra hour at the scene specifically to search for it. No luck.

But he wasn't ready to give up.

"What's got you staring at those photos for the past forty minutes?" Nolan peered over his shoulder.

Harper minimized the screen. He wasn't about to tell Nolan that he'd decided to revisit the apartment building where the goods had been stored. Nolan was too smart and would figure out what he was up to.

"Nothing. Just making sure everything is in order."

"Any plans for the weekend?"

"Nothing except taking David to the zoo and then the park."

"How's he doing?"

Harper shrugged. "The same. Therapy keeps his muscles alive, and Luis takes him out every day—the library, the park, anywhere he can get mental stimulation." He swallowed against the lump in his throat. "He's happy—or as happy as he can be. That's the best I can hope for."

"It can't be easy. I admire you."

Harper snorted. "For what? I get to walk and run and enjoy life. I'm not tied to a chair, unable to move but still alive inside."

"But you're there. Every day. Lots of people would've put him in a home, and then they'd go to visit once a week."

Sweat rolled down his back. "I couldn't."

Nolan squeezed his shoulder. "I know. But a guy's gotta live. See you on Monday."

He nodded and clicked the mouse to bring the photos up again. He'd combed through every inch of the apartment, looking for the photo of Colson's grandparents. After that night, when they'd practically mauled each other, Harper felt guilty over crossing the line with a victim. Numerous times he'd passed by Colson's house, thinking he should go up the steps, apologize for being unprofessional, and move on.

But he didn't want to move on. He wanted... *Fuck.* He wanted Colson Delacourt, but it wasn't right. Colson had touched a nerve. It wasn't professional to become involved with a crime victim, but also, he had to give everything to David. He'd learned the hard way that he couldn't have both.

Still, even if Colson was off-limits, Harper could go the extra mile to try and find the picture that meant so much to him. He closed the computer and left the precinct It wasn't something he looked forward to doing, but he was damn well going to try.

Two hours later, he surveyed the mess of garbage bags in the compactor room with disgust. He'd gone through close to a hundred plastic bags of trash, and there had to be at least fifty more. He should just say fuck it and leave. He was already late for dinner with David, but Luis had reassured him he was fine with watching him late, and David wasn't too hungry, so dinner could be postponed for an hour.

He untied another bag and wrinkled his nose at the dirty diapers and remnants of God knew what. Harper quickly retied that one and tossed it aside. Another bag contained a ton of cigarette butts and fast-food bags and boxes. Harper recalled the same trash in the apartment where they'd located the stolen picture frame. He picked out all the garbage until he saw it: the crumpled photograph of two elderly people with a smiling Colson between them.

He smoothed it out the best he could, but it would be impossible to rid the picture of all the creases.

"Bastards," he swore. Judging by the unbridled joy in all their faces, Colson had loved his grandparents and had been loved in return. Perhaps that was why he was so devoted to his neighbor, Millie Johnson—he felt a kinship to the lonely, elderly woman because she reminded him of his grandparents.

He glanced at his watch—close to seven. He had to get home to David. He was very careful to keep to their routine as David's doctor said it gave David a sense of security, but with his job, that wasn't always possible. He slipped the photo into a Redweld file he'd brought along and left the building. On his way home, he sent Colson a text.

Are you around tonight?

An answer popped up a few minutes later.

Yes, why?

Harper bit his tongue while typing.

I have something to show you. Can I come by after dinner?

I'll be here.

Harper had to get something off his chest before he saw Colson later.

Listen, I'm sorry I stepped over the line. I've never done that before.

It took a moment for Colson to respond, but it felt like an hour.

I know you're a professional and I'm sorry too. We can talk about it face to face.

More than relieved that he and Colson were on the way to making amends, Harper increased his stride. His good mood didn't go unnoticed by Luis when he came home.

"You're looking pretty happy about something."

"Just that we wrapped up our case and found a majority of the stolen goods."

Luis broke out in a big smile. "That's great news. I'm sure the neighborhood is relieved."

"Yeah, and the captain and the chief are very pleased." He sighed and rolled his neck, enjoying the air conditioning. "I'll be down in a few minutes." He needed a shower after being in that enclosed room with heaps of smelly garbage.

He took the stairs two at a time, stripped off his clothes, and got into the shower. Clean and dried off, he put on athletic pants and a T-shirt and joined David in the kitchen. He'd already eaten half his dinner—roast chicken cut in small pieces, french fries, and steamed vegetables. Harper kissed David's cheek and made himself a plate.

"How was your day?" He chewed and swallowed, then took a sip of the beer Luis gave him. "Thanks. I need it."

"I'll bet. We went to the aquarium and saw the penguins and the otters. David wanted pizza, so we had that, then came home, had a cool bath, and watched a movie."

"Sounds great. Better than my day." He ate some more. "Would you like to go to the zoo tomorrow, watch the seals?"

David's eyes grew wide, and he moved his mouth.

"Yes, we'll go for feeding time. I know you love to hear them talk."

He finished dinner and told Luis he'd read David his story. "You worked overtime today."

"I don't mind, Harper. I've got some stuff to do anyway, so if you want to go out after David goes to sleep, don't worry. I'll keep an ear out for him."

He chewed the inside of his cheek. "Uh, well, as a matter of fact..."

"Yeah?" A huge knowing smile spread over Luis's face. "Awesome. Go ahead."

"After David's bedtime."

They finished dinner and watched half of an action movie before David started getting drowsy. He lifted David from his chair and put him into bed, straightening the sheets around him. The story was one where Superman and Batman joined forces to battle the Joker. David's eyes grew heavy, and he yawned, making a small noise.

"Tired, buddy?" David blinked and licked his lips. "Okay. A drink of water, then you go to sleep. Tomorrow we have the whole day."

Harper lifted him and gave him the straw from the bottle next to the bed. David sighed and closed his eyes as Harper settled him onto the pillow.

"You know," Luis said from behind him after he'd shut David's bedroom door three-quarters of the way, "David isn't going to suffer if you have a personal life."

Harper's jaw tightened. "We've been through this before."

"No. What you've been through is a guy who wasn't worth your time. That doesn't mean you give up."

"I've got to go. I have to bring something to someone." He picked up the file he'd left by the front door. "I shouldn't be home too late."

"Take your time. Have fun," Luis called out after him.

It was summer and close to eight thirty at night, which meant the sun hadn't yet set and the streets were crowded. The cafés were filled with outdoor diners, having drinks and dinner, laughing and sending each other long loving looks.

Harper didn't know whether to be envious or nauseated. When he turned onto Colson's block, he texted him.

Be there in a few.

Colson didn't answer. Maybe he was in the bathroom. Harper walked up the steps and rang the bell. No answer. He knocked and knocked.

"Colson? Colson, it's Harper. Harper Rose."

A minute later, Colson appeared, sleepy-eyed, his hair messy, as if he'd just woken up. Did he have somebody with him? That thought annoyed him.

"Did I interrupt you? I did say I was coming by."

"No. I was watching something on television and must've fallen asleep."

"Another wild Friday night?" Harper razzed, and Colson flushed and thrust his jaw out. Harper enjoyed teasing Colson—maybe too much.

"You said you had something to show me?"

"Can I come inside at least?"

Colson hesitated, and Harper leaned in closer. "I promise to keep my lips to myself."

"You're a better detective than you are a comedian." With a huff, Colson stepped aside, and Harper passed by him. Their eyes met, and that same sizzle of heat as the time before sprang up between them. Colson met him in the center of the hallway, and Harper gazed around.

"Well, I think I'm good at both. Nice place. Very different from the old homes, like Ms. Johnson's."

"I like wide-open spaces."

"Like your birds and butterflies?" Harper murmured.

Colson's cheeks reddened. "Haven't you ever wished you could leave it all behind and just...be free?"

He didn't know how to answer that. He had no idea what it meant to be free, and yet he wouldn't have it any other way.

He held out the file. "This is yours, I believe."

Puzzled, Colson took it and opened it. He pulled out the mangled photograph.

"Oh, my God. You found it. How...I can't...Harper." He sank to one of the bottom steps of the staircase. "Thank you," he whispered. Shiny-eyed and flushed, he blinked. "Thank you so much."

"I'm sorry it's in such poor condition." Harper's smile was wry. "It took two hours and about two hundred bags of trash until I found it."

"You're apologizing?" Colson stared at him as if two heads had popped up between his shoulders. "You've found the most precious thing to me. And I know you didn't have to do it." Colson redirected his attention to the picture. "You have no idea..."

"I think there are places where you can get damaged photos restored. Hopefully they can help."

Colson nodded, running his fingertips over the photo. "I'll look into it."

"So...I'll be going." Harper turned to leave.

"No, wait, please." Colson sprang to his feet, and Harper stayed still. "I, uh, I was going to order something to eat, but I fell asleep. Would you like to join me?"

Was he hungry? Not at all.

"Sure. I'd love to."

Colson slipped the photo into the Redweld and set it on the table by the staircase. "How do you feel about sushi?"

He wasn't a fan.

"Sounds good."

Colson handed him his phone. "See anything you like?"

Yeah. You.

"I'll let you pick. I'm easy."

"All right. Why don't we go into the living room? Want a beer?"

"I'd love one."

He followed Colson into the house, admiring the high tin ceilings, crown molding, and original inlaid wooden floors. The kitchen was ultramodern, equipped with all the bells and whistles. "Nice reno job. You obviously love to cook."

A harsh laugh escaped Colson. "No, not at all. I did it for Evan, my ex. He fancied himself an amateur chef."

Harper noted the top-of-the-line appliances and cookware. Luis would go buck wild in this kitchen. He, on the other hand, was a whiz at tuna salad, grilled cheese, and heating up tomato soup.

"What was his specialty?"

"Lying to me."

Narrowing his eyes, he frowned. "Sounds like a real piece of shit."

Colson shrugged. "I didn't realize it until he left, but I guess I wasn't the best judge of character." He handed Harper his beer. "You know how it is. You want to believe everything they say because you care about them." He took a drink of his beer. "But I can't blame Evan completely. I was suffering with burnout, producing nothing, feeling sorry for myself, and a virtual hermit. He met me at my best, and then I turned into the worst."

"He cheated, I presume?" Harper already hated the bastard. Not only for cheating, but for the fact that Colson still cared.

"Yeah. I guess about a year and a half into our relationship. I'm not a social media person—I had a personal assistant to post for me on Instagram and wherever. My focus had to be the writing. And Evan was aware of that. Turns out all those late nights at the office were more than a meeting of the minds." A crooked smile tilted his lips.

"It sucks to be lied to and taken advantage of."

"No cheating exes in the wings with you?" Colson asked.

He thought of Ronnie and how he'd wanted Harper to stick David in a home to make it easier. He didn't want to have to deal with his everyday care. In fact, he didn't want to see David at all.

"No. None at all."

The doorbell rang, and Colson left him to get the delivery.

"Ready to eat?"

Harper downed the rest of his beer. "Yeah. I'm ready."

For what, Harper wasn't certain, but he was breathless, as if he stood on the edge of a precipice, gazing into a wide-open space. His heart pounded, and he couldn't shake the feeling he was missing something. Something momentous that would change his life.

All he had to do was take that first step, and he'd be free.

CHAPTER NINE

Colson set the delivery bag on the kitchen island, all the while studying a suddenly nervous Harper. Something had happened while they'd been discussing Evan. Harper had said he had no exes—unsurprising to Colson, as he presumed from Harper's behavior he was a lone wolf. And yet Colson sensed he was hiding something.

Did Harper think he was looking for something permanent between them? They needed to set that straight, especially after that mind-blowing kiss.

"I feel like I should say something because I think you're mistaken about me."

Harper took another swallow of his beer, set the bottle on the island, and crossed his arms. "How so?"

"I think you believe I'm looking for another relationship, while the exact opposite is true."

"Is it?" Harper cocked his head. "You lived with your ex for how long—almost three years?"

Colson so didn't want to talk about Evan. He walked away. "Yeah, so? Everyone's entitled to make a mistake."

Harper followed him. "Are you sure that's what it was?"

He whirled around. "Why are you so interested in my ex? It's over and done with. He's gone, and I'm fine with it. I've moved on."

Harper searched his face. "Just making sure. Because the first time we met and your hands were all banged up, you said it was because you found out he was with someone else." A surprisingly tender smile rested on Harper's lips. "I'm nobody's boyfriend, but I sure as hell don't want to be a stand-in for who you really want to be with."

Irritated, Colson attempted to explain. "You're not a stand-in for anything or anyone. Yeah, I was upset. Wouldn't you be if someone you loved and thought loved you, up and left one day? And then a few months later, he's happier than he's ever been." Colson's lips thinned. "His words, not mine. I wouldn't write something so cheesy. And you don't have to convince me. I know you're not boyfriend material."

Harper's eyes glittered. "And you came to this conclusion how?" He took a step forward. "Because we were talking about your ex and I said I had no exes?" A predatory smirk tipped his lips up. "Or was it because of what happened last time?"

Colson glared. "You kissed me first. And also, it takes two sets of lips to tango."

"I'm not into dancing," Harper murmured, his arms encircling Colson's waist.

Like the first time Harper had touched him, Colson lost sense of everything else except the point of contact where Harper's skin touched his. Their mouths were a mere inch apart, yet it was already enough to trip his heart into overdrive, and his breath stuttered.

"What are you into?" Colson asked, taking Harper's full lower lip between his teeth and tugging.

Harper covered his mouth, and Colson slid his arms around Harper's neck, anchoring him in place, while he pushed his tongue between Harper's lips. Harper pressed him against the island, hands kneading his ass.

Colson released him for a moment, his fingers pulling at the waistband of Harper's track pants, tugging the clothes past his hips. His cock hit Colson's belly, and he grasped it.

"I'd like to be in your mouth. That's what." Harper nipped his lobe, then stuck his tongue inside the shell of his ear, and Colson lit up.

"I think that could be arranged." He sank to his knees and licked the glistening crown of Harper's dick. It was exactly as he'd imagined—its solid heft, the sweetness of the precome trickling from the slit, and the incredible heat rising from Harper's skin, twisting his mind so nothing existed but the sheer hungry need to take him in his mouth.

"Oh, yeah." Harper threw his head back and hissed. Colson gazed up at him, lost in the sight of Harper unraveling. Openmouthed and panting, his chest heaving as if he'd run a mile. Colson liked seeing the normally sardonic and put-together detective lose control.

He swirled his tongue while sucking and added his hand to the action. Soon Harper was clutching Colson's hair, thrusting his hips, and Colson, who loved sucking cock, took it all.

"*Mmm*," he hummed, tickling the slit and cupping Harper's balls. They were tight, and Colson knew it wouldn't be long before he'd be tasting Harper Rose's come in his mouth. "So good. Sweet." Again, he sucked deep while slipping a finger into the cleft of Harper's ass, and that was enough.

"Oh fuck, Jesus." Harper gasped and came, shooting hot and heavy down Colson's throat. He sagged onto the barstool, and Colson licked him clean. Hazy-eyed and smiling, Harper pulled him up, then teased his long fingers against the bulge of Colson's thin shorts. "Time for me to make you feel good."

Harper reached inside, and his large, warm hand gripped Colson tight. Colson wriggled the shorts and briefs down, eyes riveted on his dick sliding in and out of Harper's fist.

"Come here." Harper leaned forward, crushing their lips together. He moaned into Harper's mouth, and Harper sucked his tongue while jerking his dick harder...faster. Harper bit at his lips, one hand working Colson's throbbing dick while the other teased at his hole. A desperate, hungry need shot through him. Like an animal in heat, he was ready to roll over and take Harper's dick right there in his kitchen.

"God, oh God." His hips bucked, and stars burst behind his eyes. He came, and Harper held his gaze while he licked his fingers.

Harper patted Colson's softened dick, giving it a final stroke before tucking him into his briefs and shorts. He put an arm around Colson, who rested in his arms.

"I have a confession to make." Harper nuzzled his hair.

Basking in the afterglow, Colson rubbed his eyes, his immediate reaction one of suspicion. "What is it?" He tried to shift away from Harper, but to his annoyance, Harper held him firm.

Harper's lips touched his ear. "I don't really like sushi."

A *whoosh* of relief left him, and he laughed. "You could've said something."

"I didn't care. I'd eaten dinner earlier. I came to give you the picture."

"And?" Colson prodded.

Harper's grin turned wolfish. "And this was something I hoped for but wasn't going to push. Especially after what happened the other night."

Colson winced. It was the elephant in the room and needed to be dealt with. "I'm sorry. I didn't mean it."

"I think you did."

Damn. From the little he knew of Harper Rose, the man wasn't a bullshitter and liked to cut to the chase. He eased out of Harper's arms. "Okay. I meant it, but it came out the wrong way."

Harper sat on a barstool. "How about you explain it to me? The right way this time."

Knowing they needed to clear the air, Colson took a stool next to him. "Look, I was completely wrong to accuse you of using your position to take advantage of people. And I apologize."

"It was. I've never stepped out of line performing my job. An accusation like that could damage my career." Harper grew more agitated by the moment. "I could lose my job."

"Whoa, Harper, wait a second. Slow down." Colson scrambled away from him and put the span of the island between them. "How did one little, stupid remark become this mess?" He gentled his voice. "I'm sorry. It was mean and nasty, and I apologize. I don't believe you're like that. And what I said was in the privacy of my home, with only the two of us around. How could anyone possibly find out?"

Harper ran a hand through his hair. "Maybe you'd talk about it with your friends. I don't know. You have a habit of saying things in public that shock people. Did you forget those ladies in the coffee house?"

"Oh, Christ." He groaned. "Come on, Harper. That was *once*, and specifically for their benefit. I knew they were being nosy, and I wanted to have some fun with them. I was playing a game."

Obviously, he and Harper had a different idea of fun, because Harper wasn't smiling.

"I can't afford to take my job lightly. I shouldn't have kissed you. It just happened."

There was something Harper wasn't saying, but he didn't elaborate, remaining tight-lipped.

"I understand you're very dedicated. I'd never tell anyone what happened while the case was being investigated." Colson didn't want this–whatever "this" was that he and Harper had growing between them–to end before it had a chance to be explored further. "But the case is over." He waited.

The darkness in Harper's face lightened. "So it is. And the night is young."

Colson grinned. "And I'm hungry. So you may not like sushi, but I'm going to have some of this."

"Not to worry. I can watch television while you eat your raw fish." He wrinkled his nose, and Colson laughed.

"What do you have against sushi?"

Harper shuddered. "I don't like eating raw things. Food is meant to be cooked."

"What about veggies?" Colson popped a salmon-avocado roll into his mouth.

Harper rolled his eyes. "That's not food. That's grazing. Totally different." He turned on the set and found an old black-and-white romantic comedy, which to Colson's surprise, he settled in to watch.

"You like classic movies?"

Harper's smile was wistful. "Yeah. My mom used to watch them."

Colson slowed his chewing. This was the first time Harper had mentioned his family or anything personal. He swallowed.

"My grandparents did too. Bette Davis was their favorite."

Harper's eyes glowed. "She was the greatest. *Dark Victory, The Little Foxes, Jezebel.* People would say my mother looked like her when she was young." He shrugged, as if suddenly aware how much he'd revealed. "Anyway, yeah. I'll just sit here while you eat."

Dammit. Every time he thought he was getting a bit closer to the enigma that was Harper Rose, the man threw the walls up.

Colson finished a roll, and though he was still hungry, he decided not to waste time eating sushi when he could have Harper Rose in his mouth.

"Are you sure you don't want to try?"

He plopped himself next to Harper on the large sectional sofa.

"I told you—*mmph.*"

His mouth hit Harper's. "Taste me." Harper sucked his tongue, and Colson wondered if he could come from a simple kiss. He was beginning to realize, though, that nothing about Harper Rose was simple.

"That wasn't so bad." Harper licked his lips. "A little salty and a little sweet."

"Like you." Colson nudged Harper's cheek with his nose and trailed kisses along his jaw. "But this is ginger and soy sauce. They play well together."

"Like us. How about we take this off," Harper whispered in a husky voice that sent a thrill up his spine. He tugged at the hem of Colson's shirt. "I'd rather play with you."

"Yeah?" Colson peeled the polo off and flung it aside. In the shadow of the light from the television, Harper's eyes gleamed as he ran his hands over Colson's shoulders, dipping past his abs to tease at the line of hair disappearing beneath the waistband of his shorts. Colson wet his trembling lips. "Like what you see?"

More ink covered his chest—birds and butterflies in flowers, and sunrays over one pectoral muscle. Harper's heartbeat accelerated, and Colson felt him grow hard. His fingers plucked at the points of Colson's nipples, and he moaned.

"Not fair," he gasped, pulling Harper's T-shirt over his head, his mouth watering at the dips and planes of his lightly hairy chest. He buried his face in Harper's neck and sucked hard, nipping at the fluttering pulse. That earned a grunt, and Harper cupped his ass.

"This feels damn fucking fair to me. More than that. Perfect." He slipped his hands inside Colson's shorts.

Maybe it was moving fast, but Colson didn't care. Life was fucking short, and he was going to take what he was given. "It would be even more perfect upstairs, where we have more room." Colson met Harper's eyes and rolled off him. Harper followed him up the steps, and into his bedroom, Colson pulled off his shorts and Harper stepped out of his track pants.

They lay next to each other, and Colson took their hard shafts in his hand. With Harper thrusting hard, Colson listened to the sounds they made—bare skin slapping against bare skin, breathless cries rising in the air, and his hand slick with precome rubbing their aching cocks.

"Fuck," Colson groaned. "Oh God, fuck me."

"Yeah, that'll be happening," Harper stiffened and came, his dick pulsing out hot sticky streams across their bellies. Colson followed a minute later, and they lay plastered together with sweat and come. Colson kissed Harper's naked shoulder, wondering if he'd now make an excuse to grab his clothes and leave.

"That was incredible, Harper."

Harper held him close, another surprise as Colson didn't take him as a cuddler. "*Mmm.* It was. A nice surprise. You're not only into blood and guts, are you? The murder and the macabre?"

"No, I'm really not." Deep down, he was a romantic, looking for someone to care about him. He might not talk about it, and he certainly wasn't about to share it with Harper, whose picture was next to the word "cynic" in the dictionary.

"Just gonna rest a moment." Harper's lids fluttered shut, and Colson held on, rubbing his shoulder, wondering if Harper would stay the night.

CHAPTER TEN

At two in the morning, Harper felt guilty leaving Colson sleeping, but nothing, not even the very delicious mouth of sexy Colson Delacourt, would keep him from spending the day with David. At home–but still thinking about the incredible sex–he shot off a quick text to Colson.

Thanks. I had fun.

Even though he'd come home late and it was his day off, he was up before the sky brightened to dawn. He made coffee and planned the day around their visit to the zoo and feeding time, as it was David's favorite thing.

He made them peanut butter and jelly sandwiches– heavy on the jelly for David since Harper worried about him choking on the sticky spread. Also turkey and cheese, blueberries, and cut-up nectarines. They'd get ice cream afterward, and then Harper would take him through the park and let him see the petting zoo.

As a special treat, he'd take David for a frozen coffee drink, and they'd have pizza for dinner and watch a movie. It was a routine they followed, and both looked forward to it.

Yawning and stretching, Luis walked into the kitchen. "*Mmm*, do I smell coffee?"

"Yep. Help yourself."

Luis poured a cup and joined him at the table. He took a sip and sighed. "I'm surprised you're up so early." He grinned into his cup. "Considering you came home so late. Have a good time?"

Avoiding the question, he asked one of his own. "I could ask you the same. It's your day off. You should be sleeping in."

Luis shrugged and drank more coffee. "I'm always up with the sun. And I have some stuff to do. So, did you have fun?"

If getting his brains rearranged by Colson's wicked tongue could be considered fun, hell yeah, he did. It took Harper an hour after he'd gone to bed to come down from the high of the evening.

"I guess so."

"Gonna see him again tonight?"

Harper, who'd been thinking about when he could pay Colson a visit, worked his jaw. "There's no one and nothing to see. This is my day with David."

Luis gave a weary sigh. "It doesn't have to be mutually exclusive. You can have a special someone."

"Been there, done that," he clipped out. "You know how it ended."

"Yeah, because Ronnie wasn't the right guy."

Harper set his mug on the table. "But I thought he was. And I brought him here into David's life, thinking that maybe...I don't know."

"Yes, you do," Luis pressed. "You wanted to be a family. There's nothing wrong with that."

"I misread him. How could I have been that blind?"

He'd met Ronnie while testifying at a trial. One of the perps he'd collared had been accused of attempted murder, and Ronnie DeMarco was the hotshot defense attorney. Initially, during the case, Harper had been antagonistic toward him, but once it was over, they'd found common ground, especially in bed. It was the first time he'd been pursued with flowers and dinners at restaurants he'd only read about, and Harper, starved for human affection, had opened himself up and fallen in love.

The only sticking point in their relationship had been the time he gave to David. Ronnie would say he understood, and when he met David, treated him kindly, yet after they'd been together three months, he'd begun to drop subtle hints that David would be happier in a group home where he could socialize with others like him. He'd try and get Harper to visit places where he said David could live and Harper could see him on his days off. Harper would look at the brochures and toss them into the trash.

The final straw happened at the park one day. He'd left David with Ronnie to use the restroom. He'd come back to find David sitting alone, parked by the side of a bench. After fifteen minutes, Ronnie had returned with the excuse that a client called and he'd had to meet him at the park entrance to receive some critical evidence.

"Come on, baby. He doesn't even know what the hell is going on around him. He was fine."

Shaking with rage, Harper pointed a finger in his face. "*You left a defenseless person alone. Anything could've happened to him.*"

"*You're obsessed with taking care of someone who's one step from being a vegetable.*"

Stricken, Harper took David, put him into the van, and left. He'd deleted Ronnie's number and blocked him.

That was the last time he'd allowed anyone into his heart.

"When you want something badly enough," Luis said, "you miss the cues. I believe he cared about you, but he cared about himself more. But there are other good people out there."

"I can't afford to trust again. You remember how upset David was that day. Being pushed into a corner, left alone...he could've been traumatized. And he liked Ronnie—I could tell he didn't understand why he was here one day and gone the next."

"I think you don't give David enough credit. He understands how much you love him and that you would never let anything hurt him." Luis rinsed his cup. "But I also think he wouldn't want or expect you to spend your life caring for him to the detriment of your own."

"He needs me," Harper maintained stubbornly.

"You have to fill that well at some point. You're not a machine, Harper. All you do is work, come home, and take care of David. Yeah, you love him more than anything. But that doesn't mean you don't deserve to find someone to love you."

Harper closed his eyes for a moment, recalling Colson's kisses and the heat of his skin, how his blue eyes glowed when he came.

"I'll be fine. I *am* fine."

"Maybe if you keep telling yourself that, you'll believe it's true." Luis imparted those words of wisdom before leaving the room.

He glared at Luis's back, but the effect was lost as he disappeared.

Harper knew better. He saw the worst of humanity every day. People were shit and would always disappoint you. That was why he loved spending time with his brother. David's pure innocence and sweetness made him believe that all wasn't lost, that there was still some good in the world. He glanced at the monitor showing David's room and saw that he was up.

"Time to rock and roll."

"Look, David. Look at that big guy up on the rock." Harper pointed to the big black seal lying in the sun.

David moved his head and made barking noises.

"That's right. He sounds just like that." Harper set the baseball cap on David's head to shade his face from the sun. "And here comes the person with their food."

A park employee walked into the seal enclosure with two buckets of fish. All the animals began to bark and swim in circles. From experience, Harper knew it would be a show. It was what they'd come for, and Harper loved seeing the excitement on David's face.

"Mommy, I can't see. I wanna see."

At the tap on his shoulder, he faced a young blond woman, her hair pushed off her face by a pair of oversized designer sunglasses. She was decked out in head-to-toe high-end athletic wear.

"Excuse me, but my son wants to stand by the gate to see the seals being fed."

Harper shrugged. "I'm sorry, but my brother wants to see them too." He figured that was polite.

She, however, wasn't finished. "But that's not fair. He doesn't even understand what's going on. I mean, look at him."

"I wasn't aware you were privy to his medical records and understood the extent of his brain injury. Now if you'll excuse us." He turned around, and David was smiling at the seals jumping in the air.

"Unbelievable. I've never met anyone so rude. Come on, Mason. We'll find a space over there."

"But this is the best spot," the kid whined.

"I know, but this man doesn't care. He's being selfish."

"Excuse me?" Harper knew he shouldn't respond but couldn't help it. "I'm being selfish? Look in the mirror. It wasn't me who started this. Now please leave us alone."

They finished watching the seals and traveled throughout the zoo. Unfortunately, everywhere they went, the woman and her child were there, and she encouraged her son to run up to the front before David could get to a good viewing spot.

At lunchtime, Harper took David to the picnic area, and they ate their food. He cut up David's sandwich into small pieces and fed it to him, then gave him some fruit. While wiping David's face, he saw tears in his eyes.

"What's wrong, buddy? Does something hurt?"

David frowned and made a whining sound. It broke Harper, knowing David's mind was alive, yet he couldn't make his needs known. He had a feeling it had to do with what had happened at the seal feeding. David was extremely sensitive to the emotions of people he came into contact with.

"Mommy, I want ice cream now."

Harper's nerves twisted in a knot. It was that little boy again with the obnoxious mother.

"Mason. Stop staring."

Of course, little kids never did what they were asked.

"What's wrong with him?" The kid pointed at David. "How come he can't walk? He makes funny noises."

Harper's eyes burned. He hoped the mother would have some decency and tell her son that wasn't a nice thing to say.

"Mason, come here. Now. Stay away from them."

The contempt in her voice was like icy water thrown over him. He packed their things and tossed the trash into the bin. As he wheeled David away, tears were running down David's face.

"Hey, buddy, it's okay. Don't be upset." He made it out of the zoo and into their van. "Let's go for our coffee drink." But David wasn't having any of it, and Harper recognized the signs. David was in a full-fledged breakdown. A rare occurrence, as David was a sunny, good-natured man. The last time that had happened was after he'd told him their mother was dead.

Harper decided to head home. Hopefully the familiar surroundings and quiet would calm David. One of his favorite movies always put him in a good mood. On the drive home, Harper cursed the woman whose insensitivity had set this off.

It was a struggle to get David inside, and Harper tried to settle him with the promised movie and some juice. None of it worked, and Harper couldn't stand to hear the ugly sounds of him crying and wailing.

He stood in the kitchen, careful to keep an eye on him while remaining out of David's line of sight. As rare as it was for David to have a tantrum, it was even more shocking for Harper to lose control. The weight of everything crashed into him, and he leaned against the wall, his head buried in his arms.

"What happened?" Luis put an arm around him, and Harper, embarrassed at being caught out, rubbed the wetness from his face.

"Long day." He forced a smile.

"Come on. I know you can fake it better than that."

Harper allowed Luis to steer him to the table. "Sit. I'll go check on David."

"No, Luis. It's your weekend off."

"Shut up, man." It was said with such affection, Harper was ready to burst into tears again.

Luis returned. "He's sleeping. I emptied his colostomy and urostomy bags and cleaned him up."

"Shit. I can't believe I forgot to do that." Furious with himself, he banged his fist on the tabletop.

"Harper, it's okay. Tell me what happened."

As he relayed the story, Luis's face grew dark with anger. "I swear some people shouldn't have kids. I don't blame the little boy. He learns from the parents."

"David got so upset, and it was such a good day until that point. But how long should he sit there and listen to cruel jabs and people talking about him like he doesn't exist? I can't blame him for getting upset. Anyone would. I should've gotten him out of there sooner."

"He'll be okay," Luis soothed. "It happens. Sometimes you get children who are kind and loving, their parents good, decent people. Like the two little kids we met in the park a while ago. They talked to David naturally. They looked *at* him, not right through him." A sly grin crossed his face. "Their father is friends with your victim."

"Which one?" Harper asked distractedly. "I have a lot of satisfied customers."

"I told you—Colson Delacourt."

Harper was proud of himself for not moving a muscle. "Oh, him."

Luis rolled his eyes. "Yeah, him. The tattooed hottie."

"Listen, I'm going to take a shower and go for a walk. I'm still too upset to sit around. Can you watch him for an hour or so?"

Luis took him by the shoulders. "Take as long as you need—I'll keep the monitor on just in case. I have no plans for tonight. All I'm gonna do is watch the game on television. And your screen is bigger than mine." He winked. "Stay out as late as you want."

"Yeah, sure, whatever." He stood, then bent to give Luis a kiss on the cheek. "Thanks for the talk."

Upstairs, he took a cool shower, which washed away some of his anger but not all. Still edgy and restless, he put on shorts and a T-shirt.

"Going out. Be back soon."

"Take your time."

He stopped by David's chair. "Hey, big guy. How're you feeling?"

David smiled and made kissing noises, and Harper was relieved to see he'd returned to his usual calm frame of mind. When their mother died, David had withdrawn for a month, refusing to let Harper lift him from the bed, barely eating. Afraid he was going to waste away, Harper had broken down and cried, begging him not to leave him as well. They'd clung together, and Harper had promised never to leave David alone. Together forever. He'd always have a home with Harper.

"You want me to stay home with you? We can order pizza."

Luis waved him out. "Me 'n David are watching the game. You go ahead. I've already ordered a pizza, and there's chocolate pudding. It's going to be a party." He held Harper's eyes. "We're going to be fine."

Harper kissed David's cheek. "I love you. I'll see you when I get home."

Shoulders hunched, he walked out into the steamy night. He took a detour through the park, walked up Squibb Hill to the promenade, passing the tourists hanging by the railing, pointing at the famous skyline of the city and the span of Brooklyn Bridge.

None of it moved him.

Eventually, he found himself at the base of the stairs to Colson's town house. He should be home. David needed him. He should—

"Harper?" He looked up to see Colson standing at the open door. "Are you okay?" Colson descended the steps. Worried blue eyes met his. "What's wrong? You're sweating like crazy."

He stood still, and Colson held a hand out. "Come on."

He took Colson's cool hand in his overheated one, and they walked inside the air-conditioned house. They remained in the foyer, and Colson continued to hold his hand.

"I was sorry you left before I woke up."

"I had to get home."

"Why?"

Harper curved his hand around Colson's nape and pulled him close. "So much talking when we could be doing this."

He covered Colson's mouth with his.

CHAPTER ELEVEN

He should stop this.

He deserved an explanation.

He'd ask Harper why he left.

In a minute.

He sucked Harper's tongue and grew dizzy when Harper's erection rubbed against his belly. Heat poured off him, and Colson grew faint from the heady smell of sweat and soap and Harper's desire. He clung to his biceps.

"What's going on...ohhhhh." Colson sighed as Harper yanked his shorts to his ankles and sank to his knees. His hot, wet mouth took him deep, and it was like liquid fire engulfing his cock. "Oh fuck, fuck." He held Harper's face steady while his hips thrust hard and fast. "There, right there," he croaked and came so hard, he lost his footing and had to grab Harper's shoulders.

Harper continued to suck and lick his shaft until he pushed at him.

"Too much, please."

Harper pulled him down and kissed him again, and Colson tasted his saltiness on Harper's tongue. Harper continued to kiss him, swallowing his moans, biting and sucking his lips, his neck and jaw.

"Need you," Harper whispered, and Colson's heart squeezed, knowing instinctually that Harper didn't say those words often.

Colson led Harper upstairs, where Harper peeled off his clothes and pulled Colson to him on the bed. He turned Colson over and kissed the globes of his ass, then spread them apart.

Colson shivered but stayed still. Harper stuck his tongue past his rim and the wet sucking sounds caused his cock to stiffen, and soon he was humping the bed, craving the friction on his dick, while Harper's slick tongue worked his hole.

"Don't stop, please. Don't ever stop." Harper fucked his hole with his fingers and mouth. "Oh, God." Colson writhed under Harper, and his dick throbbed out a smaller, almost painful climax.

He felt the thick, heavy length of Harper's shaft rub between his ass cheeks and thighs, Harper moving in quick, hard thrusts. Hot sticky liquid poured over the small of his back, and Harper released a gusty sigh and covered Colson's body with his.

"This was a surprise."

"*Mmm.* This was incredible." Harper kissed his neck, and Colson rolled him off so they faced each other.

"I meant it, though. You left me and sent a text that said, 'Thanks. I had fun.' "

Harper reached out and traced the tattoos on his chest with his fingertips. "I did have fun."

When people used to smoke, there would be ashtrays to smack them over the head. Now all he had was a plastic water bottle.

"Ow." Harper rubbed the side of his temple. "What'd you do that for?"

"For being an obtuse idiot. We have sex, and you leave and send a text I could get from my sushi delivery guy."

Harper raised a dark brow. "You have sex with your delivery person? I don't know about you, Delacourt."

This time he threw a pillow at Harper. "You know what I mean." Why did he get so damn flustered with Harper?

Because aside from him being an annoying idiot, you like him. A lot.

"No. I don't."

About to go off on him, Colson peered at Harper and shut his mouth. Harper was telling the truth. He thought that four-word text after their night together was fine. Colson thought hard about it and decided...maybe it was. They were two guys, with an insane sexual attraction, and they acted on it. It was...fun.

Why did it have to be anything else?

"You know what?" He shifted closer. "Forget about it. I don't feel like wasting time talking about that."

Harper's silvery-gray eyes were bottomless pools of light, and he brushed their lips together. "I don't feel like talking at all."

"What do you want?" he asked.

Harper's cock twitched and thickened against his thigh, and Colson shivered. Harper skimmed those long fingers over his face, mapping his jaw, his cheekbones and lips.

"I can't promise much. Or anything. I keep odd hours, and my time isn't my own."

A horrible thought crossed his mind. "Are you married or living with someone else?"

"Hell, no." Harper's absolute denial settled that question. "It's just that I don't want the same thing as you."

"How do you know what I want?" Colson nuzzled into Harper's neck, drowning in his scent. Jesus, he wanted to rub up all over him naked and have it soak into his pores. "Maybe I do."

"Yeah?" Harper nipped at his ear, his deep voice rumbling through Colson. "Tell me, Boy Scout. What do you want?"

"You."

A deliciously wicked smile curved Harper's lips. "Looks like we're on the same page." He lay flat and checked his watch. "I have to go."

Why? Stay with me. Where do you have to be at ten p.m. on a Saturday night?

"Sure," he said, keeping it light and easy. "You want to shower first? I know I have to." Visions of a wet, soapy Harper played like a fantasy in his mind.

"I'd better not. I'd just have to put my same smelly clothes on again."

Disappointed, he nodded. "Oh yeah, that makes sense."

From his place on the bed, he watched Harper get dressed. He stuck his feet into his sneakers and stood over him.

"I'll see you."

"Yeah, sure. See you." Colson slipped on his shorts.

"Don't forget to lock up and set your alarm."

He followed behind Harper and opened the front door. "I won't, Detective. Night."

Harper hesitated a moment, then kissed him on the lips. "Bye."

Colson watched him walk away and disappear into the night.

What the hell are you hiding, Harper Rose?

Like his first two bestsellers, this book flowed as if it wrote itself. Too keyed up to sleep, he stayed up well past two in the morning and wrote two chapters. Halfway through, he still hadn't decided if his detective would have a romantic relationship and sent an email to Luis to ask if he'd had a chance to beta read the chapters.

With that done, exhaustion hit like a brick wall, and he fell into bed. He awoke to the sun and his phone buzzing with a call from Hogan.

"Yeah, what?" He stretched.

"I didn't catch you in the middle of something—or someone—did I?"

Colson didn't know if Hogan was being annoying or hopeful.

"Ha-ha. Only a yawn. I'm still in bed." He squinted into the phone. "Ugh, it's almost eleven already?"

"Yeah. Time for you to get that lazy ass out of bed and come over for brunch. We've got a margarita pitcher with your name on it."

Keeping Hogan on the line, he checked his texts. Despite their conversation to keep it light between them, stupid him had hoped to have gotten a text from Harper, but his messages remained empty. And since he had nothing scheduled for the day, it was either stay in his house or hang out with Hogan.

"Okay, sure, why not?"

"Try not to overwhelm me with your enthusiasm."

"Yeah, yeah. See you soon."

He ended the call and glanced over at the empty side of the bed, then forced himself to get up and shower. No matter how much he liked it, Colson doubted Hogan and his family would appreciate him showing up smelling like sex, sweat, and Harper.

Of course, it didn't matter. As soon as Hogan opened the door, he busted out a big grin. "Had a good night?"

He'd tried to cover up the red spots on his neck, but damn Harper for having a thing about marking his throat. It was sexy as hell while happening, but now he looked like he'd been mauled.

"I don't know what you're talking about." He pushed past Hogan to hug Bea. "Hi, beautiful."

Her sparkling dark eyes danced. "Don't think you're going to play that game with me, mister. I know a hickey when I see one...or three."

"Can we not? Please?" He glared. "I came for margaritas and conversation and hopefully your fabulous eggs Benedict."

"All three are on the menu," she said, taking his hand. "We have the table on the deck set up."

They walked through the cheerful and sunny main floor of Hogan and Bea's home in Cobble Hill. Not too large, but not small either with three stories and a spacious backyard and deck, the house was his home away from home when he first started writing. It was one of the reasons he'd moved to the neighborhood. Hogan and Bea were more of a family than his own ever were.

The kids swarmed him, chattering about everything and nothing. He nodded and smiled at them, still disbelieving that his best friend had helped create two lives. Once outside, the kids left them to go play on the swings and slide set Hogan had put up. The large picnic table had the promised pitcher, a fruit salad, chips and guacamole, and a cheese board.

"Expecting a small army?" he joked.

Bea and Hogan exchanged glances, and he tensed. "What did you do?"

"Nothing. Really," Hogan insisted.

"Meaning?" He sighed. "You are the worst liar. Always have been. Who is he?"

"A very nice guy I work with," Bea rushed to explain. "I promise it's casual. He's about thirty, just got his PhD, and teaches the other first year psych class." Bea was a child psychologist and taught college students in the city.

"Would've been nice if you'd mentioned it earlier," he grumbled.

"So you could refuse?" Hogan glared at him. "You liked being a couple. We're just trying to help you out."

"Yeah, but maybe I'm not ready. Or maybe I don't want another relationship. I'd rather—"

"What? Fuck around?" Hogan tipped his chin toward him. "Is that what those marks on your neck are about?"

His annoyance had zero effect on his damn inability to keep from blushing. "That's not your business."

"I'm making it mine. You go from being a monk to...whatever that is."

"Nothing. I already said, not your business." He knew Hogan would frown upon his booty-call relationship with Harper. He didn't understand it himself, but that didn't stop him from wanting Harper to text him again.

"Anyway"–Bea shot Hogan a warning glance–"Danny will be here soon. No pressure, just see how it goes."

"Please don't ever sandbag me." He crunched some chips and washed them down with more of his margarita. "I'll be nice."

Bea looked relieved. "Hogan tells me you're writing a new book?"

He sipped his drink. "It's coming along. I'm debating a new angle to draw in more readers."

"Yeah?" Hogan popped some cheese into his mouth. "Like what?"

"A romance. Between the detective and–"

"A suspect?" Hogan grinned.

"No," he snapped. "That would be unethical of the detective."

"But it would make it juicy," Bea said. "Forbidden love and all that jazz." She grew animated. "You'd have the stress of solving the case and the stress of people finding out about the relationship."

He stared at her. "You sound like you read that kind of stuff."

"Yes. I do." She raised her chin. "That kind of stuff, as you call it, is an almost billion-dollar industry run by women, read mostly by women, so of course it doesn't get the respect it deserves. Authors I read are also lawyers, doctors, engineers, teachers, housewives...and I sense your disdain for some reason." Her eyes flashed. "If you plan to write about something, don't denigrate it. We'll see right through your attempt to cash in. There's nothing bad or trashy about writing love stories. Or wanting to find love."

"Ooo...kay. Jeez." He put up his hands. "I didn't mean to set off a firestorm. I'm not against love. I'm just seeing how it's all going to work out. The romance angle came to me as I was writing it, and I want to explore it."

Hogan chuckled. "I love it when she gets passionate and professorial."

"I just want Colson to realize it's not a joke to write about." She sipped her drink.

"I'm realizing it. I promise. I even have a beta reader who's going to let me know what he thinks of the romance—someone who's read my other books. He'll tell me if it fits in."

"How about letting me read it?" Bea suggested.

He wrinkled his brow. "You don't like crime thrillers or murders."

She patted his hand and refilled his drink. "For you, I'll make an exception. I've read tons of romance. I can tell you if it works for me or not."

"Even if it's two men?" At her raised brows, he explained. "My detective may have a romantic interest in another man."

"Well...I don't see why not. Can you?"

"No. And it's only a subplot. Right now, just thoughts and feelings."

Hogan gazed at him thoughtfully. "What brought this on? You've never been interested in that kind of storyline."

"The industry is completely different from when I last published. As Bea said, romance is huge, and I'm looking to attract new readers."

"Send it to me tonight. I'll let you know." The doorbell rang. "Remember." Bea wagged a finger at him, and he scowled.

"Yeah, yeah. Nice. I'll be nice."

He didn't want nice. He wanted…Harper.

"So who's the guy?" Hogan asked.

"Bea said—"

"Not Danny. The one who had you for dinner last night."

Recalling the animal-like noises he made when Harper ate him out, Colson pressed his lips together. Hard.

"So it's like that." Hogan rose to his feet as Bea approached with his setup, and Colson followed his lead. "At least give this guy a chance."

Bea stepped out on the deck and made the introductions. "Colson, this is Danny Forman. Danny, this is Colson Delacourt."

"Hi, Danny. Great to meet you."

Big, blond, and blue-eyed, Danny Forman extended a hand. "You as well. Bea, this is for you." He presented a bottle of wine. "I remembered you like Chardonnay, and this is a great year." He smiled at him and Hogan. "My ex was a sommelier. He taught me everything I need to know about wine."

Colson needed another margarita. It was going to be a long afternoon.

CHAPTER TWELVE

Busy tonight?

Harper chewed his lip, waiting for a response.

What the hell was he doing?

It was six o'clock, and Nolan had left a few minutes ago. He'd offered Harper a ride home, but he'd declined, claiming he needed to finish up the reports he'd let slide for a few days.

That was his bullshit excuse, and he was sticking to it.

The truth was, he'd typed out the text and had been waiting for Nolan to leave to hit Send. It had been three days since he'd been with Colson, and he was hoping they could get together. Luis had texted that David was at a birthday party for one of his friends in his therapy group.

No need to rush home. Go out and have some fun.

Then he'd added a winky face, making Harper roll his eyes. "Everyone has an opinion on my personal life."

His phone buzzed, and he grabbed it to read the text, not even bothering to deny the curl of excitement in his belly at Colson's answer.

I am now.

Whistling to himself, he slipped on his suit jacket and closed his computer. He left the precinct and walked outside, barely noticing the heat or humidity. All he wanted was to be in Colson's house, trading barbs and banter, knowing he could reach out and touch him at any time. After a day filled with nothing but negativity and bad news, he needed to grab whatever joy he could find, and while he loved being with David, the few times with Colson had set off a craving in his blood for something more.

He walked up the steps to the town house, and before he had a chance to ring the bell or knock, the door opened. Colson stood there in only a pair of boxers, a tempting smile on his handsome face.

"I figured why bother, since we're just going to get naked anyway?"

Harper's cock swelled, and his breath grew short. "I need to lock up my gun."

"Come with me."

He followed Colson to an office, where a free-standing safe stood in the corner. "I keep my papers in here. It's the best I can do." He opened it, and Harper slipped his gun inside, and watched Colson lock it. When he stood, Harper claimed his mouth in a kiss. Colson responded by pulling off Harper's suit jacket and undoing his tie.

"I'm glad you weren't busy." Harper slipped his hands past the waistband of Colson's boxers to knead his round ass. God, he was perfect.

Colson flung the tie aside and undid his shirt, pressing kisses to his throat and collarbone. "I'd just finished when I got your text."

"*Mmm*, lucky me for perfect timing." He yanked Colson's boxers off while Colson undid his belt and pants. He kicked off his shoes and let the clothes fall to his ankles.

"I think we're both pretty damn lucky." Colson rolled his hips, their erections rubbing. "I was wondering if I was going to see you again this week." His fingers played along the length of Harper's dick, squeezing and rubbing. He gazed at Colson's slick hand fisting his dick and groaned.

"You keep doing that, and you can see me anytime." He licked his fingers and slid one into Colson, followed by a second, pumping them in and out of his hole.

"Upstairs," Colson whispered, and Harper hoped his legs weren't too shaky to walk, but he made it up the steps. They climbed into bed, and Harper found himself under Colson, who gazed at him with a tender expression. "I'm really glad you're here."

"I am too." Harper reached up to cup his face, and he guided their lips to meet in a kiss. Their tongues swept together in velvety hot slides, and Colson nipped his lower lip. He trailed kisses over his torso, swirling in his navel, and licking up the precome from the swollen head of his dick.

"Taste so good," he breathed, and the hot air over his sensitive flesh drove him wild with longing. Seeing his dark head between his thighs, the muscles flexing under the colorful tattoos, Harper moaned and tangled his hands in Colson's waves.

"I need you. Please."

Colson gave a final lick up the length of his shaft, then took a condom from the night table and rolled it down Harper's dick. "Fuck me hard."

Harper watched as Colson rose over him, and slowly, inch by inch, took him into his body. His head flung back, teeth catching his lip, and a face filled with bliss, it was the most sensual and erotic sight he'd ever witnessed. Being inside Colson was more than a joining of two bodies—Harper could feel the tight walls suck him in, making them one.

"Oh, God." Harper sighed and held Colson's ass in his hands as he rode Harper's dick, rising and falling ferociously until Harper pulled out and got Colson on all fours.

"This way, baby."

Colson spread his legs and arched his spine. "Fill me. Come on," he begged. Blue eyes pinned him, blazing with lust. "Fuck me. I want you so fucking bad."

Harper slid his cock in, bit by bit, pushing halfway in, kissing and nipping Colson's neck before thrusting hard and at a furious pace. Colson wailed and rocked his hips into Harper while frantically working his cock.

The smell of sex and sweat rose around them, and Harper lost himself in a dizzying whirlpool of pleasure where the only thing that mattered was him and Colson. He held on to Colson's hips, plunging in and out of his silky heat, knowing the exact moment Colson came as he jerked and twitched beneath him.

"Take it. You want it, don't you?" He sank his teeth into Colson's neck and rolled his hips, driving deep, burying his cock to the root, even as Colson moaned. "You're incredible."

"Fuck me, Harper. Oh God, please."

Hearing Colson beg for more even as he came spiraled him to a level of desire he'd never reached. His dick swelled and throbbed, held within the confines of Colson's hot, tight ass, and his climax rushed over him, leaving nothing but scorching heat in its wake. He closed his eyes, his whole body trembling. Colson sighed, and Harper rubbed his cheek against his sweat-soaked nape.

"I can't move just yet."

"You think I can with you on top of me?" Colson chuckled, the movement stimulating Harper's overly sensitive dick, and he hissed with the pleasure-pain.

"Wiseass," he grumbled with a smile he couldn't keep off his lips.

"Perfect ass, amazing ass, and now adding wiseass to the list." Colson shifted, and Harper slid out of him.

"You're all that and more." Harper knotted the condom and tossed it into the trash. He gazed down at Colson lying naked and deliciously rumpled, blue eyes heavy and lips kiss-swollen.

Mine, he wanted to say. *What you are is mine.*

But Harper knew he didn't have the right to make that claim. Colson wasn't his. He couldn't be because Harper couldn't give a single piece of himself away. Everything he had was to make sure David would always be protected.

"Can you stay?" Colson propped up on his elbows. Refusal sprang to his lips, and perhaps Colson saw it because he rushed to add, "It's only seven thirty. I doubt you'll turn into a pumpkin before midnight."

"Move over, Boy Scout," he growled, and Colson grinned.

They'd dozed for an hour when Harper woke up to a gurgling in his ear. "Hungry?" he teased, and Colson turned an adorable shade of pink.

"Well, yeah. I worked all day, straight through breakfast without lunch. Then you came over and attacked me."

Harper snickered. "You answered the door half-naked. You knew exactly what you were doing." He pinched Colson's ass, earning a yelp. "If you wave something pretty in my face, I'm going to touch it." He squeezed a cheek. "Or kiss it."

Colson rubbed his cheek against Harper's chest, and contentment flowed through him like warm honey. He wished...he wished he could split himself in two and be both the brother and lover he wanted to be.

"Since I picked sushi last time and that wasn't your thing, why don't you pick tonight?"

"How about burgers and fries?"

"Sounds good. Make mine well-done."

"Okay. So now I know that aside from having a fabulous ass, you like to chew shoe leather." Harper pulled up the delivery app, found the burger place they always ordered from at home, and put in Colson's address. "All done."

"You think you're cute, huh?" Colson pretended to glare as he slipped on a pair of boxers and pulled on a T-shirt. Damn, he hated Colson covering up those gorgeous tats. If he had his way, the man would walk around naked all the time in front of him.

"Nah," Harper shrugged. "I know I am. My clothes are downstairs. You know, in that room where you couldn't wait to get me naked?"

Colson rolled his eyes. "How do you and that massive ego fit through the door?"

"That's not all that's massive. I see you walking funny." Harper winked and cackled before taking off and running. He found his clothes and grimaced at the wrinkled state of his shirt and pants. "Good thing I have other suits."

"Water or beer?" Colson asked.

"Water, please." Colson took out a pitcher, filled it with ice, then water, and poured them each some. "How did you decide to become a police officer and then a detective?"

Harper took his glass but didn't drink. "I don't really know. I grew up with a lot of cops and firefighters, and at different points in my life, they helped me. I didn't have the grades or desire to go to medical or law school, and I figured what the hell, I'll take the police exam. I passed, and the rest is history."

Hopefully that explanation would suffice. When David was injured, so many police officers had responded and stayed with his parents at the scene and checked on his progress at the hospital, they became very close. Some had brought them food and arranged for him to be picked up after school and taken to the hospital to see David. At Christmas they'd brought gifts and a tree, as his parents had neither the strength nor the desire to celebrate the holiday. The officers became like a second family to him, and joining the force was his way of giving back.

But Colson was no fool, and those blue eyes pierced right through him, searching to the bottom of his shattered soul. Luck was on his side, as the bell rang.

"Food's here." He smiled and took a sip of his water. "I'll put out the napkins."

Colson shot him another searching look, then left him. Harper blew out a relieved breath and had the place settings on the kitchen island by the time Colson returned with their food. As they ate, he decided to do a little personal digging of his own.

"So I have to ask—what's behind the name Colson? You have to admit it's not something you hear every day."

Colson made a face. "It was my mother's maiden name. A few people call me Cole, because let's face it, Colson is a mouthful."

"I know that. I have it on firsthand knowledge." He finished his burger. "Speaking of mouths…"

"Were we?" Colson asked with a wicked grin and a twinkle in his eye. "I thought we were talking about my name."

"Be quiet, I'm trying to segue." His hunger sated, Harper pulled Colson's stool over with his foot until they were close enough to share the air between them. "Your mouth has a bit of ketchup, right there." He leaned in and licked the tiny dip at the top. "*Mmm.* Delicious."

"Thank you for being my personal napkin," Colson teased.

"I'm not finished yet." He slid his tongue in to meet Colson's, and they sat kissing as the sun set outside.

"I should go."

"You should?" Colson bit his earlobe, and his dick filled. "I don't think so."

"Yeah, I really should." But he didn't move. He couldn't leave. Not yet.

"Why? You could spend the night."

One last kiss to Colson's sweet mouth, and he rose to his feet. "I can't. I've got to get the rest of my clothes and my gun. Could you open the safe, please?"

Colson slid off the stool, his mouth set in a grim line. "Can I ask you something?"

"Ask away." He shoved his hands into his pockets.

"You said you're not married, but...are you involved with someone else? Getting out of a relationship? I'd rather know than not."

Harper frowned. "No. I'm not like that. I'm not sleeping with anyone else."

Colson opened the safe, and Harper reached in for his gun. Fully dressed, he could still see doubt etched on Colson's face.

"I don't know what else I can say. I'm not married, and I'm not with anyone else but you. I don't want to be." He didn't know how else to let Colson know he wanted only him.

But Colson was stubborn and wouldn't let go. "Yet you can't stay the night. Do you have young children at home to take care of? Is that it?"

Little by little Colson was chipping away at the walls protecting his damaged heart, but Harper still couldn't give in to what might be nothing more than physical desire. Several nights of amazing sex weren't enough to let Colson into the tumult of his life. He sensed Colson was a good man, not someone to play with his affections, but recalling how Ronnie had fooled him so badly and upset their family dynamic, Harper still rebuffed him. "No. I don't have children. Is not spending the night together a deal breaker?"

"I just don't understand. We've had sex—you can't be more intimate with someone than sharing your body—yet you won't share my bed. Make it make sense."

"I-I can't. This is how it has to be." The damage Ronnie had done to his trust in people might be the death knell of anything possible with Colson, but Harper couldn't make himself take the chance to let Colson into the most important part of his life. "I'll talk to you."

His head hung low, he was halfway to the door when Colson called out to him.

"Harper?" He peered over his shoulder. "Feel like getting dinner soon? In a restaurant?"

And despite the serious conversation they'd had, Harper couldn't resist teasing him. "Are you asking me on a date, Boy Scout?"

Colson made it to his side in three long strides. "After everything we've done together, you're still calling me that?"

Harper debated and tapped his cheek. "*Hmm.* Well, their motto is 'Be prepared.' And you are very well prepared."

"And you're impossible."

Laughing, Harper opened the door. "The answer is yes. Text me ahead of time so I can check my shift. And by the way, I prefer Colson. The full mouthful. Good night."

He could hear Colson laughing as he locked the door behind him.

CHAPTER THIRTEEN

"I have to tell you, Cole, initially I wasn't sure what to make of this new book when you told me about the romance angle."

It had been over three years since he'd last sat in his agent's office. He'd been Ned Thatcher's first author, and the two of them had become close, working long hours together to make sure his debut novel was ready. Once he'd sold it for foreign rights and hit all the bestseller lists, Ned had acquired other thriller authors in his roster, but the two of them had a special relationship, and Colson knew Ned would always give him a straight-up opinion, whether he wanted to hear it or not.

"No? How come?"

Ned made a face. "Come on. You write gruesome shit. I was leery that people would want to read about someone thinking about sex after viewing dismembered bodies."

Thinking of Harper and all he'd seen, Colson shrugged. "I don't know. I think it's life. Sex and love can often play against violence and the ugly."

Ned narrowed his eyes. "Are you speaking from experience?"

Dammit. He should've known Ned would want more than a cursory response. Colson shifted in his chair. "Well, yeah. My house and a neighbor's were broken into, and I've become friendly with a detective on the case."

A tiny grin worked its way to Ned's lips. "Oh, yeah? Friendly as in getting inside info for the book?"

"Uh, well, we haven't really gotten to that yet."

Ned whooped. "Is that because you're too busy getting it on? Halle-fucking-lujah."

Colson stared at him. "Whoa. Okay. I had no idea you were so invested in my personal life."

Ned grew serious. "I hated seeing you struggle. Burnout is the worst, and you're so talented, I know you have more in you. It was Evan's fucking around, am I right?"

God, he hated dissecting his personal life, even if it was with someone he knew well. He might be right to attribute part of the problem to Evan, but it was more than that. His first two books had flowed from his mind to the page, and when he'd struggled with the third, he listened to the demons in his head whispering, *not good enough, not strong enough, not man enough.* His parents had shut the door on him, and his grandparents were gone. It was easier to retreat than fight those ugly internal voices.

"I mean, I don't know. It was definitely a combination of a lot of different things that sucked my confidence dry. But this thing is only casual. Nothing serious." Although he seriously wanted to see Harper again and not have to wait a week.

"Whatever it is, I'm all for it. The more I read of the story, the more I liked it. I could tell there was something different in your writing. I don't think I've ever read emotion from you like this." Ned met his eyes. "I like it. Yeah, your detectives have had personal issues, but romance, even if it's closed-door or sweet, whatever the heck the industry is calling it, adds depth and another dimension to the plot."

There was nothing like a little validation to shore up one's confidence, and Colson wasn't above lapping up the praise.

"I'm glad you like it. I hope the readers respond the same way."

"Being honest?" All joking aside, Ned put on his agent hat. "I won't lie. Some readers won't appreciate a romantic relationship."

"Because it's gay?" he challenged.

Ned snorted. "More likely that it's any type of romance. You've never been into writing that genre." A slow smile crept over his face. "I know you're saying it's casual and blah, blah, blah, but maybe you're feeling things you haven't in a long time, and it's something you want to celebrate in your new book."

"Slow down, lover boy. I haven't put out anything new in three years. I need something to draw in new readers, and romance is a huge seller. I'm itching to try something new, and this came so naturally to me. Hogan's wife, Bea, read it, and she said it worked for her."

Assessing his response, Ned seemed to accept it. "Okay. You know I represent all genres, especially from an own voices author, and I have to admit, I'm enjoying this book even more with the romance you've put in like breadcrumbs. It humanizes the detective and makes him relatable on a different level than just another police procedural. Tell me more about how it's going to play out."

Relieved that Ned understood, Colson was happy to share. "As I'm seeing it, the two men will work together to solve the case, while at the same time filling the emotional space inside each other. One's never experienced love, and the other is recovering from a failed relationship."

"And is there going to be sex in the book? Just thinking ahead to marketing."

Colson pondered a moment. "I don't think so. It's not necessary. I can show the physical part of their relationship without getting explicit. It's really how they learn to interact with each other emotionally."

"Good, good." Ned took some notes. "It needs some polishing here and there and a little work on them evolving from more than a physical relationship. Right now it sounds like they're basically in it for the sex, and I'm not sure how that's going to work with your readers." He peered over his glasses. "I'm sensing this is more true to life than fiction. You don't have to answer."

From his burning cheeks, Colson knew he didn't need to. Ned knew already.

"Now, tell me about this new guy. A detective, huh?" Ned's smile broadened. "Nothing like a man in uniform. Or someone who has a big...gun."

Groaning, this time he buried his burning face in his arms. "I can't believe you said that."

Ned laughed. "Yes, you can."

Colson raised his gaze to the ceiling. "God, you're right. I've forgotten your sense of humor. The crazy thing is, he thought I was planning a murder and almost arrested me for trying to kill my neighbor."

"You've got to be shitting me."

"Nope." As he relayed the story of his first meeting with Harper, Ned's face ran the gamut of expressions, from shocked to incredulous and finally amused.

"That is one hell of a story, and it belongs in a book, because no one would believe it in real life."

Colson could joke about it now. "You're telling me. And every time we've met since then, there's been this strange...attraction. At first I didn't let myself think too much about it."

"But eventually you did, and *boom*, huh?" Ned snickered.

He and Ned had always talked freely. They were of a similar age, and Ned had grown up in the neighboring town of Westport, Connecticut. He understood how Colson had grown up and why he'd run away from that life.

"Yeah, well, whatever. We hit it off. But like I said, we're not in a relationship. We see each other when we can."

Ned shrugged. "It's okay to experiment and step outside your comfort zone. If this booty-call arrangement works for you, don't sweat it."

"Okay, well, getting back to the book," he said, steering the conversation away from his personal life, "I'm hoping to have it finished within a few months. I have someone giving it a thorough read-through chapter by chapter."

Ned nodded his approval. "Sounds good. When it's ready, send it to me, and I'll give you my take." He seemed to hesitate, and Colson braced himself. "I'm happy you're writing again. I've missed working with you. I have plenty of other authors who can write and have great sales, but you were my first. You'll always be special to me."

"Damn you for being so nice," Colson pretend-grumbled. "And thanks. It's been a hard road of return, but I think I'm finally on my way." Knowing Ned had always been straight with him, Colson was curious to get his opinion on Harper. "Can I ask you something?"

"Fire away." Ned checked his notes.

"It's not about the book. It's personal. About my situation with the detective." He couldn't help it. Harper not spending the night bugged him, and Colson wanted a second opinion.

Ned set the computer mouse aside. "I'm all yours. What's up?"

"What would you think if you were with someone and they said they couldn't spend the night, ever?"

"I'd say they were married," Ned answered promptly and frowned at the implication. "Is that what's happening with you and the detective?"

"Yeah, but he swears he's not married, not in a relationship, and has no children. All he says is that it's complicated."

"Sounds fishy to me. And you believe him when he says he's not married?"

"I don't know why, but I do. Am I a fool?"

Ned sighed. "No, of course not. But you might be willing to give him more of the benefit of the doubt because he's the first person you've been with since Evan and you're lonely."

Colson's smile was wry. "You mean I'm a sucker."

Ned didn't laugh. "No. And there's obviously something there that you find worth pursuing. But you've always been too trusting. That's why you have me, to run interference for you, at least when it comes to your books." Colson could see Ned's mind spinning.

"Does he only want to see you directly after work? That's a dead giveaway."

"No, that's the thing. We've seen each other on the weekends *and* during the week. One time he stayed until around two in the morning, then left."

None of it made sense to Colson, and he knew there was something Harper deliberately wasn't telling him. The little he did know of Harper, if he pushed too hard, Harper wouldn't push back. He'd simply walk away.

And losing Harper wasn't a risk Colson was willing to take.

Ned steepled his fingers in front of his face, and Colson waited. He'd always appreciated Ned's insights. He'd been the first to suggest—gently—that no, his books weren't a fluke because he was stuck on a blank page. The success he'd had was so unexpected, and the resulting pressure to perform played tricks with his head. Ned had told him to take as much time as he needed to figure out how to breathe again.

"I think...you like this man. More than like. You're interested in him. You're not one to have sex so easily, so the fact that you're willing to accept his terms means you see something worthwhile in him and possibly something growing between you." He paused. "Aside from what has to be great sex—because let's face it, that's what you're *not* telling me but has to be true, otherwise you'd tell him to take a hike." He grinned, and Colson fervently wished the floor would open up and swallow him. "But all kidding aside, you must feel like there's potential for something more permanent with him. Am I right?"

"I don't know. It's funny. We started off on the wrong foot, and yet for some reason, we keep returning to each other. When he leaves, I say to myself, 'Next time I'm going to say no.' " He sighed, frustrated at being so weak. "But somehow no becomes yes."

Ned's eyes were shrewd. "You know, there are tropes in romance for a reason. People laugh, but it's true. And two of the favorites are enemies to lovers and lust to love. Think about it."

He was about to ask Ned what the hell he was talking about, but they were interrupted by a call. Ned made a face. "It's the president of the agency. I have to take this. I'll call you after I've read the manuscript a second time, with a more critical eye. The first time is to see if it hooks me. Enjoy yourself with the detective, and don't get too caught up in the hows and whys. Eventually it will either run its course, or you'll find out the reason behind his secrecy. In the meantime, have fun. You deserve it." He winked, and Colson left with a lot to think about.

During the car ride home, he sent Harper a text.

Dinner tomorrow night?

He didn't receive an answer until he was home.

My tour ends at eight. Is that okay?

Colson sighed. Harper couldn't be with someone else yet come to him directly from work.

Yeah. How about Italian?

He named a restaurant in Dumbo with a view of the river.

Sounds good. Meet u there about 8:30.

OK

Dinner in public was safe. No getting naked within five minutes of seeing each other.

"This is nice." Harper glanced around the restaurant. They'd gotten a prime seat by the window, where they could watch the twinkling lights on the bridge and appreciate the Manhattan skyline. "I don't usually get out for dinner."

Colson sipped his wine. "No? You eat at home every night? You must be a good cook."

Harper finished chewing a piece of bread. "I'm usually too tired."

Their server appeared, and he ordered the eggplant parmigiana while Harper ordered the rigatoni Bolognese, and they split an appetizer of fried zucchini.

"I hadn't noticed." Colson grinned. "You seem to have plenty of stamina when you come by."

Harper's eyes gleamed in the flickering candlelight. "I guess the thought of you naked gives me superpowers."

Colson choked on the wine. "Jesus," he muttered, but he couldn't deny the thrill that shot through him at Harper's wolfish grin.

"I will admit that as hot as you are without clothes on, you're looking pretty damn fine tonight." Harper's gaze devoured him, and Colson shivered but held strong.

"You don't look half bad yourself, considering you've been chasing bad guys all day." Colson figured turnabout was fair play, and he ran an appreciative eye over Harper. He wore a well-fitted charcoal suit with a blue-and-white checked shirt and a bright-blue silk tie that brought out the icy blue in his glittering gaze.

"Do you like being a detective better than a beat cop?" he asked.

"A uni? Yeah. I wouldn't want to be out on the street these days. I'm glad I'm not in Homicide, though."

"Are you in a special division? I've worked with some detectives in Major Case and Homicide when I was researching for my books."

Their appetizer came, and more wine was poured. Harper crunched on a piece of zucchini. "I'm in Central Robbery, which handles a wide variety of cases, and I was lucky to be able to get assigned to a precinct near my home. Once I gain more experience, I can move if I want, but right now I'm fine where I am." He stared out the window. "I've seen enough death in my life."

Stricken by the sight of what he believed to be tears glistening in Harper's eyes, Colson covered Harper's hand with his. "Hey. I'm sorry. I didn't mean to bring up sad memories."

Harper turned, showing him a face filled with so much pain, it hurt his heart. But then a hesitant smile curved his lips, and he turned his palm up to slide his fingers with Colson's. "Maybe it's time to create some new ones. We can start after dinner?"

His intention was to have a night of talk and discovery. There was so much more Colson wanted to learn about him, but it was impossible with Harper's hand in his. His touch warmed every part of Colson numbed by his own loss and pain. They'd taken a first step tonight, and he wanted miles more.

"Come home with me."

CHAPTER FOURTEEN

Days later, he couldn't stop thinking about that night. They'd gone home after dinner and hadn't even made it upstairs before he'd gotten Colson naked and riding his dick on the living-room couch. After, he'd sucked Colson off and spent another hour licking every patch of skin, inhaling his scent, imprinting the taste of him on his tongue to last him until the next time they met.

They'd finally made it upstairs and fallen asleep. He'd awoken with a start and gotten dressed, then stood by the bed, watching Colson sleep. For the first time, he regretted having to leave.

And so that afternoon, he'd done the unthinkable.

"Could you work late and give David dinner?"

A wide smile broke over Luis's face. "No problem, man. It's a beautiful night. We'll take a little drive and come home and watch the Mets."

He hated making Luis work overtime—he gave them so much already—but the need to see Colson was like a fever in his blood. He and Nolan had made some headway on their cases, and a few of their perps had gotten stiff sentences, so Harper counted it as a win and wanted to celebrate.

He took a chance and picked up a bottle of wine, some sushi for Colson, and teriyaki for himself. It didn't occur to him to text ahead of time and he cursed his stupidity when he rang the bell and no one answered.

He set the bag on the stoop and texted.

Hungry? Open the door.

Too late he remembered Colson's warning that he didn't pay attention to his phone while writing.

"Dumbass idea," he grumbled and picked up the food. He could always make the excuse to Luis that they knocked off early. Halfway down the steps, the door opened.

"Harper?"

He stopped and turned around. "In the flesh."

"What're you doing here?" Barefoot and looking as if he'd been up all night, Colson stood in the doorway. His hair was messy, he was unshaven and dressed in a white T-shirt and boxers.

And desirable as fuck.

"I brought you dinner."

Colson rubbed his face. "Dinner? What time is it?"

Harper grinned as he retraced his steps. "After six." He leaned in and kissed Colson under his ear. Colson's breath hitched. "You'd better eat first. You're going to need your strength for what I've got planned." The silky flutter of Colson's lashes teased his cheek, and he continued to press kisses to his face.

"If you keep doing that, I can't be responsible for what happens," Colson murmured but leaned in closer, and a very hard, thick dick pressed against Harper's belly. "But I'll give you a hint. It would definitely get us arrested if we continue in public."

Harper pulled him inside. "Don't worry. I have an in."

The door slammed behind them.

"I don't know about you, but I'm ready for the weekend." Nolan flicked on his computer and took a long swig of his coffee.

"You know it."

Guilty over not giving David the attention he was used to and having Luis put in too much overtime, Harper had stayed home the rest of the week. Colson had texted him a few times, and though he longed to get together, Harper had declined, claiming work had piled up.

You let me know.

But Harper didn't. He went silent, figuring it was for the best. He shouldn't want what he couldn't have, so it was better to end it now, before that ache in his chest grew any stronger and he did something stupid, like fall for Colson.

Several days passed without Colson texting. Harper figured he must've grown tired of the excuses and moved on. That put him in a lousy mood, and he buried himself in his work to try and forget the sexy Colson Delacourt.

"Let's get to it," Harper said. "Bad guys are having a party at our expense. New gang, old story. I thought our leads would pan out. I'm pissed."

"Same. They never learn, do they?" Nolan read the reports. "Punching people for their phones and purses, pushing them over while they get their keys out to open their front doors...man. Sometimes I wonder." Nolan stared out into the distance, and Harper set his cup on the desk.

"Wonder what?" Unease settled in his chest.

Nolan glanced around, then wheeled his chair over to Harper's desk. "Have you ever thought of hanging it up when you hit your twenty years?"

A chill ran through him. Nolan was forty-five, ten years older than him. "Are you? You've only been a detective for four years."

Nolan's mouth drooped. "Ay, there's the rub."

He chuckled. "You're quoting Shakespeare in the squad room. I bet that's a first. His smile faded. "You really want to leave?"

"Every once in a while I think about it, but I love the job. Just sometimes all the shit gets me down. I think, why bother? Then it's like, oh, because these assholes think they're smarter than us. And it makes me want to collar every last one of them."

Relieved, Harper laughed. "Yeah. I get it. But nothing gives me more pleasure than slapping the cuffs on them. Except seeing them go away for eight to twenty-five."

It was Nolan's turn to laugh. "Now that's a problem if collaring bad guys is your only pleasure." He eyed Harper, who braced himself, knowing what was coming. "Are you sure you're not interested in one of Gina's friends? She knows a guy–"

Alarmed, Harper cut him off. "No, it's fine. I'm not interested."

"Why?"

"I'm just...not." Avoiding Nolan's penetrating gaze, he clicked to bring up the case files. "We have three witnesses to interview and surveillance video to watch. You want to handle it together or split it up?"

"Together." Nolan knocked his foot. "You're not going to dump hours of staring at videos on me. Nice try."

Smirking, Harper drank his coffee.

At six, he powered down the computer, just as his cell phone rang. Seeing it was Luis, his heart pounded.

"Harper?"

"Yeah, what's wrong? Is David okay?"

"Chill out. He's fine. In a great mood, in fact. One of the therapists brought pizza, so he's already eaten dinner."

His panic attack averted, Harper blew out a breath and ran a hand through his sweaty hair. "Oh, great. Thanks for telling me. It's been a long day."

"Just letting you know, in case you wanted to make plans, you don't have to rush home."

"Thanks." His desk phone rang. "I've got a call. I've got to go."

"Take as long as you want. I'm not going anywhere."

God help him if Luis ever did.

He set his phone on the desk and answered the call. "Detective Rose."

"Hello, Detective. This is Millie Johnson. Do you remember me?"

He smiled into the receiver. "Of course. How are you? Is everything okay?"

"Are you finished for the day?"

"I was about to go home, yes."

It was a struggle not to text Colson, and an ache formed in his chest, knowing it was for the best, but the bleak loneliness waiting for him at home was almost too much to bear.

"I was wondering if you could come over."

"Is something wrong?"

"I'm not sure, but I came home from the bank, and something didn't feel right." Her voice lowered. "I think I was watched."

He stood and stuffed his phone, keys, and wallet into his pockets. "I'll be right over. Do not let anyone inside. Do you understand?"

"Yes. I hope it's nothing."

"Me too," he said grimly.

The streets were crowded–Thursday summer nights tended to start the weekend–and Harper threaded his way around people. He reached Millie's house and saw her peeking through the lace curtains. She beamed when she saw him on the steps.

"Thank you for coming so quickly." She peered over his shoulder, then closed the door behind him. "Come into the kitchen. It's very cozy in there."

He followed her and sat at the island. A plate of cookies was set in the middle with a vase of fresh roses. It reminded him of his mother–she'd loved baking, and after school or baseball practice, she'd always have something freshly made, either cookies or brownies. Enough for all his friends. Grief threatened to overtake him—the last time he'd had the team over, David had pestered him, and he'd begged his mother to get rid of the brat.

If only...

"Why don't you tell me what happened?" His voice was tight and scratchy.

"Would you like a cup of tea?"

"No, I'm fine." From his past encounters with her, Harper knew he'd need to finesse his questioning, as Millie liked to go off on tangents. "Now, about what you told me on the phone? You think you were followed?"

"Yes. I took out money, like I do every week, and came home. I had a feeling...like someone was following me. I would stop occasionally and look around." She lowered her voice as if someone was eavesdropping. "It was creepy."

"And? Did you see anything? Anyone?"

"Well...yes. There were a lot of people on the street coming home from work."

He bit back his frustration and placed a smile on his face. "So why do you think you were being followed?"

She met his gaze. "I've always been told I have very good senses."

"I'm sure you do, but it's hard to investigate on just your senses. I will look around outside, if you don't mind, to see if I can find anything to indicate someone was on your property." The sun hadn't set yet, so he should be able to see any footprints or other evidence of trespass.

"Thank you. I appreciate it." She opened the kitchen door, which led to the yard. "You can get to the garden this way."

He put on his nitrile gloves and began a thorough inspection of the deck. Nothing. He checked each step and took photos of the footprints, and at the bottom of the steps, in the shadow of an evergreen, he picked up a cigarette butt. Millie had been watching him, her head peeking out the window. He held it up.

"I know this doesn't belong to you."

"Definitely not."

He slid it into an evidence bag he pulled from his suit jacket pocket. "I'll take it and have forensics run it. Do you have gardeners?"

"Well, yes, but I've told them constantly there is no smoking. It's bad for my roses."

There went that theory. He'd bet his shield it was a gardener.

After twenty minutes of eyeballing grass and finding nothing, he gave up.

"I'm happy to report I don't see anything."

"Oh, that's good. I'm glad. Now please come inside."

"Well, I need to check the front."

"Oh. You can't get to it from the garden."

He traipsed up the steps of the deck, through the house, and out the front door. Like he did in the backyard, Harper searched through the bushes.

"Hey, what're you doing?" a familiar voice shouted. "I'm gonna call the cops."

Harper straightened up and faced Colson, who stood on the sidewalk at the base of the staircase to Millie's house. At his side was a big, good-looking, blond man. Harper crossed his arms and leaned against the brownstone's balustrade. Well, now. Was Colson on a date?

"Excuse me?" He smirked. "I think it's okay, don't you?"

Colson flushed. "Oh, hi."

"Oh, hi," he repeated and waited. Colson obviously felt uncomfortable, but Harper didn't understand why. They weren't a couple and had made no promises. Still, Blondie needed to put a little space between himself and Colson. He was practically on top of him.

"Th-this is Danny. Danny, this is Harper."

"Detective Rose," he corrected. "I'm here at Ms. Johnson's request."

"I see. We won't keep you, then."

Danny-boy smiled at him. "Nice to meet you."

The pleasure was all Danny's.

He watched them walk across the street and up the steps to Colson's town house. His jaw tightened. He and Colson might not be dating, but that didn't mean he liked knowing Colson was going to have sex with someone. Danny-boy had that gleam in his eyes, and who could blame him? Colson was hot as fuck in his button-down with the sleeves rolled up, showing off those tats and sexy, strong forearms. His faded jeans looked painted on to his thick thighs and fabulous ass.

"Detective?" Millie's voice pierced through his haze of angry lust.

"What? I'm sorry. I don't seem to have found anything out of the ordinary."

"Come back into the house, please."

Colson had found someone else. It was what Harper had wanted...wasn't it? He'd made it clear there was nothing between them but sex, so seeing Colson with another man, someone who could give him all the time and attention he deserved, shouldn't hurt. He shouldn't want to punch the guy in the nose and tell him to get away from Colson. That he was with Harper.

God, I'm so fucked.

Harper needed to leave. Or throw up. He should take a long walk to release the tight knot of misery in the pit of his stomach. Instead, he walked up the stairs and into the kitchen, where Millie gave him a cup of tea and pushed cookies in front of him.

"I wouldn't worry about Colson and that man."

He choked on the tea. "I'm sorry, what?"

Her eyes twinkled. "I may be old, but I still have eyes. And the first time you were here with Colson, you couldn't take yours off him." Her kind face glowed.

"I-I don't know what you're talking about."

"I'm sure you do, but I'll respect your wishes if you can't talk about it. I'm assuming you once had a bad relationship, but you can't let it keep you from opening yourself up again."

It was definitely time to leave, but he couldn't do what he wanted, which was bolt out the door and start running. Because Harper knew, with the first step taken, he wouldn't be able to stop. Over the years, he'd learned the one thing he couldn't run from was his life.

"I'm sorry, Ms. Johnson, but you really are wrong. Mr. Delacourt and I are...I mean, we aren't..." He sighed. "There isn't anything to say." He'd obviously lost his ability to speak and form sentences.

"That's unfortunate."

A laugh escaped him. "And why's that? I'm perfectly fine as I am."

"I know you think I'm an old lady who says and does silly things." She became serious. "When I was young, I danced with a world-famous ballet company in Europe and lived a dream life. All the doors were open to me, and I mingled with royalty, as well as artists and designers. I had my own money and wasn't beholden to anyone. I picked my lovers and did whatever I wanted. I thought it would last forever."

Fascinated, Harper asked, "What happened?"

"Life, dear boy." She gazed at her swollen hands. "I grew older, and they replaced me. Once I was no longer onstage, memories of my accomplishments faded, and so did I. People moved on and stopped inviting me. I was left alone, with my pictures and faded dresses and dreams."

"I'm sorry."

She shook her head, and her expression turned surprisingly fierce. "You're young, and I hate thinking of you alone."

"I'm not alone." Now that the first words had been spoken, he couldn't stem the flow. "I have a brother. He's brain-damaged and wheelchair-bound, and he lives with me." Millie's evident shock was nothing compared to his own and the knowledge that he was revealing this most intimate part of his life to someone he barely knew. And yet Harper couldn't help feeling it was the right thing to do. "He's been like that since a bus accident when he was five. David's twenty-five now. I have someone who cares for him when I'm not there." His chest heaved as if he'd run a marathon.

"Oh, Detective. I'm so sorry." Millie looked truly stricken. "Your brother is a very lucky man to have someone so caring. And you keep him at home with you? You've never considered having him live in a specialized facility?"

"Never," he responded, swift and firm. "He's my brother. I promised to always take care of him."

"Promised who?"

"My mother." He blinked as if he'd woken from a fog. "I have to go. I'm sorry. I'll get that cigarette butt to the lab and let you know if we find anything."

To his relief, this time Millie didn't insist he stay. As much as he liked her, Harper didn't think he could face her again. She was a sweet lady, but if she called, he'd make sure Nolan handled it. Her suggestion that he and Colson could have a relationship...Millie's own loneliness had precipitated that remark. The wishes of a lonely lady trying to live vicariously through him.

But he knew better. Colson might say he was a homebody, but he would want a life that included dining out and travel. Events and parties. Things couples did. Things Harper couldn't do on the regular.

Passing by Colson's house, he gazed up and saw the light was on in the bedroom. Were they in there together? Naked and touching each other? Kissing?

His ragged breath roared in his ears, and his hands balled into fists. Harper had a vision of going in, pulling that jerk off Colson, and kicking him out of the house.

Then the bedroom went dark, and Harper stood there, ugly thoughts swirling in his mind, his emotions battering and bruising him from the inside of his heart. He put his head down, and unwilling to think about what might be going on between Colson and his date, he walked away.

He strode the length of the Promenade and back, wrestling with the devil on his shoulder. It was eight o'clock, and he needed to get home to David and say good night. The love of his brother was the only thing Harper needed. Everyone else could go to hell. But that didn't stop him from walking past Colson's house on his way home. No lights were on. He kept on moving.

CHAPTER FIFTEEN

Colson knew the date was a mistake. The more Danny mentioned his ex, the more Colson knew Danny Forman was not his type of guy. Not to mention, Colson had promptly forgotten all about him after they'd met at brunch. Harper was the only man on his mind. And in his bed.

Except he wasn't.

Colson had thought they were becoming intimate. Not only sexually, which was insanely hot and passionate, but they had an emotional connection. He was making inroads with Harper, getting glimpses behind the walls, and it was those times—when Harper let his guard down and showed him a sweet, tender side—that Colson could see himself falling for this man.

Yet days had passed with Harper giving him a litany of excuses why they couldn't see each other, then going silent. Realizing he'd been ghosted, Colson alternated between being heartsick over a man he barely knew and angry that he'd dared to dream of possibilities.

It was only because he was still in his head about the book that he'd said yes to dinner with Danny Forman. He'd fallen asleep at his desk, and the phone's ringing woke him. He'd automatically hit Accept Call.

That was how they'd wound up at some expensive sushi restaurant in the neighborhood, where Danny had tried to impress him with stories about his trip to Tokyo with his ex and the fabulous meals they'd had. He'd talked about all the other countries he'd been to, and Colson had listened and nodded in all the right places but wished he were home. He'd never enjoyed the résumé building on dates and preferred things to come naturally. Finding Harper in Millie's front yard, an overwhelming desire had hit him to leave Danny and go sit with Harper in Millie's cozy kitchen and eat something homemade and full of sugar.

Dammit, he missed his grandparents.

And Harper.

He hadn't planned on inviting Danny inside, but the man had followed him up the stairs, and Colson had felt he'd had no choice.

"Coffee?"

Danny stopped wandering around and flashed him a grin. "Sure. If you don't have anything stronger."

They'd already had a few beers with their sushi. The last thing he wanted was Danny getting drunk. Colson mustered a faint smile. "Uh, I don't. Haven't gone shopping in a while." He filled the pot and set it to brew.

"Let me know when you plan to restock. My ex hooked me up with some great places where I can get you a good deal."

Having done a mental tally of how many times Danny had mentioned his ex, Colson could now round it up to an even ten.

Time to wrap this up.

"You know—"

"Hey, I was wondering if I could see that signed Stephen King book you mentioned. I'm a big fan of his."

Colson's lips twitched. Danny hadn't even pretended to have read one of his books. "Sure. I'll be right back. Help yourself to coffee when it's ready." He left Danny sitting on the couch and ran upstairs.

In his bedroom, Colson opened the closet, took out the box where he kept his collection of signed books, and retrieved the Stephen King. Closing his eyes for a moment, he recalled Harper stretched out on top of him, kissing him, licking him...

"Stop it. You're acting like a teenaged, lovesick idiot." Colson made a fist and banged his thigh, angry with himself for falling into the trap of thinking that what he and Harper had was anything more than the urge to scratch an itch no one else seemed to be able to satisfy.

He shut the light and returned to see Danny sprawled on the sofa, coffee cup in hand, completely comfortable. A domestic scene Colson could see playing out for years. If he wanted, Colson knew he could fall into a relationship with Danny. He'd be the type of partner who'd come home for dinner every night and go out to brunch every weekend. Football in the winter and baseball in the summer. Hamptons parties and summer trips to Mykonos.

Colson would know exactly what to expect.

There'd be no vibrating presence, sucking up all the air in the room. No sarcastic banter or teasing. No loss of control from a single kiss.

He wasn't Harper.

"Here it is."

Danny's eyes lit up, and he thumbed through it. "So cool." He set the book on the coffee table, and to Colson's shock, grabbed his face and planted a wet kiss on his lips. "I've been wanting to do that since I met you."

He pulled away, trying to hide his grimace as he wiped his mouth. "Oh, yeah? I'm sorry, but when I'm writing I don't allow myself any distractions."

Danny's brow furrowed. "Sex isn't a distraction."

"It is for me. I'm sorry. I'm on a deadline, and I'm afraid I have to call it a night."

At his crestfallen expression, Colson almost felt bad for the guy, but he wasn't about to kiss someone to make them feel better.

"Sure. I–I understand."

"I'll be pretty tied up with the book for the next couple of months."

Danny's lips quirked. "That's writer talk for thanks but no thanks, huh?"

Colson shrugged. "I just believe in being up front. I had a nice evening."

Danny winced. "Ouch. Nice is the kiss of death." He leaned in and kissed Colson on his cheek. "I enjoyed meeting you. I hope to see you again."

He walked out, and Colson locked the door behind him, then headed upstairs to write.

"So it was a no-go with Danny, huh?"

He and Hogan met for a late afternoon coffee several days after the ill-fated date.

"That was pretty quick. He told Bea we went out?"

"Yeah. He said you had dinner, then gave him the brush-off—nicely, but you weren't interested. Still hung up on the other guy?"

Yes, dammit.

"No. And I just wasn't feeling it with Danny." He played with his cup. "And tell Bea thanks, but please, no more surprise setups. I'm okay, and I need to concentrate on this book."

"So that's going well? I'm really happy you're in the groove. Even more so because it got you out of the house."

"Yeah. I'm loving the book's trajectory. And I'm not sure how much a two to three block radius counts as out of the house. But I'll take it." He finished his coffee. "Where's the rest of the crew?"

"At the park. I'm going to meet them. Wanna come?"

As much as he loved Hogan and his brood, Colson had little desire to spend another Saturday in the park, surrounded by screaming kids.

"I, uh—"

"Gotta find a good excuse to say no?" Hogan's booming laughter drew attention from the other coffee drinkers. "Can't say I blame you. But you know, there are a lot of single fathers out there. You never know."

His phone buzzed, and he saw it was a text from Harper. His heart kicked up.

Wanna meet up?

Was he kidding? He should say no. Why the hell did Harper think he could waltz back into his life after ghosting him? But he was already anticipating feeling

Harper's mouth on his, and a throb of lust hit him in his belly.

Yeah. Give me half an hour.

"I gotta get going."

Hogan's brows shot up. "Hot date with your mystery man?"

Colson's face grew warm, but he shrugged. "I have things I have to get to."

"*Mmhmm.* I'll bet. You have fun."

He left Hogan, and when he rounded the corner to his block, Colson broke out into a jog. Once home, he showered and put fresh sheets on the bed, laughing at his stupidity, since he knew they'd only mess them up. A shiver of anticipation ran through him.

The bell rang, and he answered it in shorts and no shirt, knowing how much Harper liked his tattoos.

"Hi." He leaned against the door as Harper passed by him, and he admired his firm ass and strong thighs. Harper wore a black T-shirt and gym shorts. Dark hair curled at his neck, and those beautiful pale eyes glittered.

"Hot day," he murmured, and Colson crossed his arms.

"About to get even hotter, I'm thinking." He closed the door, and to his surprise, Harper didn't kiss him, instead standing silent, with that penetrating, intense gaze.

"How was your date the other night?"

Was Harper...jealous? Colson kind of liked the idea of the big bad wolf left wondering.

He gestured toward the kitchen. "Want a drink? I have beer, wine...whatever."

"A beer is fine."

He took two bottles out and handed one to Harper, then leaned his hip on the kitchen island. "Why?"

"Why what?" Harper looked nonplussed.

"Why do you care?" If he had to drag a confession out of the man, he was going to have him admit he was there for more than sex.

Harper blinked and rubbed the back of his neck. "Uh, I don't...I mean, it was strange seeing you with someone, that's all."

"Why? I'm single, right? You let me know that when you couldn't be bothered to answer my texts."

"I knew this was a mistake," Harper muttered and set his bottle down, but Colson wouldn't let him run. He planted himself in front of Harper.

"Why? Because you don't want to admit what you're feeling?"

A pink flush rose up Harper's cheeks. "I don't know what you're talking about."

Colson leaned in and put a hand over Harper's heart. It pounded, and Colson's lips curved in a smile. "Yeah, you do. I feel it." He rested his forehead on Harper's and heard the sharp inhale of his breath. "You want me."

"I've never denied that."

"It's more than just sex, though. Isn't it?"

"The sex is amazing." Harper tried to kiss him, but Colson refused to let him take control.

"Stop it. Talk to me."

Harper stilled. "I–I didn't like it," he whispered.

"You didn't like what?"

They were so close, he swore he could hear the rush of Harper's blood through his veins and the rapid pump of his heart.

"You with that guy. I hated seeing him next to you. All I could think of was the two of you here...him touching you...kissing you."

"Never going to happen." Colson slid his arms around Harper's waist. "I didn't want him. I want you." He pushed Harper against the island and slammed their mouths together. A groan escaped Harper, and that harsh sound fueled Colson's lust.

"Say it," he demanded, his voice rough with restrained passion. "Say you want me too. Only me. Say it, Harper."

"Yes, goddammit. I want you. With me. Only me. No one else gets to touch you."

Harper's hands roamed all over him, and Colson soaked in his heat, reveling in Harper's touch. This was what he'd wanted all along. There was no use denying it, and so he gave in to the fire licking through his blood.

"This is all I could think about. You. With me." Colson sucked Harper's neck, leaving a mark. It excited him even further, and he moaned as Harper bit his shoulder and tweaked the stiff peaks of his nipples.

"How about this scenario?" Harper cupped his ass and put his lips to his ear. "Me. Inside you." Colson's dick swelled and throbbed, and Harper stuck his tongue in his ear. "Yeah. You like that thought, don't you? Want my dick in you?"

Colson molded his hips to Harper's. "Let's go upstairs."

They raced to his bedroom, shedding clothes on the way, and tumbled naked onto the bed. Colson took the lube and condoms from the nightstand, and Harper grinned.

"I'm glad you have a full stock." He stroked himself to firm thickness, and Colson ached to feel him. "Once won't be enough, I'm thinking."

"Less thinking and more doing," Colson growled and pulled him down for a kiss. Harper sucked and teased his tongue while the friction on their shafts sent Colson into orbit. "Fuck me." He clawed at Harper, and Harper hissed and licked the straining cords of his neck and flicked and bit his nipples. "Boy Scout turned wildcat."

"Just fuck me." He writhed, his cock spurting out precome. God, he'd missed Harper's touch, his mouth...his everything.

"You like that, huh?" Harper slipped a cool finger past his rim. "Damn, you're sucking me in like you're never going to let me go."

I don't want to.

Colson lost it again as a second finger moved in and joined the first. His cries and pleas rang in the air as Harper massaged the spot that had him ripping at the sheets. When he pulled out, leaving him empty and aching, Colson growled.

"What the fuck. Get over here."

"Shh, I'm going to give you what you need." Harper rubbed the wide head of his dick against his hole, and Colson's hips angled to take him in, but Harper played with him, teasing him, entering only an inch, then pulling out.

"Bastard," he whispered as he tried everything to take Harper deeper, but Harper continued to edge him with short, shallow thrusts. "Oh God, please, please, please."

"*Mmm*, I like hearing you beg me for it."

His entire body was on fire, and he opened his mouth to curse Harper, but Harper's mouth covered his and he drove in deep, filling him, splitting him in two. Colson moaned and locked his legs around Harper's waist, sending him all the way home. "Fuck," he panted and grabbed Harper's thick biceps. "Move, dammit."

Harper rolled his hips and thrust hard, over and over, slamming him into the bed. He reached between them, and at the touch of Harper's large hand on his dick, Colson blew apart and came.

"You're the sexiest fucking thing I've ever seen," Harper murmured and continued a slow, deliberate slide in and out of his twitching, boneless body, wringing every last bit of pleasure from him. "And you're all mine."

His dick throbbed at Harper's possessive, husky growl, and he dug his fingers into Harper's shoulder and rubbed their cheeks together. "*Mmm.* You're mine too."

Harper stiffened and gazed down at him, eyes glowing and Colson reveled in the possessive hold Harper had over him. He tightened his grip on Harper's thick shaft inside him, and Harper shivered.

"Yeah."

His heart leaped at Harper's admission. Their lips met, Harper's movements grew more frantic, and Colson watched him falling apart as his orgasm hit. He was wild and so damn beautiful. Colson held on to him, not wanting to let him go.

Harper nuzzled into his neck. "You're going to kill me, aren't you?"

"Arrest me, Detective. I'm your prisoner."

"Don't tempt me to bring my cuffs the next time." Harper's dick pulsed, and Colson squeezed him. "I'd like to see you spread out under me."

His heartbeat accelerated at the thought. "I wouldn't mind."

A smile spread across Harper's face. "I'll remember that."

A kiss to his cheek, then Harper slipped out of him and got rid of the condom. Colson held his breath, wondering if Harper would get dressed and leave. To his shock, he slid under the covers and tangled their feet.

"Did I pull you away from anything important? Like your gruesome new book?" Harper wrapped an arm around him and kissed his ear.

Colson laughed. "Just so you know, when I'm writing, nothing will disturb me, not the doorbell, the phone..."

"Not even me?" Harper spooned him, his soft dick nestling in the crease of his ass.

"Nope, not even you, Detective. I have to concentrate, so I block out all distractions. No matter how delicious they might be, writing is my first priority."

"*Mmm*, so I'm number two, huh?" Harper bit his ear, his hands roaming over Colson's chest.

"Depends. For lovers, you're number one."

Harper tweaked his nipples, teasing them into hard peaks. "How many on that list?"

"Only one. You." He wriggled his ass, and Harper grunted. Colson turned to face him. "Give me a few to recuperate, and we can go for round two." Harper's grin was all the answer he needed.

Colson's phone rang, and he closed his eyes. "I'm not answering it." It stopped, and he sighed with contentment as Harper encircled his waist and pulled him closer.

"Good."

A minute later it rang, stopped, then started over. "Shit. I'd better see what the hell this is, because it looks like it's not going to stop."

He checked the screen and saw it was his mother's number. A chill ran through him. "Goddammit."

Harper sat up. "What's wrong?"

"It's my mother."

The phone lit up again with the fourth call.

"Well, are you going to answer it?"

"No. Trust me, nothing good will come out of this conversation."

Too keyed up to sleep, he got out of bed and went to the bathroom to shower. Harper was waiting when he opened the glass door. "It rang a few more times."

He dried off and walked naked into the bedroom. Figuring the fun was over for a while, he put on a fresh pair of briefs and shorts. "And I'm still not going to answer it."

"There are several voice mails."

"Thanks for the info, Detective. I sense you think I should talk to my mother. Do you know the last time I did, she told me it was time to end my little experiment of gayness and come home and be normal?"

Harper winced, and to Colson's shock, held him tight. The last thing he would've expected was for Harper Rose, hardass detective, to be soft-hearted. Not that he was complaining. Colson sank into Harper's broad chest.

"I'm sorry."

"Do you? Think I should talk to her, I mean?"

"I'm not the right person to ask." Harper's voice rumbled through him. "I got along with my mother. She never said a negative word about my being gay."

"You're lucky."

Harper stiffened, and laughter that was anything but humorous burst from his lips. "Oh yeah, I am one lucky son of a bitch. You have no idea."

Colson cupped his jaw. "Care to talk about it? I happen to be a good listener."

Harper kissed him hard, leaving him breathless, his mouth tingling. "Not on your life. I didn't drag you away from writing your bestseller to talk."

Colson rubbed up against Harper's rapidly swelling erection. "Well, you're better than my friend Hogan. That's who I was with when you texted."

"Oh, yeah?" Harper eased off his briefs and shorts while kissing his neck. "And you left him for me?"

"Yeah." Colson threw back his head and hissed with pleasure as Harper took their full cocks in his hand and began to pump them. "Can you imagine wanting to be sitting in the park all afternoon watching a bunch of kids run around instead of here with you?"

Harper stopped, his lust-filled gaze turning flat. "I have to go."

Colson blinked and rubbed his face. "What? Why? I thought–"

"Wrong. Whatever you were thinking was totally wrong."

Harper pulled on his clothes and left him standing in the middle of the bedroom, wondering what the hell happened. The door slammed, and Colson had a sinking feeling it was the last time he'd be seeing Harper Rose.

CHAPTER SIXTEEN

"Harper, you want a drink? Harper?" Luis kicked his foot. "What's going on? You've been in a funk all week."

They were in the park with David, sitting in a shady corner. It was late Saturday afternoon, and he hadn't stopped thinking of that disastrous last meeting with Colson.

"I'm fine. Just busy. And I'll take one of those club sodas." He took the ice-cold can from Luis and opened it.

"You're not busy at work. You've been home at a normal time every night. With the same sad-sack face, I might add."

"I said it's nothing."

Luis drank some of his soda and held David's juice box for him to take a drink. "Well, I had an interesting week."

"Yeah?" Harper drank more club soda. Could he have been so wrong about Colson? Luis had even said he was kind to David and treated him well. Maybe he'd overreacted. There was no doubt he was overly sensitive about David, and when Colson had mentioned not wanting to be in the park, all he could think of was Ronnie, and he wouldn't, couldn't, let himself be with another man who pretended to care.

And yet Colson had texted him twice during the week, asking if they could talk.

I'd really appreciate it, Harper. Please?

Bastard that he was, Harper ignored Colson's pleading.

"Colson Delacourt asked me to preread the book he's writing."

Harper met Luis's eyes. "Oh, yeah? How'd that happen?"

"It was a while ago. I guess I forgot to mention it." Luis gave David some of the squeeze yogurt. "David and I were sitting here, and he showed up one day and started talking to us. I was rereading one of his books, and he said he'd need someone familiar with his work to look through the book he's currently writing to see if the new angle worked. Of course I jumped at the chance."

"So you've been doing it for a while now?"

"Yeah. He sends me chapters, and I give him feedback. Not gonna lie, it's pretty cool."

"I'm sure." Harper had read some of the critical reviews of Colson's work, and they were impressive. "You never mentioned you worked for me?"

"No. Why would I?" Luis moved David out of the shifting angle of the sun and into the shade. "He mentioned the break-in, but I wanted him and me to be strictly about the book. This one's a lot different than his other two."

"You said he had a new angle?" Harper asked. "He writes gruesome books about murders. What could be new?"

"Yeah, but now he's trying to put a romance in the book." Luis's grin threatened to overtake his face. "Between the detective, Harrison Rosa, and the Chief of Forensics, Calvin Diller. Notice anything about those names?"

Yeah, it was about as subtle as a brick to his face. Which Harper felt he'd been hit with the more he listened to Luis.

"Harrison Rosa is a grumpy detective, annoyed at the world and completely closed off. He's focused solely on his career to the detriment of anything and anyone else. Calvin Diller is a guy who's been burned in relationships. They're thrown together because of a series of murders, and the more time they spend with each other, piecing the case together, the greater the attraction grows."

"Fascinating." Harper pretended disinterest. "Hopefully he doesn't have them doing anything inappropriate in the precinct. Too clichéd."

Ignoring him, Luis continued. "I got the newest chapter this week. Calvin's got a problem. Years earlier, his parents kicked him out because he's gay, but he gets a call that his mother's sick, and he doesn't know if he should go see her or not because they're in the thick of the investigation."

Shit. That must've been the call Colson had gotten the night they were together. Shock rippled through him, and this time he was unable to conceal his concern. Luis, who noticed everything, slapped his thigh and cackled.

"I knew it. Don't think you can hide it from me anymore. You've been seeing Colson Delacourt, and it has nothing to do with his break-in. Admit it."

He couldn't lie to Luis. He lifted a shoulder. "Uh, well, I don't know if you'd call it seeing each other, but...yeah. We've been together." He chewed the inside of his cheek. "But it's over, so it doesn't matter."

Was it truth or fiction that Colson's mother was ill? Should he reach out, just to see if Colson was all right? Despite their estrangement, whatever news he'd received must've been devastating. It pained Harper to know Colson was hurting and had asked to talk, and Harper had remained a ghost to him. God, he really was a shit human.

"Why? What happened?" Luis prodded him. "He's a nice guy. I think you two could be good together. He's not like Ronnie."

Guilt made him snappish. "How do you know? Because he was kind to you and David a few times?"

"That's more than most people," Luis said softly. "And I'd think after all the years we've known each other, you'd know I was a better judge of character than that."

Rightfully shamed, Harper hung his head. "I'm sorry. I know you are."

"But...you're confused. Or is it something else?"

He so didn't want to talk about this.

"Something else? Like what?"

"That's on you to figure out."

Enough of the guessing game. "It's getting late. Don't you think we should get David home?"

Luis finished his soda. "It's barely six. You have someplace to be later?"

Yeah. Talking to Colson, but Luis didn't need to know that. "No. But you know David has his routine."

"Eh, David's enjoying himself. You're here, and he gets to see the kids playing. I think it's all good."

Dammit. Not that he didn't want to be with David, but he had a lot to explain to Colson, and he had to be in early the next morning. "I need to do something. It won't take long. Can you stay with David for about an hour?"

"I've got the whole night. You know I don't stand on regular hours. I enjoy my time with you guys. When you need me, I'm there."

Luis was the rock of their unit. Harper needed him as much as David did.

"Thanks." He crouched by David's chair. "Hey, buddy. I gotta go for a few, but I won't be long. Is that okay?"

David's fingers twitched. His type of paralysis—a C6 spinal cord injury—allowed for limited movement of his arms and shoulders, some of which the doctors tried to tell him were involuntary, but Harper refused to believe were anything but David wanting the reassurance of touch. He placed his hand over David's and squeezed.

"I love you." He kissed David's cheek and readjusted his baseball cap. "I won't be long."

"I'm gonna make a baked ziti tonight. And we have ice pops for dessert. Cherry."

"Yum, right, David?"

David licked his lips and made humming sounds. He left them and walked to Willow Street and up the steps to Colson's town house. He knocked on the door several times and rang the bell, but no one answered. Knowing Colson had a video camera monitoring the entrance, Harper gazed directly into the lens and waved, then pointed to the door and knocked a second time.

Radio silence.

Well, looks like I fucked it up.

"Detective? Oh, Detective Rose!"

Bracing himself, Harper turned. Millie Johnson was waving to him from her stoop. While the last thing he wanted was to talk to the gregarious lady, he couldn't ignore her. He schooled his face in a pleasant expression and crossed the street.

"Good evening. How are you? No more feeling as if strangers are watching you, I hope." He stayed at street level, hoping against hope the conversation would be quick.

He should've known better.

"Come in. I have brownies. Just out of the oven."

"Oh, no, I can't. I have to get home."

"You were going to spend time with Colson, but he's gone. So now you can have a little visit with me."

Damn she was sharp. Objecting was futile, and Harper heaved a sigh and trudged up the wide steps of the brownstone, again admiring the beautiful interior.

"How long have you lived here, Ms. Johnson?"

"Please. You must call me Millie. And I bought the house in 1965 for a laughable amount. It wasn't the hot spot it is now, but Brooklyn Heights has always been home to bohemians and entertainers. The creatives. Did you know Truman Capote lived just down the block? The poet, W.H. Auden had a home on Montague Street. And Norman Mailer lived on the next block, Columbia Heights."

"Yes, lots of authors and artists." He stood in the kitchen. "You said Colson was gone? Did he go out for the day?"

"He stopped by to ask if I needed him to get anything for me before he left. He's such a nice man, always thinking of others." She set a cup of coffee on the island with the plate of brownies. "Come and sit."

Unable to refuse, Harper did as told and pulled out a stool. "Do you know when he'll be back?"

"Well, no." She thought for a moment. "He said he'd be gone for a few days but couldn't be sure."

He sipped the coffee. "Did he happen to tell you where he was going?"

Millie peered at him over her reading glasses. "Detective, is there a problem with Colson? Are you investigating him?"

He drummed his fingers on the island. "Well, no," he admitted. "His case has been closed."

A twinkle lit her eyes. "Then I'll assume this is personal."

Jesus, she should be on the force, the way she so smoothly picked him apart. "Uh, I don't–"

"Detective. You shared the intimate details of a life I think has made you a hard man. But from our meetings, I can tell you're also a good person. And very kind."

His lips twitched. "Now I think you're trying to butter me up, but for the life of me, I can't figure out why."

She didn't join his smile with one of her own. "I'm an old lady. I know you have much better things to do on your day off than sit here and waste your very limited free time with me. So that speaks to your integrity." She clasped her hands. "Life is very short. One minute you're young and beautiful; then you blink and you're alone. In the dark. Dependent on others to do what once came naturally. No one to talk to except the memories in your head. We're all here for a moment in time. Don't waste one precious second."

He stared into the depths of his coffee cup. "I'm not...I have responsibilities I can't ignore."

"Your first responsibility is to yourself."

"No." His hand clenched into a fist. "It's not." His voice quavered. "I told you about my brother."

"Yes, but taking care of him to the detriment of yourself isn't helping either one of you. You may end up resenting him."

"Never," he lashed out. "I love him. Everything I do is to make sure he knows he's safe, and I don't think of him as a burden." He rubbed shaky hands over his face and gentled his tone. It wasn't Millie's fault. "So you understand now."

She cocked her head. "No, I'm afraid I don't see what your brother's tragic story has to do with you. And Colson."

"David has to come first. And people don't want to be with someone whose focus isn't on them, but it's okay. I'm used to it."

"But Colson isn't like that. He's caring. Which you already know—it's that sense you have about people that helps you in your work. I'm certain you don't believe Colson would be cruel. It's why you keep coming back to see him."

"I thought...maybe he was different. But I need to straighten out some things with him."

Millie bit her lip. "Well...he didn't tell me not to say anything. He went to Connecticut. He received a call that his mother was ill, and after some soul-searching, he made the decision to go."

So he'd been correct in thinking Colson had injected his real life into his novel. "Thank you." He checked his watch. "I should get going."

"Please don't give up," Millie implored. "I think you might find what you're looking for." An impish smile curved her lips. "Or in this case, who."

She walked him to the front door, and he stooped to kiss her cheek. "Thank you. And I hope you know you're not alone. Make sure you lock the door when I leave."

"You're so concerned with making sure your brother knows he's loved, who watches out for you? Good night, Detective."

He waited to hear the *click* of the bolt, then descended the stairs and headed toward home. Millie's words hit him harder than he'd thought, and as he walked through the streets, he wrestled with his conscience.

What did he want? The answer was obvious. Colson. But was it for more than what they'd had before he'd screwed it up? He waited at a red light, staring into the windows of the café at the corner. All the people enjoying their dinner and drinks. Happy people, laughing, holding hands...he'd ignored it all for years after Ronnie, convincing himself that his focus needed to be on David and making sure he was safe. He watched a couple lean in and kiss, and a jolt of yearning hit so hard, it left him breathless.

Would Colson understand him keeping David at home? He'd never forgotten the look in Ronnie's eyes when he'd met David for the first time. The shock. The fear. Harper couldn't take the chance of opening his heart and letting Colson in, if he'd only walk out.

Thunder rumbled in the distance, setting the mood for the tumult rising inside him. But according to Millie, being with Colson didn't have to mean putting David second. Having a relationship with Colson could be as important as loving his brother. His desire for Colson wasn't diminished by his love for David. Could they somehow share his heart?

Maybe Luis was right, and he was simply afraid of trying again and getting hurt. A faint smile crossed his lips. Some badass detective he was. He could chase down armed criminals in the dark, but telling someone he cared left him scared shitless.

Before he turned the corner to his block, he sent Colson a text.

I'm sorry I've been MIA. I've been trying to work some things out in my head. I know you went to see your mother. If you need to talk, call me.

He didn't expect Colson to answer. He put away the phone and joined his family for dinner. The baked ziti was a success, and he, Luis, and David decided to watch the original *Star Trek* television show from the beginning. By ten p.m., David was half-asleep. Harper waved Luis off.

"Go to bed. Thank you for everything."

"Did you see who you needed to see and get your head on straight?"

He thought for a minute about his conversation with Millie. "Yeah, I did. And I appreciate everything you said."

"No problem. You have to learn to recognize happiness sometimes. You've had it rough and let the past make you hard. It's time to show everyone the real Harper Rose. That man has a lot of love to give."

"How about you?" he asked Luis, aware the man spent most of his free time with David. "Are you happy? You know how important you are to me, and not just for what you do for David."

Luis nodded. "I know. But see, I had the love of my life. I'm not interested in that again. Don't worry, though, 'cause I get my share of attention and have my fun. So yeah. I'm happy. I've got good friends and a family right here."

"I love you, Luis. You know I couldn't do any of this without you."

They hugged. "Good thing is, you never will. You're stuck with me. Now lemme ask you something." Luis crossed his big arms and directed stern brown eyes at him. The man spent much of his free time working out and needed those muscles, carrying David and dealing with his wheelchair. "You make it right with Colson?"

He shrugged. "I'm trying. It's up to him now. Hopefully I didn't screw up too badly."

"I think if you explain everything to him and stop holding back, it'll work out."

He wasn't as confident as Luis, but he put up a good front. "I guess we'll see. I'm going to give David his bath. Thanks for the talk and advice."

"Anytime."

He took care of David and put him to bed.

"I love you. I've never regretted anything. Not one moment with you."

David made kissing noises and moved his mouth, and Harper cupped his cheek and pressed his lips to David's stubbly jaw. He turned on the monitor and flicked off the light.

"Sleep tight, buddy. I'll see you for breakfast."

Harper shut the door. The living room was silent, which meant Luis had gone down to his apartment. Harper got into bed and checked his messages, but there was nothing from Colson. He turned off the light, wondering if he'd screwed it all up. Colson had every right to say to hell with it and him and stay out of his life for good.

CHAPTER SEVENTEEN

Colson sat on the edge of the bed in his hotel room and watched the sun rise. He'd left home around five, and after several frustrating delays with the train and Metro-North, didn't arrive in Greenwich until after eight. Too late to make an appearance at his parents' house, so he'd checked into a hotel in town and tried to collect his tumbling thoughts.

What did you say to people you hadn't seen in fifteen years? Especially when you knew they didn't give a damn about you. He was probably stupid to have made the trip, but after sitting with Millie and listening to her talk about chances she regretted not taking, he'd decided it would either be something new and better, or the end. He hoped it would be the former, considering his mother had called him. He'd know in a few hours.

Then there was Harper.

Damn him.

They might've started out seeing each other to scratch an itch, but like a damn mosquito, Harper Rose had burrowed under his skin, and Colson couldn't ignore him. Harper turning growly and possessive had ignited a flame that burned like whiskey streaming through his blood. He'd developed an unquenchable thirst for Harper's mouth on his, those strong hands holding him down as he took Colson apart piece by piece. He liked sitting with him and trading barbs, and he enjoyed Harper's shrewd, sharp intensity.

Yeah, he was a little obsessed with the man.

He gazed at Harper's message from the night before, and his finger hovered over the Delete button. Millie Johnson was a sweet lady, but she didn't understand. He ran a hand through his hair.

"What the hell did he mean, things to work out?" he grumbled. As a writer, Colson didn't like vagueness. "If he has a problem, he can tell me. It's not like we're strangers."

But the more he thought about it, the more Colson realized he was wrong. They might've been intimate with their bodies, but they'd rarely shared what was in their heads or hearts. He knew as little or as much about Harper Rose today as he had the day they'd first met.

Except how hot and demanding his kisses were. How hard Harper thrust deep inside him so that even thinking about it set off mini explosions inside Colson, rendering him dizzy with desire.

"It's him who held back. I told him about myself." Colson paced the room. "He needs to open up and tell me why he freaked out and ran. And why he can't spend the night. Because he's hiding something important."

But he'd never get an explanation if he deleted Harper's message and ignored him. If he wanted to know, he'd need to give him another chance, but he wasn't going to make it easy for him. He decided to answer.

Thanks.

Colson pressed Send and turned off his phone. He wanted no distractions with what he had ahead of him that day, and if there was one thing Colson was certain of, it was that Harper Rose was the most frustrating, annoying, distracting man.

He lingered over his cold brew at a café on Main Street. Things hadn't changed much since he'd last been there—a few stores had moved in, along with two more coffee houses. He looked as out of place with his earring, longer hair, and tattoos now as he'd felt as a gay kid pretending to be straight, terrified that people might find out his secret.

As a teenager, he'd sneak away on the weekends with a fake ID and hang out at the clubs. Sex wasn't hard to find, and at nineteen, he'd lost his virginity in the back of a dirty Chevy Impala. For a few brief moments under a naked stranger calling him baby, he'd gotten more love than he'd ever received from his parents.

He sipped his coffee and caught a few glances from businesspeople stopping to get their drinks before boarding the train to the city. Maybe they recognized him from the profile picture on his books. He also didn't miss the interested side-eyes from some women and even a couple of men sitting and drinking their coffee or tea.

Maybe things had changed enough that his parents were willing to open a dialogue. If that was the case, he'd be agreeable to start fresh with them and put the past with all its hurt behind him. He could be the better person. He finished his drink and tossed out the cup. He was getting ahead of himself. First, he had to be let in the house. He called for a car, and with sweat dampening his shirt, sat in the air-conditioned coolness, peering at the rolling lush lawns of the great estates.

It was almost a half-mile drive up the path to the entrance of his parents' huge mansion. He'd always preferred his grandparents' ranch-style home, which while still large, was less ostentatious than his parents' massive Tudor. He wiped his hands on his shorts and rang the bell. To his surprise, it wasn't Amalia the housekeeper answering the door, but his father. Having not laid eyes on him since he was twenty-two, Colson shouldn't have been shocked at how he'd aged. For some reason, he'd expected the great Hamilton Delacourt to have remained untouched by the passing years, like in *The Picture of Dorian Gray*. God knew he had enough skeletons to hide in the attic. Instead, he'd turned gray, his skin a collection of lines, like the weathered clapboard on the house they owned on Nantucket, a product of years spent on the Sound.

"Well. To what do we owe the great honor of a visit from the prodigal son?"

"Nice to see you too, Dad."

Colson's gaze was direct, meeting his father's blue eyes. They flashed and after scanning him from head to toe, dismissed him with undisguised contempt.

"I see nothing's changed." He gave Colson his back and walked away.

Colson followed, considering it a win when his father didn't ask him to leave.

"Not true, Dad. Since I left, I've had two number one *New York Times* best-selling books. And I'm working on another. I'm a successful author."

"Obviously, that didn't translate into you dressing like one. Or is unwashed vagrant the in look these days?"

Flushed with anger and frustrated with the conversation, Colson chose not to engage. "Where's Mom?"

"Probably in her room. Why?"

His parents hadn't shared a bedroom for as long as he could remember. "Because I want to see how she's feeling. Never mind. I don't need your permission to go speak to my mother."

"She's fine. Dramatic as always."

He left his father and ran up the wide staircase. At his knock, his mother answered.

"Come in."

Pale as an angel, she lay in bed, thinner and frailer than he'd ever seen her.

"Mom?"

A faint curve of her lips greeted him. "I was right. The only way to get you to come see me is to say I'm dying."

He perched on the end of a wooden chair by the side of her bed. "Are you?"

She lifted a bony shoulder. "Who knows? The doctor said my heart is weak. Are you surprised?" Her blue eyes glowed fiercely, the only spot of color on her white face. "My only child broke it and left me."

"You're kidding. Left *you*?" His head spun at how she'd twisted the narrative to make his banishment from the family about her. "I didn't leave, remember? I was kicked out, told I didn't belong. You both told me you didn't accept who I am. How could I stay?"

"Yet you lived at your grandparents' house."

"Because they loved me. When they went into assisted living, they told me I could stay in their home as long as I wanted. That it was my home too."

"I often wondered if you'd given them a sob story about having no place to live after you left, and that's why they gave you the house in their will." A meticulously styled brow arched high. "As well as all their possessions. Normally, that would go to their next of kin." She sniffed. "It's not like you're going to need any of your grandmother's jewelry for a future wife."

It wasn't surprising that his mother showed no emotion concerning her parents. Or anyone else except herself. Grace Delacourt was the most self-centered woman he'd ever met. Colson believed some intrinsic part of her that would've allowed her to love was missing. He contrasted her with Millie, who'd showed him more kindness than his mother ever had.

"Next of kin. Meaning you." Colson's laugh was bitter as he swept his arm out in front of him. "Because you have so little. You're almost destitute. I can tell."

"There's no need for sarcasm. I'm not supposed to have stress."

He bowed his head. "Sorry," he muttered. He truly didn't wish her ill will.

"Did you come alone?" Her hands played with the edges of the comforter.

"Yes, why?"

"I wondered, that's all."

"No. I'm not married. I would've told you that when I called you. I'm not even seeing anyone." At that news, her expression became cunning. "What is it?" he asked.

"It means there's still a chance."

Dread crept through him at the implication of her words. "A chance for what?"

"You people can get married now, and you haven't. You don't have a…a boyfriend." Her lips pursed. "So that means you're not so sure."

"You people? Really, is that how you think of me? And what am I not sure about?" He couldn't believe what he was hearing…and yet he could.

"Being homosexual," she hissed. "Did you have to make me say it?" Distaste dripped from her words. "My son, being with other men." She shuddered. "The thought of what you do together…makes me ill. I'm positive that's why I had a heart attack. It's not normal. It's wrong."

"Then don't think about it. Because there's nothing wrong with me loving another man." Maybe the lack of sleep was affecting him in more ways than one, but he refused to allow her to put him down. "I told you before, I *am* normal, whatever that means in the twisted dictionary of your mind. Maybe I don't want to be married. Whatever I want and decide, it's my choice."

She pushed herself up to sitting, her cheeks pink. "But you'll stay now."

"Why? Do you accept who I am? Or you think because you've been ill, that means I should forgive almost fifteen years of neglect from you?"

"I'm your mother. Doesn't that mean anything to you? I gave you life."

"And I'm your child. You're supposed to love me no matter what. But you can't do that, can you?" He brushed at his wet lashes. "You gave me life, but that doesn't mean you get to decide how I live it. Or who I love."

"I need you."

"No, you don't. You have everything here. Nothing's changed since I left, including your attitude. All these years, it's always been me who reached out, never you. You say you need me? You have a funny way of showing it because in over fifteen years, it was always me who made the first call. I was the one who'd call at Thanksgiving and Christmas. There was never an invitation to come home. You never knew when I had a bad case of the flu and was home alone with a high fever, or in the hospital when I broke my leg skiing. You never once bothered to call me to see if I needed you."

He would not let her destroy everything good in his life—the career he'd made for himself, his friends, Hogan, Millie, and maybe...Harper. His agent was more than someone who made money off him. Tens of thousands of fans read his books and loved them enough to make them bestsellers. People cared about him.

"I have to go. Bye, Mom. I hope your recovery goes well."

She made no move to stop him.

At the bottom of the steps, his father waited. "Leaving so soon?"

Ignoring his father's question, Colson said, "Let me ask you something. Did you ever give a damn about me?"

His lips curled in a sneer. "I saw weakness in you early on, and when you revealed who you were, it all made sense. In this world only the strong survive."

"That's where you're wrong, *Dad.* I'm not weak. I'm strong as hell. Because I can live knowing I have two of the coldest, most unfeeling people as parents, and yet still have room in my heart to love. But I didn't learn that from you. Grandmother and Grandfather taught me."

"Two old fools. They never should've given you all that money."

"But they did." He narrowed his eyes. "And while it enabled me to have this extraordinary, easy path in life, I've been selfish and not given back. As soon as I get home, I'm going to set up a trust for gay, houseless youths and make sure my grandparents' names are front and center." His grin broadened. "And yours as well."

He walked out and down the path, past the large circular driveway, and called for a car. By the time he reached the main road, the car was waiting, and he sank into the seat, grateful for the air conditioning cooling his overheated face.

If it wasn't so sad to see how enraged his father became as he spoke—veins popping out, his face almost purple—it would've been funny. Of course, he had no intention of disgracing the project with his parents' names. But he'd long thought about what to do with so much, aside from yearly donations. Now he had a plan.

At the hotel, he was shocked to see it was only eleven o'clock. With no reason to remain, he packed up and checked out. On the train ride home, he tried to read, but his mind kept wandering. As it was the middle of the workday, he debated calling Harper, then decided he didn't—couldn't—wait until the evening.

"Detective Rose."

"Hi."

"Colson?" The deep voice dropped a pitch lower. "Is that you?"

"Yeah. I know you must be busy, but—"

"No, it's okay. I-I'm glad you called. How's your mother?"

He thought for a second. "The same." Any explanation would take too long for a phone call and required a face-to-face conversation.

"Oh. I thought she was ill? That's what Millie said."

The train sped along the tracks, the landscape outside the windows a blur of buildings and roadways. "It's...complicated. But nothing's really changed." A thought struck him. "Wait. You spoke to Millie? Why? Did something happen? Is she okay?"

"She's fine." Harper cleared his throat. "I...uh...she saw me at your door and told me you were away."

His lips twitched. "From all the way across the street?"

"Wiseass," Harper growled. "I was concerned because you said you didn't have the best relationship."

He wasn't about to discuss it in public. "I can't talk about it now. I'm on the train home. I should be there by early afternoon."

"I'm off at six." He waited, but Colson wasn't going to ask. If Harper wanted to see him, he'd have to make the first move. "Can I come by later?"

Relief along with a bit of giddy excitement tumbled through him, but in no way would he make it easy for Harper or show how eager he was to see him. "Yeah, sure."

"Won't be until probably around ten."

"I'll be awake. See you when you get there."

"Bye."

Colson stared at the dark screen. What was Harper doing for the hours between six and ten, and who was he doing it with?

CHAPTER EIGHTEEN

"What was that about?" Nolan asked.

"Nothing." Harper swiveled around to face his partner. "Now, about those burglaries–"

"You are such a bad liar." A gleam brightened Nolan's eyes. "I heard you make plans for later tonight. You got a date?"

"No, I don't have a date."

"The *worst* liar." Nolan snickered. "You're a tough guy when it comes to the perps, but you're just a big ole softie everywhere else."

"Can we please get to work?"

"Nah, this is more fun." Nolan leaned back in his chair.

"Glad my personal life is amusing to you," he grumbled, cringing at the realization that he'd played right into Nolan's suspicions.

"Aha!" he crowed. "I knew it. Listen, I'm glad you finally have a personal life."

"I'm not sure what it is. I still have concerns."

"About David, you mean?" Nolan's brows knitted. "Has the guy met him yet?"

"Not really." He chewed his lip and explained Colson's chance meeting in the park with Luis. "But he doesn't know I'm David's brother, and he has no idea what taking care of David means. The last time, I made the mistake of bringing Ronnie in too soon. I thought I knew who he was, but I was wrong. I don't want David to become attached only to have the person disappear again."

"That's a tough one," Nolan sympathized. "But what's the alternative—being alone because of one mistake? That's not fair to you."

But Harper was used to life not being fair. He'd seen it at work, with so many unsolved cases, leaving the bad guys to roam the city without consequences. And he'd had more than his share of personal pain at home. David's accident, robbing him of a full and active life. His parents' deaths and assuming sole responsibility of David. Every day he woke up and thanked God for Luis, who lightened the load, but in the end, David was his brother. And while he wouldn't ever regret the decisions he'd made, the time he spent with Colson gave him a taste of a life he'd almost forgotten existed.

A life he yearned for. And felt guilty for imagining.

"I'll deal with it. I just have to figure some things out."

"Don't take too long," Nolan warned, his tone indicating he'd made that mistake. "It can cost you."

Harper's curiosity got the best of him. "Speaking from personal experience?" He and Nolan didn't often delve into their private lives, and as far as Harper knew, Nolan and his wife were rock solid.

"I met Gina in college, but I wasn't interested in settling down and walked away from her. When I joined the force, I had no shortage of women—you know how some love the uniform and the badge. But it started to get boring and empty. Every face was the same. I missed Gina. So I looked her up and called her. She told me she wasn't interested in being with someone who wasn't serious about making her and a relationship a priority. And I thought about it and realized she was right. Eventually I'd be older and alone. And I didn't want that."

"But you're happy, right?"

"You bet your sweet ass I am." Nolan's gaze was steady. "And if you have that chance, grab it. Don't waste ten years like I did."

"Rose, Martinez. My office," Captain Poole called out, and startled, they jumped to their feet.

"What do you think it is?" he asked Nolan.

"Who knows."

They entered Poole's office. "Shut the door, please."

Captain Ira Poole was a grizzled, thirty-year veteran who rose through the ranks and had the respect of everyone under his command. He'd been offered the Chief of Detectives numerous times but preferred being with his squad and getting his hands dirty. Harper admired the man tremendously, not only for his work ethic, but also for how he'd handled the situation between him and Lombardi.

"What's up, Cap?" Nolan leaned against the small conference table.

"A new robbery ring." Poole sighed and scrubbed his face. "You'd think maybe these bastards would get tired and try something legit. Anyway, here's their MO. They have someone in their posse follow the vic on their way home. They wait until they're at a corner, and *bam*, someone rides up on a scooter and rips their bag, phone, or even one of those expensive little dogs right out of the vic's hands. They ride away and disappear."

Harper made a face. "Jesus, that's cold, stealing a dog." He thought of Millie. "Where have they hit so far?"

"The whole of downtown plus–Dumbo, the Heights, all around Fulton to Flatbush...those scooters make it easy."

"Okay. Any description?"

"Just vague." Poole consulted his notes. "Usually they ride in pairs. They wear hats pulled low to try and hide their faces, but the consensus is late teens, early twenties. Light-skinned Hispanics or White. One has a tattoo of the devil on his arm, and another has multiple earrings, all the way up to the cartilage. Braids to the neck."

He and Nolan took notes. "You've sent us the case files?" Nolan inquired.

"All yours. That's all."

He and Nolan returned to their desks and opened the files. "You want to hit downtown first, then work into the Heights and Dumbo?" he asked Nolan. "With all the banks and the courts, they should have plenty of video footage for us to watch."

"Yeah. I'm going to need glasses by the time I finish this one," Nolan muttered, and Harper cackled, knowing how vain his partner was about his appearance. Nolan wore only designer suits, monogrammed shirts, and you could see your reflection in his shoes. Harper loved to tease him.

"Don't worry, you're still adorable." Harper blew him a kiss, and Nolan threw him an evil look.

"Oh, yeah? I'm not the one who has the little old ladies in love with him."

Harper glared. "Whatever. Let's make some phone calls. I'll take the courts and you take the banks."

"Whatever you say, lover boy."

"Long day, Harper?" Luis questioned as they ate dinner. "We had fun—it was story time at the library, and then we took a ride to Coney Island. We played arcade games, and I won David a stuffed bird. Then we went on the boardwalk and got custard and watched the ocean."

David was still chewing the piece of chicken Harper had given him, and he waited until he swallowed.

"Did you like it? It's fun, and you can do a lot of people-watching. Plus, the smell of the ocean. I always loved it."

David blinked and his mouth opened. No matter what the doctors told Harper about the severity of David's brain injury, Harper fervently believed he understood what was going on around him. He lived with David, not the doctors.

He fed David the rest of the chicken and some string beans. In physical therapy they were working on seeing if David could gain enough strength and mobility to use a fork, but Harper was afraid of pushing him. Plus, he enjoyed the bonding time.

Once the table was cleared, they watched a little television until David's bath time. Harper put him to bed, kissing his cheek.

"You smell nice and clean. I'm glad you had a fun day."

David kissed him and sighed, closing his eyes.

He left the room after shutting the lights and went to take a shower. Luis was still watching television, having turned on the ball game, and his eyes lit up when he saw Harper had changed clothes. He put up a hand.

"Don't even ask. As I've mentioned many times, your TV is twice the size of mine, and you have better snacks." He popped a pizza roll into his mouth. "I know 'cause I bought them. So I'm happy to stay up here and keep the monitor on." His eyes crinkled shut with laughter.

Harper rolled his eyes. "Oh, for God's sake. Everyone has an opinion about my life."

"Only because we've been waiting for you to wake up and start living."

"Has everyone I know started working at a greeting-card company? I don't know what you all think I've been doing, but I don't need a relationship to feel alive or validated. I love being with David. Nothing brings me greater happiness than seeing him happy and knowing he's secure."

"And do you know how David feels?"

In the middle of sticking his wallet and keys into his pocket, he stopped and stared at Luis. "Huh? Of course I do. I know he loves me."

"David wants you to be happy too."

Harper's eyes burned. "What're you talking about? You talked to David about me dating someone? You shouldn't have."

"Why not? Sometimes it seems like you're using David as an excuse for hiding."

"Hiding from what? That's ridiculous."

"No. It's not. Everyone you've loved has hurt you in some way, either by accident or deliberately. Your father died young, your mother took her own life because she couldn't deal with the stress of taking care of David on her own for the rest of her life, Ronnie broke your heart by pretending to care for David only to try to move David out of your life."

"You haven't ever let me down. You're the one person I can count on."

"And I'll be here, but you need to be good to yourself. I thought we had this talk and you knew what you had to do?"

Saying it was one thing. Doing it was another, and Harper hadn't reached that level in a very long time.

"I'm fine," Harper mumbled. "I've always handled things the best way I knew how."

Luis squeezed his arm. "That was then. Try another way now. Let people in."

On his walk to Colson's, he ran through a slew of conversations in his mind—what to reveal and what to hide—but when Colson opened the door, he knew there was only one thing that needed to be said.

"I missed you."

Colson's brows shot up. "Come in."

Head bowed, he walked straight into the living room and sat on the couch, with Colson beside him.

"I have a lot to say, but please let me speak without asking me any questions."

"Okay."

He concentrated on the wood grain of the floor, the fringes on the rug...anything but Colson's curious face.

"I live with my younger brother, David. He's brain-damaged and a quadriplegic from an accident that happened when he was five. We have a live-in aide who cares for him while I'm not home and is basically like a father to him and an older brother to me. David's ten years younger than me, and I would do anything to protect him—I have since both our parents are gone." He raked a hand through his hair. "Three years after the accident my father died suddenly, leaving my mother as David's sole caretaker. She—she couldn't handle my brother's injuries. It changed her. She became depressed and withdrawn." He swiped at his face. "I'd just started college and was living at home, trying to help her out. She thought having an aide to help her meant she wasn't a good enough mother. Of course, no one else thought that, but she sank lower and lower, and despite all the help she got with therapy, I came home one day and..." His voice caught. *Dammit.* He hadn't thought he'd get this emotional about it after so many years.

Colson pulled him close. "I don't care if you told me not to interrupt. Harper, dammit, I'm so sorry."

"I knew you wouldn't listen to me," he groused, but didn't mind and settled into Colson's arms. It felt so damn good to be held. He couldn't remember the last time he'd let someone touch him without it leading to sex. Not that he didn't want Colson, but now was a time for baring souls, not bodies.

"Get used to it," Colson murmured against his temple. "What a terrible, horrible thing to have happened."

"I wish...I wish they could see us now. David is so happy, it's so hard to see him trapped in his mind and body. I'd like to think I've helped him feel loved and protected."

"I'm sure he knows," Colson soothed. "He's your brother. You have a special bond."

He shifted away from Colson. "Six years ago, I had a relationship, and he pretended to be in sync with me and how I was taking care of David. I was wary but thought he cared. I thought it would be okay. So I allowed him to meet David, and after several months, he started to hint that a special home would be best and David wasn't getting the best care he could with me. That he should be with other people like him."

He coughed, and Colson touched his knee. "I'll bring you some water."

Light-headed, he nodded and waited, drawing deep, ragged breaths. Colson pressed a cold glass into his heated palm. The condensation made it slippery, and he clutched it tighter, his knuckles turning white. His hand trembled slightly. He took a sip and set it on the table. Without saying anything, Colson held him again.

"When I told him no, that David stays with me, he grew angry. Then I found he'd left David alone in the park when he should've been watching him. I knew he didn't understand. It's been just the three of us since."

Much in the same way he comforted David, Colson rubbed his back, and Harper wished he could stay there, listening to the thump of Colson's heart under his cheek. It was nice for a brief moment in time to think of no one but himself. His wants. His needs.

"I think I've met your brother. His aide's name is Luis?"

Harper's lips twitched. "Yeah. He told me he talked to you."

"Why didn't you say anything?"

Harper disengaged from Colson and captured his gaze. "Because of everything I just told you. I couldn't risk bringing someone into David's life again who might hurt him. As much as we...mesh."

"Is that what you're calling it?" Colson's lips curved in a grin, but his eyes were tender, and Harper's heart gave a funny bounce. "I hope you know I'd never do anything to hurt David. From the few times I've met him, he looks happy and well-loved."

"He is. He has Luis and me. We'd do anything for him."

"I can tell. So where do we go from here? What happens now? Because I had time to think on the train going to my parents' and coming home, and I'm not satisfied with only half of you. I don't want to be shut out of your life. I'm a greedy bastard. I want it all."

"That's why I'm here. I'm ready to take the chance. If you want to."

CHAPTER NINETEEN

Colson's heart broke for Harper. Who knew behind that arrogant smirk and brittle facade lay a man so shattered, he survived by sheer courage and love for his brother? He sensed that any pity or sympathy would be met with a chill rivaling the Antarctic, but that didn't keep him from wanting to hold on to Harper and warm him up, soften the hard lines on his face with gentle kisses. Colson wanted to show Harper that what he believed to be a roadblock was in reality a door, opening up a new, fuller life.

"Meaning what? You're willing to take a chance on something more for us?" Colson hoped that meant a forward step together, but with Harper, he couldn't be sure. And it wasn't as if he were an expert in healthy relationships. He'd rushed into living with Evan after only knowing him for a short while, caught up in the frenzy of lust and passion. By the end, he'd been clueless as to the distance that had grown between them, and Evan's cheating.

"I-I guess. But I should ask if that's what you're interested in." From Harper's wary eyes and furrowed brow, it was apparent that he had no idea Colson wanted the same thing. He was so busy thinking up reasons to keep himself at a distance, he was clueless as to how desirable he truly was. All the trauma he'd learned to deal with had caused him to retreat, tortoiselike, into a protective shell where no one could reach and hurt him.

"I know I make my living with words, but as the saying goes, actions speak louder." Colson leaned forward and pressed a kiss on Harper's lips, then traced the little constellation of freckles dotting the juncture of his neck and shoulder. "Does this answer your question?"

Finally a smile broke through, reaching Harper's eyes. "Yeah. It helps. I know you've met David a few times, but this will be different. Like I said, I don't bring people home or into my life. I don't want David to become attached, only for them to disappear on him. I can't be sure he'll understand, and I'd never want him to think he was the reason. Because as far as I'm concerned, if someone doesn't believe what I'm doing is right, that's their problem, not mine, and I don't want that kind of negativity in our lives."

It made sense, but Colson knew from their previous interactions that Harper had little faith in people. "You must get overwhelmed sometimes. It can't be easy to have that constant worry on your mind." After his parents had told him to leave, he'd lived with his grandparents, and it broke his heart to see their health slowly deteriorate. He had no choice but to agree with their doctors to move them to a place where they'd be looked after by people better equipped than him to handle their increasingly complex medical issues. They needed care he couldn't give. Even years later, the memories were still too painful, which was the main reason he'd never gone back to the house they'd left him in Connecticut.

"I don't think of him as a burden. He's just so pure and happy for the most part, how can I feel sorry for myself? He's the one who's had a raw deal in life."

"Do you think you're anticipating negativity?"

Harper shrugged. "I've had a lot of practice. However..." He paused and worried his lip. "I'd like you to come to my house and see exactly how we live."

Colson knew that few people were allowed into Harper's personal space. "I'd like that. I consider it a privilege to learn more about your brother."

"Enough about me." Harper laid heavy hands on his shoulders. "Tell me about what happened with your mother."

As emotional as Harper's story had left him, Colson was oddly detached relating his conversation with his parents.

"She hasn't changed. Neither of them has. My father was quick to point out again that he'd sensed my *weakness* from an early age, while my mother lives in a fantasy world about my sexuality." If only he could rid himself of his bad memories of them. "She continues to try and force me to admit that I could date women and be 'normal.' Anyone who thinks bigotry is the stuff of books and movies is fooling themselves. I'm living that life." Now it was Harper who held him against his broad chest. "You want to know something funny? Not funny ha-ha, but something so outlandish that if I put it in one of my books, no one would believe it?"

"Of course. I want to learn everything about you."

Simple words that did something complicated to his heart.

"It was the year I turned eighteen, and all the kids were having high school graduation parties, but not me because my parents couldn't be bothered." Harper's arms tightened around him. "It's okay. My grandparents took me out to the theater and an incredible dinner. Anyway, I was at my friend Kit's house, using the bathroom. When I opened the door, Kit's father was waiting for me. His much older, extremely conservative father who'd never said more than five words to me."

"Did he—"

The walls closed in on Colson, but Harper's presence remained a force field of kryptonite to keep those walls from crushing him. "He was drunk, I could smell the liquor on him, but he still had the strength to pull me into a spare bedroom. Told me he'd seen me cruising the gay bars in Bridgeport. I was terrified at that point of being outed and didn't say anything."

"That bastard," Harper swore, and Colson loved the outrage on his behalf.

"He said he'd noticed me for years during pool parties. That I had a sweet ass, and how he'd like to be the first to break it in." Almost twenty years had passed, but his skin crawled at the memory of those pudgy, soft hands on his body. That afternoon had been the source of nightmares for weeks after, but now he could repeat the events as if they'd happened to someone else.

"We were in a bedroom, alone. I could hear the splashing and laughter from everyone in the pool right outside the window. Even if I screamed, or fought him, it was his house, and he was a hedge fund billionaire. His staff would make it go away. And he was right. I had been at the bars down there. Maybe he'd been there as well, but who were they going to believe? He had enough money to pay people to say what he wanted."

His breath hitched, and he grew cold even as sweat dripped from every pore.

"He assaulted you?" Harper's deadly tone shocked him to awareness.

"He tried, and I froze. It was almost like I was asleep and caught up in a nightmare. I could feel everything happening, but I was watching it from a distance. He had me pinned beneath him on the door, my face pressed against the wood, and I could feel him rubbing between my legs. When he reached to unzip his pants, I woke up and smashed my heel into his foot, my elbow into his stomach, and ran like a fucking bat out of hell."

"Did you tell anyone?" Harper smoothed those big hands over his shoulders, back, and neck, as if to wipe away any remnants of that day. Their strength sent Colson into sweet bliss.

"No. Only you know. I haven't even told Hogan. At the time, there was no one I could trust. Certainly not my parents, who wouldn't have believed me anyway. I loved my grandparents, and I didn't want to upset them. I was alone."

"Good thing you don't have to worry about that anymore."

He met Harper's intent gaze. "No?"

"No," Harper repeated. "I'm here. You're not alone."

Their lips met, and hunger blazed through him, hotter and brighter than any time before. Harper's tongue flirted with his lips, then demanded entrance, and Colson granted it, sucking its velvet softness ravenously. They played cat and mouse with their kisses, alternating licks and nibbles, until Harper placed shaky fingers on his cheek and pulled away. Regret played out over his handsome face.

"I hate to do this, but I have to go home. I swore to myself that coming here tonight would be only to let you know how I feel and to see if it was mutual. That it was more than sex."

Aching with pleasure, Colson gathered his wits. "I think we've come to that conclusion." He stole another kiss, ending it by holding Harper's full lower lip between his teeth and tugging. "Although I want you."

"God, you're killing me," Harper groaned and put several feet between them. "I don't want to leave, but I have to."

This was such a different Harper than the frozen-faced, snarky man who'd once thought him a murderer. Harper's face was flushed, his mouth swollen and well-kissed, and his moon-bright eyes glowed with undisguised passion.

"I have to get in early. We have a new robbery ring that's going around on scooters. But I'd like to see you this weekend." Looking vulnerable, he ran a hand through his hair and seemed to be running something through his mind, then came to a conclusion. "Maybe you can come by and meet David then? He can get used to seeing us together."

"Is that what you're planning to tell him? That we're together?" He held his breath. Hoping. He'd fallen hard for Harper, and it was more than sexual. His passion and commitment to his job were a massive turn-on, the kindness he'd shown Millie was a reflection of a deeply sensitive man who'd spent his whole life in service to others, and his single-minded devotion to his brother indicated a heart overflowing with love.

Oh, yeah. He was head over heels, shut the front door, in it to win it.

"I'd like us to be." The intensity of Harper's stare devoured Colson, and his lips tingled as if he could feel Harper's mouth on his.

"Me too."

The following evening, he spoke to Hogan and filled him in on the trip to his parents and some of what happened with Harper.

"Wait, so that man in the wheelchair the kids were talking to, that's Harper's brother?"

"Yeah. Small world, huh?" Colson grinned at Hogan's snort.

"You could say that. Let me ask you something. And don't take it the wrong way."

"I will if you're going to be negative."

Hogan released a long, drawn-out sigh. "It's not being negative so much as I wonder if you understand what you're getting into."

Of all the people in his life he'd expected to understand, Hogan was at the top of the list, which was why his comment stung.

"Explain what you mean by 'getting into.' Because I'm not liking what I'm hearing."

"Don't get your ass in a sling. I think it's great that Harper has dedicated his life to taking care of his brother. It shows tremendous strength of character on his part. But are you willing to do the same? Do you want the responsibility of a third person in your relationship? Especially one who'd require so much care?"

It was a fair question, and he'd spent hours since Harper's visit asking himself the same. But he'd concluded that Harper was who he was because of how the circumstances of his life had shaped him. Losing his parents and caring for his brother were what made him a superior detective and gave him a caring heart. He had an innate sense of fairness, right and wrong, and compassion.

"I'm not mad you asked me that. But I look at it this way. Would I leave my husband if something happened to him and he'd need lifelong help? What kind of person would that make me?"

"But you're not married to him. This is a choice you're deliberately making to step into a situation."

Colson smiled. "Yeah, I am. You didn't see the passion and fierce love in his eyes when he spoke about David. Anyone who has such a big heart is the kind of person I want in my life. And if you're thinking I'm going to be missing out on things, don't. I'm a homebody at heart. I don't need to travel to the ends of the earth to find what matters to me. I'm not changing who I am to fit my life to Harper's. I'm rediscovering me. I'm more than someone who writes books. That burnout opened my eyes. I need something else in my life other than words on a page. I'm finding a family. A home."

"I hope so. You deserve the best. That's all I want."

"Then wish me luck. Because it's all I want as well."

"Okay, so now, dude, what the fuck is up with your parents? Did your mother really think because she had a heart attack that you were going to change who you are?" Any other time, Hogan's outrage would be funny, but not concerning his parents.

"Lifestyles of the absurdly rich and extremely self-absorbed, what can I say?" he deadpanned. It had taken him years to get over their abandonment yet only minutes for it to rush over him like a tidal wave, threatening to knock him over and drown him. "And from the way she argued with me, I wonder how sick she is. She's always been the queen of manipulation and selfishness." When his grandparents died and left him their house, a nine-room estate with six acres, she'd tried to get him to give it to her, since he was so young and lived in New York. She'd couched it in terms of doing him a favor and taking away the burden of taxes and upkeep, but he'd refused.

"I remember," Hogan said darkly. "She never liked me, that's for sure, and tried to break up our friendship."

Colson winced. "Yeah. She had her opinion on who she wanted me to be friends with and didn't appreciate my refusal to join the fraternity her father had belonged to."

"Especially in favor of hanging out with the scholarship kid from Brooklyn. That was a real fuck-you to her." Hogan chuckled.

"But that was never the reason. You understood me. You felt like you didn't fit in because everyone was rich, while I had my sexuality to worry about."

"And now we both have what we want."

Thinking about Harper and David, Colson smiled. "Yeah, I think maybe we do."

CHAPTER TWENTY

"So you're finally taking the plunge?" Nolan asked.

He and Nolan had spent five straight hours watching videos and taking notes. Harper's eyes burned, and he'd thought he was ready for a break, but now he wasn't so sure, if discussing his personal life was how they'd spend it. They closed the computer and removed the flash drive. Harper put it into the evidence file, and they returned to their desks.

"I don't know what you're talking about. Colson is coming over on Saturday to meet David. That's all. You make it sound like we're getting married."

"Yeah, but for you, having someone to the house to meet your brother? That's huge, man. Come on," Nolan said, sounding genuinely happy. "It took you close to a year before you allowed me to come over." Nolan blotted his face. The air conditioning in the room wasn't the best, and Harper pressed the cold can of soda against his forehead.

"Yeah, well…I guess we'll see." He was trying not to get too worked up about it. He'd only told David he was bringing home a friend, and David had shown little reaction.

"What's there to see? Colson seems like a good dude, and now he knows the score about your home life and isn't running."

"It's one thing to be told, another to see it. I'm being cautious, is all."

"Okay, I get it," Nolan agreed. "Still, at least he's willing to try. You have to learn not to be so negative."

Not exactly an easy thing to do when you hadn't had much positivity in your life. The phone on Nolan's desk rang, and he picked it up. Harper finished his drink and entered his notes on the case.

"Let's go." Nolan sprang out of his chair. "We got another one. Same MO. Two riding on a scooter. The lady was with her two little kids, holding her phone, and the jack-offs sped past and grabbed it out of her hand. Two unis on the scene now. Corner of Henry and Remsen."

They took off and made it to the scene in less than fifteen minutes. A woman in her midthirties was talking to two officers. Two little kids waited by her side, and the younger one was crying.

"What do we have?" He flashed his badge, earning wide-eyed stares from the children. "Detective Rose and my partner, Detective Martinez."

"I was telling the officers that I was standing on the corner, waiting for the light to change, talking to my children, when this motorbike turned the corner and almost knocked me down. One of them grabbed my phone right from my hand." Her brown eyes flashed with anger. "And scared my son."

"I wasn't scared, Mommy," the older boy piped up, and Harper grinned to himself.

"You weren't?" he asked. "Do you know what these bad men looked like?" Sometimes kids were better witnesses than their parents.

"Yeah. One wore a black shirt with a smiley face on the back of it and white sneakers with a gold swoop on them. He had long braids." The little boy scrunched up his face. "Oh, yeah. The guy driving had a tattoo, not like Uncle Colson with birds, but, um...a face...with like horns and stuff out of its head. It was ugly."

Harper pulled out his phone and brought up a picture of the devil tattoo one of the other victims had identified on their assailant. "Like this?"

"Yeah, that's it," the boy said excitedly.

Not to be left out, the younger one had recovered and nodded. "Uh-huh, like that."

"You didn't see it, Mikey. You were too scared."

"Did so."

The two little boys continued to argue, and Harper was curious about the Uncle Colson remark. He approached the mother, who was busy giving a statement to Nolan.

"Your sons gave a great description of the people who stole your phone. Better than many adults."

Her expression was one of wry amusement. "I was afraid they'd be too scared, but I guess they're braver than me."

"It is scary," Harper rushed to reassure her. "But we have enough of a description to know they're part of a gang running around this area. Your boys don't seem to be suffering any ill effects." He glanced over at the two children, who were still trying to one-up each other about who saw what, complete with hand gestures and very loud voices.

She groaned and rolled her eyes. "You see that? They're going to argue all night now about who saw more and brag to my husband." She made a face. "Oh God, I don't even have a way of telling him what happened. And I have credit card info stored on the phone."

"We can call him for you, if you'd like."

"Would you mind? His name is Hogan Carmichael, and he works at Pomerantz and Co."

Harper chuckled. "This is the second time I'm calling your husband. The first time was when we suspected Colson Delacourt of planning a murder. We were wrong, of course, but when your son mentioned an Uncle Colson and his tattoos, I figured it had to be him."

Her jaw dropped, and she let out a hearty laugh. "That was you? Oh, I heard all about it. Too funny because Colson is the sweetest, most gentle man. The boys adore him."

He made the call and gave her his phone to speak to her husband. When she finished and handed it to him, her smile was one of pure satisfaction. "Thank you, Detective Rose."

"We'll be in touch, Mrs. Carmichael. Here's my card if you need to reach me."

She tucked it away in her purse. "Thanks. Or I guess I could just ask Colson?" Knowing eyes met his, and not for the first time he cursed how small the neighborhood was. Whoever said New York City was anonymous didn't know what the hell they were talking about.

"We're friends, yes." And he intended to get even friendlier that weekend if everything worked out well.

"Tell him I said hi. I think you'll probably be seeing him before I will." She couldn't conceal her grin, but he remained stoic, his answer bland.

"We'll be in touch, Mrs. Carmichael."

He and Nolan questioned several people on the street but didn't gather any more crucial information. At the precinct, they wrote up and filed their reports. He pocketed his keys and wallet.

"I'll see you Monday." He saluted Nolan, who called out after him, "I expect a recap."

Harper didn't bother to answer. He was too busy texting Colson.

I met your friend's wife and their children today. She was mugged.

As expected, Colson called him immediately. He stopped at the corner and leaned on a building. Walking and holding a conversation was never a good idea. Too much distraction.

"What the hell are you talking about? Bea? She's okay? And the kids? What happened?" He was tripping over his tongue in an effort to get the words out, and Harper waited for him to run out of air.

"Slow down. She was the victim of one of those scooter robberies that're plaguing the area. They were waiting on the corner, and she had her phone out. The perps zipped by and grabbed it right out of her hand. She was shaken up, but the kids were incredibly detail-oriented in their descriptions." His lips twitched. "I could use witnesses like them more often."

"They didn't get hurt, did they?" Apparently Colson didn't appreciate his attempt to lighten the situation, as his joke was ignored. "She's okay? Does Hogan know?"

"Yes. I gave her my phone to call him." He hesitated. "Seems she knew we're...friendly?"

"I told Hogan we've gotten close and that I'm going to meet your brother. Is that a problem? Were you planning on keeping it a secret?"

Colson's annoyance came through loud and clear, and Harper rushed to cut it off.

"No, of course not. I just figured...maybe we should wait and see how it works out first. You know..." God, he hated having to say it, but there was no guarantee Colson would stay after spending the day. Like ripping off a bandage, the pain of potential failure was obvious. At least to him. He knew Colson's nature was—as Bea claimed—sweet and gentle, something Harper had seen firsthand with Millie Johnson. But Harper also knew the reality of his daily life was demanding. As hurt as Harper had been when Ronnie walked away, he almost couldn't blame him.

Perhaps with Colson, he'd been holding his breath, anticipating failure.

Life had punched him down, again and again, and he'd learned to take it on the chin and accept the blows.

"No," Colson said, "I *don't* know. Are you expecting me to walk away?" he demanded. "Is that what you're thinking?"

"I have no expectations." What he wished for and reality were almost always two very different things. Harper had learned to live with the pain of disappointment.

"Then I guess you don't know me very well. I don't give up when I want something badly enough."

"I like it when you get demanding," Harper murmured.

But Colson wasn't having it. "I'm serious, Harper. Just because someone else wasn't willing to be a decent human being doesn't mean I'm the same. I think we have the potential for something good here, but you can't start out thinking we're going to fail."

"I'm trying not to. I'm heading home now, and I'll see you tomorrow. After breakfast is good?"

"Yeah. I'll be there, and I hope you won't be so negative."

"I'll try." It was the best he could do.

Over David's favorite meal of pancakes, Harper explained again that a friend of his was visiting and wanted to meet him. David appeared to listen and didn't respond negatively. Harper leaned in to give him a kiss, and he returned it.

Luis had wandered in during the last half of the conversation for some coffee and to give his opinion.

"Hallelujah. Colson is a great guy. Really sweet and gentle with David." Luis met David's eyes. "Remember the man who helped you with the ice cream?"

David's fingers twitched, his eyes widened, and he grunted.

Harper took that as a positive. "Yes, buddy. That's who's coming. He and I are good friends. Maybe we can take a walk in the park today. Would you like that?" To his relief, David smiled.

Across the kitchen, Luis's grin threatened to overtake his face, and Harper rolled his eyes. "Don't you have something to do on your day off except spy on me?"

Snickering, Luis poured another cup of coffee. "Nope. I'm going to hang out here and say hi to Colson." He removed a plate from the cabinet and took some pancakes. "I got invited to a barbecue, but that's not until the afternoon."

"That's an idea. We could do one here. Some hamburgers and hot dogs. I wouldn't mind. How about you, David?" His brother licked his lips, and Harper wondered, as he often did, if the doctor's diagnosis as to the severity of David's brain injury was correct. There were many times Harper believed David understood his conversations. "You'd like that, wouldn't you?"

This time David didn't respond and gazed at the wall across from them, and Harper sighed with frustration and shook his head. He took his plate and David's to the dishwasher. Luis drank more of his coffee, a sympathetic wrinkle in his brow.

"Sometimes I wonder myself, but I think David does understand more than I think we know. Just keep talking to him. It's like the physical therapy. You might not think he's capable, but one day he'll surprise us all."

"I will. I'm going to clean him up and take a shower." He checked the clock on the stove. "Colson will be here in an hour."

"I'll take care of David while you make yourself beautiful."

Harper glowered. "Very funny. But thanks. I'll take you up on the help."

Leaving Luis chuckling, he ran upstairs, showered and dressed, debated for a bit, and put fresh sheets on the bed. He'd never had a man in his room—Ronnie had refused to have sex in his house in case David interrupted them, so they'd always gone to his apartment.

But Colson was different. Harper wanted long nights of slow, delicious lovemaking. He wanted to live in Colson's body and feast on his kisses. Have the nights last forever. Not say good-bye when the sun came up. Harper wanted to know how it would feel to wake up with Colson in his bed and have breakfast with him.

The bell rang, and his heart picked up a beat. He laughed at himself. "Stop being an asshole."

He opened the door to see Colson standing there, wearing a simple black T-shirt and a pair of jeans that molded to his muscled thighs. Those gorgeous tats teased the eyes and disappeared up his biceps. A small gold hoop had replaced the little diamond. Desire swept through him, rendering him breathless.

God, he was so fucking sexy.

"Can I come in, or are you going to ogle me all day?" Colson quipped, and Harper felt his face grow hot. He stepped aside, but Colson stopped to place a brief kiss on his lips. "If you weren't going to do it, I was."

Harper curved a hand around Colson's nape and held him close, running his lips across Colson's cheek before taking his mouth in a possessive kiss. "I was, trust me. There's no way we can spend the day together without me touching you."

Colson gave in to the pressure of his tongue but demanded payback, and they battled, sucking and tease-tagging. "How about the night?" he whispered in Harper's ear. "I brought my toothbrush just in case."

God, he wanted that more than anything. "Let's see how it goes." He gave Colson another kiss. "But I hope so too."

They stood in the hallway, lost in each other until Harper heard a cough behind him and turned. Luis was there with a big fucking grin on his face. Freshly shaven, David was dressed in his favorite superhero shirt and light jogging pants.

Harper reached out, and Colson grabbed his hand and squeezed it hard. "David? Do you remember meeting Colson in the park? I think you had ice cream together."

David focused on Colson, opened his mouth, and made noises. His hands twitched. Fear jumped in Harper's chest, and afraid of David's reaction, he took a step forward, but Colson cut him off and crossed the room to crouch beside David's chair. The bag on his shoulder slipped to the floor.

"Hi, David. We had fun that day, didn't we? We're going to have an even better day today."

David made kissing sounds, and to Harper's shock, Colson offered his cheek to David for a kiss, then kissed him in return. No one but Luis or him had ever kissed David, not since their parents died. Tears sprang to Harper's eyes. He grew light-headed and yet had never been so grounded. At that moment, he knew he could never let Colson go.

"Hey. How about we put your stuff in my room?"

Colson's eyes glowed. "Yeah. Why don't you show me the way?"

CHAPTER TWENTY-ONE

Colson was almost as nervous meeting David as the night he'd lost his virginity, but when David kissed his cheek, all his fear melted away, and he kissed him back. Seeing Harper become emotional about that simple gesture tugged at his heart.

Inside Harper's bedroom, he set his duffel on the dresser. "So, does this mean you want me to stay tonight?" Harper pulled him close and kissed him until his head spun and his toes curled. Whenever this man kissed him, he wanted to get naked. Colson smiled against the curve of Harper's lips. "I'll take that as a yes."

Those fathomless eyes locked into his. "I do, but the choice has to be yours. Let's spend the day together, and then you'll decide."

"Fair enough. What do you have planned?"

"How about the zoo? Then we can get pizza and ice cream and a frozen coffee drink. That's usually our treat on Saturdays in the summer."

"Sounds like a plan."

Harper cupped his jaw. "You have no idea..." He blinked and turned away, but Colson caught his arm.

"Don't hide from me. I appreciate how deeply you love your brother. There's no shame in showing it." He kissed Harper. "Tell me what's in your heart right now."

"You," he said, and Colson's heart leaped.

"Show me everything. Let me walk in the footsteps of your life."

A wry grin tipped up Harper's lips. "Just a warning. There's an awful lot of stumbling."

Colson slipped his arms around Harper's waist. "Good thing I'll be there to catch you when you fall."

Harper guided their lips together, and he fell into a kiss that tasted of hopes and dreams and the promise of forever.

"I'm not sure this is real. I didn't think I'd ever find someone who understood."

"I can't promise I have all the answers, but I'm ready to try. All I know is, I want you by my side to help me figure it out." He gazed into Harper's eyes. "You and David. You see, I've never had a brother, and I always wanted one."

Harper pulled him close, the kiss possessive and demanding, and Colson almost swooned from the heat pouring off Harper's body.

"If David wasn't waiting for us, I'd have you naked and be inside you in a minute."

"All the better to wait until tonight."

Harper gave his ass a squeeze and they headed to the kitchen, where Luis and David waited.

Luis grinned. "Get all settled in?"

Harper turned a cute shade of pink and grabbed the keys hanging on the pegboard. "Yeah, ready to go, David?"

Colson caught Luis's eye and received a wink and a thumbs-up. Unsure what to do, he hung back, waiting. Harper handed him a cooler bag.

"This is David's lunch and snacks. I always bring them because we never know if they'll have what he can eat where we go."

"Gotcha." He hefted it to his shoulder.

Harper wheeled him down the special ramp, and Luis stayed behind. "He's off on the weekends, if I don't work, although half the time he's around to help. His schedule is fluid to help me. There's no one like him. Luis is a godsend."

"And a great beta reader. He found some inconsistencies, and he's really helped me with the book."

They reached the van, and he watched as Harper made sure David's chair was locked in place. Maybe one day, Harper would trust him to do this, and he'd make sure to be ready.

Colson settled into the passenger seat, Harper started the van, and they were off. He kept peeking over his shoulder at David, who stared out the window, the serene expression never leaving his lips.

"Stop worrying," Harper murmured. "He loves going for car rides and seeing people."

Colson put his hand on Harper's thigh. "Was I that obvious?"

Harper took his hand and squeezed. "Yeah, but it's sweet. You don't have to worry about making a good impression." He winked. "You already won me over."

Relaxed for the first time that morning, Colson began to look forward to the day. "I haven't been to the zoo in years."

"We'll be there in time for the seal feeding."

They parked the van in a handicapped spot, and Colson stayed on one side of David, while Harper wheeled him. They found a spot where David could see the seals. Colson noticed several people eyeing them, and when he caught them at it, they quickly looked away.

"See what I mean?" Harper murmured. "They don't want to see you, but they can't stop staring."

"That's their problem, not ours," Colson stated firmly.

The handler came out with the buckets, and the seals slid off their rocks and swam about the pool, barking. David made the same noises, and this time people moved away. Colson took the opportunity to push David closer.

"Thanks," he addressed a woman with a double stroller. "He loves to see them."

"Oh, uh, sure. Yeah." She darted a look at David, whose fingers twitched while his head moved side to side as he grunted. "What's wrong with him?" she whispered.

Angry for David and Harper, Colson leaned down to return the whisper. "Nothing. He's really okay. We're on surveillance with the FBI."

Her mouth opened, and she hurried off, clearing the way for him to bring David by the gate. He felt Harper behind him, his breath hot on his neck.

"You know, impersonating a federal agent is a felony," Harper whispered too, and Colson shivered at the touch of Harper's lips to the shell of his ear.

"Oh, yeah? Maybe you should call the police."

Harper's smile pressed against his cheek. "I'll take you prisoner later."

David began to make louder noises, and Colson jumped. Harper circled the chair and kneeled at David's side. "What is it, buddy? Everything okay?"

David's mouth opened and closed, and Colson's heart broke as he watched him struggle. He and Harper looked alike, and it was eerie to see them together. So similar, yet so different.

"Let's go sit and have something to eat. How does that sound, David?"

At the twitch of his lips upward, Colson's nerves settled. For a second he'd worried David was upset at seeing him and Harper touching, but as they found a table, he happily ate the squares of peanut butter and jelly Harper had for him. There was also cut-up fruit in containers, which they shared.

Harper took out a squeeze yogurt and handed it to Colson.

"Do you want to feed it to him?" Harper asked.

David tracked it and licked his lips.

"Really? Are you sure?"

Harper's face was tender. "Luis told me you helped him with his ice cream and did great."

"Yeah. I don't know why I'm so nervous now." He tore the end off and held it up to David's lips. David made humming noises of obvious pleasure, and soon they'd finished the entire stick. "Can we give him another one?"

Harper hesitated. "I don't know. He usually doesn't eat two."

"Yeah, but it's a special day and he deserves a treat. Don't you think so, David?" At the sight of his bright eyes, Colson appealed to Harper. "Come on. Don't be a party pooper."

"All right. All right. Nothing like two against one." Pretend-grumbling, Harper cut off the edge of another yogurt stick, and David finished that as well. "You okay to watch him for a minute? I'm just going to run to the restroom."

"Don't run. Us guys are just going to hang out and people-watch, right, David?" He hitched his chair closer to David, who looked at the crowds passing by.

Harper took off, and Colson decided he should talk to David. "Did your brother tell you I write books? They're kind of gory, but it's fun to name the characters. Maybe my next book will have a detective named David. What do you think?"

David's smile remained constant, so Colson couldn't be sure if he understood, but he kept talking.

"I really like your brother. He's a very good detective. When my house was broken into and people stole my things, he was able to get them back for me. That's how we became friends."

Harper returned. "How's it going? Should we take a walk through the rest of the park?"

David hummed, and Colson jumped to his feet. "I'll dump the garbage." Harper caught his arm and pulled him close.

"Thank you."

Colson kissed him. "You can thank me later."

The day passed swiftly, and not once did Colson feel as if David was a burden. They traversed the entire area of the zoo, and Colson took tons of pictures on his phone of David at the petting zoo, and with the stuffed seal he bought him at the gift shop.

"You're going to spoil him," Harper teased. "What's going to happen when he goes to the aquarium? Am I going to find a giant whale in his room?"

"I wanted something special so he'd always remember today," Colson explained.

Harper squeezed his shoulder. "I don't think that's going to be a problem. I know I always will." They shared a smile, and Harper put an arm around his shoulders. "Thank you for this. I can't imagine a more perfect day."

Before they left, Colson stopped to take a picture of the three of them, sent it to Harper, then showed it to David.

"The three of us."

"Ready to go home?" Harper pushed David's chair out of the zoo and to the van. "I was thinking a barbecue for dinner. Burgers and hot dogs?"

"Sounds great," Colson agreed. In fact, the day had been perfect. Walking through the park with Harper and David, feeling part of a family, emphasized how lonely he'd been.

The ride home was short, and Harper disappeared for a while to take care of David. When he reappeared, Colson took out beers for the two of them, and they sat together on the sectional in the cool of the living room. Luis was out, and the house was quiet. He rested his head on Harper's shoulder.

"David's taking a nap. I had to change his bags, and I gave him a quick sponge bath."

Colson understood Harper was telling him all this to give him all the facts concerning his daily care.

"I think he enjoyed himself today. He didn't resent me being there, did he? I wouldn't want him to think I was taking away his special time with you." That was his biggest concern.

Harper kissed the top of his head. "He doesn't. He was so relaxed and happy. I think he understands you're special." He kissed him again. "Very special to me."

Who needed the blasting music and party lights of the clubs? All he wanted was right here. Right now. "Thank you for allowing me to share today with you and David."

"I know it's not what you're used to, but it's all I have to offer."

"What I'm used to is nothing. This is more than I ever dreamed possible. Growing up, I was so damn lonely." He thought back to all those afternoons spent sitting against a tree, with a book, lost in stories of other people's lives. "And hiding who I was added another layer of solitude. Writing can be isolating too. I get caught up in my head, and while the reward is creating characters and stories people love, it's not enough. And when my ex left me, I buried myself so deep, I wasn't sure I'd ever be able to dig myself out of the darkness."

Harper toyed with his hair. "I consider myself lucky. After spending my days looking at the worst of humanity, I get to come home to David's sweetness and pure heart. He's the balance in my life."

"You are lucky."

Harper took the bottle from his hand and set it on the table next to his. "I'm lucky because I remember seeing you that morning at the coffee shop and thinking, who the hell is this guy with those sexy tats? He's hot as fuck."

Colson snickered. "And then you thought I was a murderer and wanted to arrest me."

Harper's eyes danced. "A minor technicality." He framed Colson's face with his hands. "I wanted you then because you're sexy as hell and turned me on. I want you now because I know you've got an amazing, giving heart beneath that ink. I'm never going to stop wanting you." He kissed him lightly. "Needing you." Another butterfly kiss. "Loving you." Harper's gaze held his.

If bones could melt, he'd be in a puddle.

"I love you, Harper. It's only three words that more books have been written about than any others, yet they fill my heart to overflowing. And I'll never get tired of saying them to you."

"I love you too." He trailed his fingers over Colson's face. "I've never said those words, but with you it just comes naturally." Harper's eyes clouded with concern. "You're sure you're okay with all this? It isn't always going to be this easy. He has good days but some bad ones too."

"I think if I can handle your grumpy ass, I'll be fine with David."

"I'm not grumpy. I'm focused." Harper's lips ticked up in a devilish grin. "And you'll have to wait until after dinner to handle my ass. I'm going to start the grill soon." He leaned in for a kiss, and Colson slung an arm around his neck to anchor him in place.

"Let me heat you up a little first. Give you a taste of what's in store for you later." He pushed Harper to the cushions and tugged his jogging pants below his hips, revealing a mouth-watering erection. "I'll make it quick and dirty." He licked his lips and took Harper's dick in his mouth.

"Jesus," Harper hissed and groaned as Colson swirled his tongue over the head while pumping the thick shaft. "I'm not going to last." He slapped his hand and tangled his fingers in Colson's hair.

"*Mmm,*" Colson hummed, his tongue bathing Harper's swollen cock. Pleasure-pain ripped through him from Harper tugging on his hair, and he moaned, working his mouth and hand faster.

"Colson, what the hell." His hips bucked hard, and Colson slipped a finger past his taint to rub the rim. A violent shiver rolled through Harper and he came, hot and heavy down Colson's throat.

He swallowed it all and sat back, loving the sight of Harper lying wrecked and blissful under him. One final kiss to his stomach, and Colson tucked him inside his clothes. Harper cracked an eye open and motioned with his hand for Colson to come close. He snuggled in and sighed.

"That's the first time I've ever had sex in this house," Harper said. "I always thought I'd be alone."

"And even when I was with my ex, I was lonely." Colson pressed a kiss to Harper's mouth. "Now it's all about us. Together. And we'll never be lonely again."

CHAPTER TWENTY-TWO

Harper stood at the grill and watched Colson give David apple juice and engage him in conversation about the zoo. The day had gone smoothly, and Colson had exceeded his ideal of the perfect boyfriend.

So why couldn't he relax and enjoy it?

Maybe because he was waiting for the second shoe to drop.

The smile that didn't reach the eyes.

The hand on the doorknob and the *click* of the lock as they walked out forever.

The left hook out of nowhere, landing square on his chin, upending him.

Colson's laughter rose in the air, snapping him out of his brain fog. "Hey, Harper. David and I are hungry. Are you going to put the food on the grill, or are you getting a facial over there? I called your name about five or six times."

"I'm fine. Just thinking." He busied himself with the food, and soon the smell of the burgers and hot dogs teased their noses. Out of nowhere, he remembered that the day of David's accident, they were supposed to have a barbecue. His mother had set up the grill and asked him to go to the store because she'd discovered there was no ketchup. Walking home, he'd heard the sirens, and when he'd turned the corner, he'd seen the wreckage.

They'd never had that barbecue.

"Are you all right?" Colson's hand rested on his shoulder. "Harper? What's wrong?"

He ducked his head and took the food off the fire. "Nothing."

"Nothing that's a whole lot of something terrible, I'm assuming, from how pale you are." His hand massaged Harper's neck, easing the tension gathered there. Gentle, concerned eyes met his. "Are you worried about David?"

"I'm always worried about him," he answered honestly, and Colson's gaze grew tender but with a hint of fierceness.

"I know. But who worries about you?"

"I can take care of myself." He tried a cocky grin. "I've got a gun."

Colson frowned. "That's not what I mean, and you know it. Everyone needs someone to care about them."

He nudged Colson's cheek with his nose. "I care about you."

"And I worry that you don't know how to accept love because you've always been the one to give and not receive."

"That's not true. David loves me."

"I know he does. I hope you know it's okay to admit that sometimes it can be overwhelming to take care of him. And it doesn't mean you love him any less."

He peered over Colson's shoulder to see David sitting under the canopy out of the sun. His face wore the same serene expression it had for years. What went on in his mind? It was a question Harper would never know the answer to, and it haunted him.

"I can't ask you to do what I do."

"And I'm not saying I can. All I want you to know is that you're not alone anymore. Let me help ease the weight off your shoulders. Use me." Colson's eyes twinkled, and the thoughts that sprang to his mind sent a sizzle straight to his balls.

"I intend to. Tonight."

"So this will have to hold you..." Colson hesitated only a second before kissing him, and Harper fell into the sweetness of his soft lips and velvety, hot tongue. The taste of apple and a hint of bitter from the beer and something unmistakably Colson. He smoothed his hands over the colorful tattoos on Colson's biceps.

"That was nice."

Colson stood flushed and panting, his eyes hazy, his lips red. "*Nice?*" He pretended outrage until a wicked, teasing grin curved that tempting mouth. "That's not what I intended. I'd better up my game for later."

"You'd better because I play to win." With a wink, he passed by him, holding the tray of cooked food. "Here we are. All ready." David's eyes brightened, and he watched avidly as Harper cut his burger into small pieces and dipped it in the ketchup. "Do you want to try using the fork? Like you do in therapy?" He put the utensil in David's right hand and watched him make the attempt several times and fail. He could sense the frustration and was about to tell him to forget it, but then Colson sat on David's opposite side and urged him on. Something Harper had never done.

"Wow, David. I didn't know you were so advanced."

About to tell Colson to be quiet and let David concentrate, he saw David lift his hand a fraction.

"That's amazing, David. Look at you go."

It might've been his imagination, but Harper sensed David wanted to show Colson he could do it. The painstaking journey from plate to mouth took almost ten minutes, but when he put the fork to his lips, Colson clapped. Harper almost broke down in tears.

David made whimpering noises, and Harper brushed the wetness from his cheeks before facing him. He'd never allowed himself to lose it in front of David—not even if the weight of responsibility was sometimes too heavy to bear, sending him to his knees.

"What's wrong, buddy?" He touched David's face, and at his lips moving, Harper kissed him. "Better? I'm so proud of you. Wait until we tell Luis."

"Tell Luis what?" The big man opened the screen door and joined them on the deck. "Someone having a party and didn't invite me?"

Harper saw him scan the table, and his brows rose high at the fork in David's hand.

"We're finishing dinner. David was showing us how he uses a fork."

"My man." A huge smile lit Luis's face. "I knew you'd do it if your brother asked."

"Actually, I think it was for Colson. I was willing to sit and not say anything, afraid to push him, but Colson encouraged him, cheering him on. And he did it."

"So you all had a nice day?" Luis settled into a chair opposite them. "I had my barbecue, and my buddies wanted to go out, but I'm tired. Figured I'd come home early and get a good night's sleep."

Maybe Luis could fool Colson with his bullshit, but Harper knew better. "Is that the story you're going to stick with?" He arched a brow. "You wanted to see how the day went." He gathered up the paper plates to dump them into the trash. "It was a huge success, I'm thinking."

"Never doubted it for a minute. And yeah, maybe I was a little curious to see how Colson dealt with helping you with David."

Lips twitching, Harper glanced at Colson. "Well, since one woman in Brooklyn now thinks David works undercover for the feds, I think he handled it all pretty well."

Colson shrugged, but the devil lit his eyes. "Hey, if she was going to stare, I wanted to give her something to talk about."

Luis slapped his thigh, hooting with laughter. "Awesome. I love it. And I can see how engaged David is. His eyes are bright, and he hasn't stopped smiling." A crafty grin spread over Luis's face. "It's still early. Only around seven. What were you planning for the evening?"

He looked to Colson, who shrugged. "I have no idea. Usually I just watch a movie after I finish writing for the day. Have a beer. Nothing special."

Luis rose to his feet. "Well, I had a big meal and need to walk it off. I think I'll take David for a spin to Dumbo. It's a beautiful evening, and the sun'll be setting soon. Summer's coming to an end, and there won't be many more nights like this."

Harper had to hide his face to keep from giving it all away.

Oh, Luis, you sneaky dude. You can't fool me. You don't ever overeat. You want Colson and me to have some alone time, and I am not going to stop you.

"Are you sure?" Colson's brows knitted in concern. "You just walked in, and you're already leaving?"

Luis bent to whisper in Colson's ear, and from the blush painting his neck and cheeks red, Harper could only imagine what was said.

He didn't have to wait long.

Chattering away about their adventure, Luis hustled David out of the house, and when Harper locked the door after watching them drive away in the van, Colson tugged on his arm.

"Let's go."

Amused and a little turned-on by Colson's bossiness, Harper allowed himself to be led upstairs to his bedroom. Years ago, he'd converted the house to have a master bedroom on the main floor for David, and he'd taken over the second floor.

Colson kicked off his sneakers, then pulled his T-shirt off, revealing all those mouthwatering tattoos. His eyes twinkled. "Like what you see?"

Knowing he finally had the whole night to spend licking him from top to bottom sent a rush of blood to his dick.

"I'll like it even more when I'm tasting you."

Colson's cheeks burned bright, and he stripped off his jeans. Harper quickly shed his clothes, but instead of climbing onto the bed, Colson headed for the bathroom.

"Come," he demanded, and Harper, hard as a rock, followed him. They got under the spray, and he sighed with pleasure at the hot water jetting over his muscles. Colson spread the slippery shower gel all over and massaged him.

"You're so tense. Ease up."

He groaned and rolled his shoulders. "I'll ease up in you—oh, fuck. What the hell..." He hissed as Colson's slippery finger slid along his crease and pushed past the rim. He'd never bottomed, but the feel of Colson's thick finger penetrating his hole was such an unexpected turn-on, he found himself spreading his legs wide and unashamedly groaning as Colson dragged not one but two fingers in and out of him.

"You like that?" Colson whispered, and he could only moan and whine as white-hot pleasure seared through him and his dick streamed.

"Yeah, please, more, harder. Fuck, oh God." He didn't care that he was crying out and snapping his hips to meet Colson's wicked, teasing hand. He reached down to work his cock, lost in sensation.

"Look at you. How hungry you are for me. I bet you've never been loved properly." Colson kissed along the sweep of his spine, then up again, his fingers still busy inside him, driving him wild. "You're so busy worrying about everyone, making sure their needs are met. Let me take care of you."

Harper couldn't form the words to say he was fine because he wasn't. He was upended by Colson. All he could manage was pleading and begging for Colson to never stop touching him.

"It's my turn to be here for you. You want to be taken care of, don't you, baby?" Colson removed his fingers, and he felt empty and hollow.

"No, fuck. Don't stop," Harper cried out in protest, but at the thrust of Colson's demanding tongue breaching his hole, he shouted out his pleasure. "Oh yeah, oh God, yes."

He pumped his dick hard and fast, head spinning from the wet, sucking sounds of Colson licking him out. "More, more," he gasped, and he almost lost his footing when Colson stood abruptly and shoved two fingers back in. They touched a spot that sent a jolt of electricity through him, and he was lost. His toes curled, his balls drew tight, and streams of come splattered all over the wall. He rested his overheated forehead against the cool tile, his body still twitching as Colson now held his hips and worked his heavy cock up and down the cleft of his ass.

"Fuck, you're gorgeous when you come," Colson's husky voice rasped in his ear, and Harper trembled. He rocked into Colson, who bit his ear. "Oh, God. Yeah, right there."

Harper felt Colson unload on his ass only a second before the shower washed it away. He reached out and turned off the water.

"We'll shrivel away into nothing if we don't get out of the water soon."

Giving a weak laugh, Colson reached over and stroked Harper's soft dick. "I'm not worried. This is a whole lot of nothing I'm going to want in me later."

Harper faced him, studying him. The sweep of his brows and the thick lashes curling up and almost touching them. Steady, clear blue eyes met his, and a sweet smile creased his face. Harper ran his thumb over the prominent cheekbones.

"You are so beautiful. Not only on the outside, but in here." He rested a hand over Colson's chest, feeling the rapid thump of his heart. "Where it truly counts." He pressed a kiss to his soft, parted lips. Another on the strong cords of his neck. And a third in the dip of his collarbones.

"Harper." Colson sighed. "I never expected to fall in love with you, but I can't imagine being without you now."

"And now that I've found you to love, I'm not going anywhere. Except to take you into my bed and hold you all night long."

He dried them both off, and hand in hand, they lay together in his bed. His whole life he'd slept alone, waking up to check on David, then climbing into his bed between cold sheets. Colson cuddled near, and he wrapped his arms around him.

"Who would've guessed you're a snuggler, Detective Rose?" Colson kissed his nipple, drawing it into his hot, wet mouth, and Harper gasped. No worries if he could get it up again so soon—his dick was filling fast. He reached over to grab a plump ass cheek and squeezed. "I'm going to get snug inside you. I need to."

Colson nuzzled against him and continued to drive him wild by biting and sucking at his neck and nipples. "I can't wait."

Desire pooled in his belly, but he wanted to take it slow. He pushed Colson under him, and as promised, licked a path up his calves, kissing the sensitive underside of his knees and the quivering inner thighs. The smell of Colson's arousal was a heady perfume he would willingly drown in, but he bypassed the beauty of a rapidly swelling cock to swirl his tongue over Colson's navel.

"Do you have any idea how much you turn me on?" he whispered. "All this gorgeous skin and your ink." The tip of his tongue traced the outline of each bird and butterfly. "You got these so you could fly away. Now you have a place to land. Here with me."

Colson pulled him close. "I love you. There's no place I'd rather be than here. With you."

Their mouths connected, lips seeking and touching, hands reaching and holding, each of them hungry to take and possess. They knew they belonged to each other. Colson's lips stole his heart, and his knowing tongue delved deep, leaving him light-headed and for the first time, able to breathe freely. He'd found his other half, the missing piece of a solitary existence that was lonely no more.

Harper licked around the wet tip of Colson's cock, drinking in his salty taste. He blew a stream of cool air across the head before engulfing the rigid length. Colson's moans rose in the air, and his hands clutched the bedsheets into knots as Harper rose and fell on his dick.

A spurt of precome hit his throat, and Harper pulled off.

"No. What the fuck?" Colson's outraged face brought a smile to his lips.

"I can't wait any longer." He grabbed the condom and lube from the nightstand and rolled it down his aching length, then used his slick fingers to tease and widen Colson's hole.

"Well, if you put it like that," Colson panted and writhed under Harper's touch. "Get inside me now."

"So demanding. Pushy." Harper sank in slowly, relishing the grip of Colson's tight ass on his shaft. Fully seated, he lowered his mouth to meet Colson's in a bruising kiss. "I love it. And you." He continued kissing him as he thrust strong.

"Fuck." Colson vibrated under his touch and grasped his shaft. "So good," he rasped. The slick sound of Colson's hand on his dick fueled Harper's lust, and he drove into Colson's willing body, the colors of his ink flashing like a garden of life. Sweat poured from him, and Colson's creamy-white skin grew red as he stiffened and came, his come spreading over his hand and their bellies.

"Rub it on me," he growled, feeling possessive as fuck and wanting to be covered in Colson's scent. Colson's eyes widened, and he dipped his fingers in the puddle on his stomach and smeared it over Harper's chest. "Now in my mouth."

At Colson's touch, Harper thought he'd blow apart. The harsh taste filled his nose and mouth, and with Colson having his throbbing cock in a death grip, he moaned around the sticky fingers and managed to bury himself deep in Colson, coming with a head rush that had him seeing stars.

He had no idea how much time had passed, but he managed to crack open one eye. Colson lay under him, his breath gentle puffs against his face. "I assume I'm still alive." Harper kissed Colson's shoulder where the tattoos began. He'd never get tired of admiring all the lines and swirls of color decorating all that soft skin.

"I know I barely am. God knows if I can walk straight. So to speak." Colson's snicker was cut short when Harper eased out of him, and he winced. "And we're both a mess. We'll have to take another shower."

"Not so fast," Harper murmured, and slid in next to Colson and held him tight, spooning him. "I love you. So much. Don't rush away so quickly. Lie with me a while."

Colson nestled in closer. "I meant what I said, you know. Earlier, when we were in the shower."

Harper kissed him, trailing his tongue down the slope of his neck to his shoulder, tracing the curve of muscle. "You think I remember what you said when you were twisting me inside out?" His dick twitched, and Colson shook with laughter. "And what the hell was that all about, anyway?"

"Me, making sure you know how much I love you. And to let you know I'll always be there to protect you."

"Me?" He laughed. "I'm the one with a gun, in case you've forgotten."

Colson turned in his arms, as serious as Harper had ever seen him. "Everyone needs someone to watch out for them. David has you. And now you have me."

He'd always been the strong one, shouldering everyone's burdens, ignoring his needs to make sure others were granted theirs. From the day of David's accident, he'd gone from a fifteen-year-old teenage boy with nothing on his mind but hanging out on the weekends with his friends, to a semi-adult, his childhood lost, dreams shunted aside.

"Let's take that shower before they come home."

CHAPTER TWENTY-THREE

Surprising himself, Colson woke before Harper. He slipped out from under his arm, took his keys, and dressed quickly. Within minutes he was walking down the block. Dawn had settled its bright, pale fingers over the leafy silhouette of the canopy of trees, and he drew in deep breaths of the fresh morning air that hadn't yet turned hot and humid.

Few stores were open at this hour–the bodegas were always a good bet for the late-night, after-partying bacon-egg-and-cheese on a roll, or the early morning injection of regular coffee, which any New Yorker knew was milk and two sugars. But Colson had a different stop.

It was Sunday morning. That meant bagels.

And, apparently, he wasn't the only lunatic up at the ass-crack of dawn to get their fix. He'd had to wait ten minutes to place his order, but the smell of freshly baked bread, the tang of salt, garlic, and onion, was worth it. He walked out with a dozen assorted, three kinds of cream cheese, and lox.

When he returned, he found Harper sitting at the kitchen table, his head in his hands. Luis sat with him, apparently in the middle of a heavy conversation.

"Hi. Sorry if I'm interrupting."

Eyes as pale as the morning mist widened. "You're back?"

"I didn't leave." Confused, Colson set the shopping bag on the table. "Uh, I mean, yeah, I did, and I guess I should've left a note, but I woke up and thought it would be nice if I got breakfast for everyone, so I went to the bagel store."

A strangled sound burst from Harper, and Luis squeezed his shoulder and nodded at Colson. "I told Harper you wouldn't just walk out. You had no reason to sneak away without leaving a note or anything."

Stunned by Luis's words, Colson dropped to the chair next to Harper's. "Is that what you thought? That I'd left without saying good-bye to you? Or David?" Disappointment crushed his heart. His voice dropped to a murmur for only them to hear. "After last night, is that really what you think of me?"

Luis slipped away, but Colson's attention was on Harper's ashen face and haunted eyes.

"Not you. Me. I guess I'm still waiting for the ax to drop. So many years have passed that I don't dare to dream of possibilities."

"Oh, babe. We're way past that point of maybe and hoping. We're the here and now. As real as it gets." Colson slid his arms around Harper's broad shoulders and rested their cheeks together.

"I thought you changed your mind and I lost you," Harper whispered.

And there went his heart again, doing those dangerous swoops. Throat tight, Colson nuzzled into Harper, drawing in the scent he'd cocooned in and dreamed about all night.

"You can't lose someone you can find in the dark. Knowing they are with you by the currents in the air. Some hearts just call to each other without needing a sound."

Finally, Harper smiled. "You're very good with words. You should be a writer or something."

"As long as I'm yours. That's all I want to be."

Harper kissed him, hands sliding into his hair to anchor him, and they stayed there in the kitchen, with the sunlight streaming through the windows.

Colson cupped Harper's cheek. "I'd better put the cream cheese in the fridge."

But Harper held him tighter. "In a minute. David will be up soon, and I want a few more minutes with you alone."

He had no desire to deny Harper, but as their kisses grew more passionate, he murmured against Harper's lips, "Unless you plan on me ravishing you in the kitchen, we need to stop."

Harper's cheek curved in a smile. "I'd never be able to eat dinner at this table again." With one last press of his lips, Harper put some space between them and brushed Colson's hair off his forehead. "Now go fix me some breakfast while I get David up."

Laughing, Colson rose to his feet, and Harper pinched his butt.

It had been a picture-perfect day. After bagels, they took a drive, then had pizza at Spumoni Gardens. He waited with David under umbrellas at one of the picnic tables while Harper got their food.

When a group of older men at the table across from them started shooting them side-eye looks, Colson decided to face them head on. "This is David. He loves pizza as much as you do."

One man, big and burly, with tattoos on his forearms and a buzz cut, murmured something to his buddies and swung his legs out from under their table to stand by theirs. Colson glanced up at him, a bit tense and wary.

"Sorry if we was staring. But...are you that writer, Colson Delacourt? The one who wrote *Killer Behind the Stairs?*"

His jaw dropped. "Uh...yeah. I am."

The man's weathered face broke out in a grin, and he turned to his friends with a thumbs-up. "It's him," he called over and turned to Colson. "We're huge fans. Me and the guys—that's Arnie with the Giants cap and Bert. I'm Sal. We met in a widowers' support group, and we all love to read suspense, thrillers, crime fiction, ya know?" Colson smothered a smile at the man's fast-talking Brooklyn accent. "Anyway, we got a book club, and we meet Sunday mornings over coffee, talk about the book and have lunch. We just finished reading yours this afternoon. Man, that was a wild ride."

Warmed by the praise, Colson shifted to face the other men, while still keeping David in his view. "It was.

I scared myself sometimes writing it, but I think it helped me."

Bert called out, "I slept with the lights on all week."

They all laughed, and he decided to share an update with them. "I'm almost finished writing a new book."

"Oh, yeah? This one gonna give me nightmares too?" Arnie joked and took a bite of his pizza.

Harper walked out with their pizza, his face quizzical but tense. Colson imagined he anticipated something negative. Colson took the food from him and set it between them.

"This is Sal, and that's Arnie and Bert. They're in a book club and they read my book, and we were just talking. Guys, this is my boyfriend, Harper. He's an NYPD detective. David is his brother." That he was gay shouldn't be a surprise to anyone who was a fan of his books—his bio, which he realized he needed to change, said he lived in Brooklyn with his boyfriend. Hopefully they'd read it.

"Nice to meetcha." Sal nodded at Harper, who'd put a square slice on the plate for David and was cutting it into pieces. "Is he an inspiration for your police characters?"

Harper's lips twitched, and Colson grinned. "No, not the one you've read, but..." Curious at their reaction, Colson decided to clue them in about his new book. "Let me ask you something."

"About the new book?" Sal asked, and all three men crowded near him.

"Yeah. I'm thinking of having this one be a little different—still a thriller and suspenseful with the requisite gore and blood, no worries."

Harper chuckled in the background and gave David some pizza.

"Oh, great. Another high electric bill 'cause I can't turn the lights out." Arnie groaned.

"Don't worry. Shirley will be glad to come over and hold your hand," Bert razzed him. "Shirley works at the bakery on Eighteenth Avenue around the corner from us. She's sweet on Arnie and always slips him an extra cookie."

"Shaddup, will ya? I wanna hear about the new book."

"I'm thinking of having the detective have a romantic relationship. With another man. There'd be no sex, just the talk of the two realizing the connection and growing close." Casually, his gaze traveled over the group of men. "Would you still read it?"

Sal was the first to speak. "Yeah. I would." He turned quiet for a moment. "When my Valerie was in the hospital with cancer, I'd be there with her. She always loved reading those romance books—I'd tease her about all that schmoopy stuff, and she'd say, 'What's wrong with bein' in love and having a happily ever after?' So I'd bring them when I'd come to see her, and since she couldn't hold them 'cause she was too weak, I'd read them to her." He wiped his eyes. "And she was right. It was nice to see the people happy at the end 'cause life can be shit sometimes."

"That's beautiful." Colson blinked at the burning in his eyes. "And I agree. Love has the potential to change people."

David made a grunting noise, and Harper wiped his face. Colson could see the men were too polite to ask, but their eyes were filled with questions.

"David was injured when he was a child, and he lives with Harper and his aide."

Harper acknowledged them with a brief nod as he helped David with the straw for his apple juice.

"Whoa, that's a rough road." Arnie's brow furrowed. "But I gotta give you tons of respect there. I know it can't be easy."

Harper set the juice box down and finally addressed the group. "Life isn't easy, and we're not promised anything. But he's my brother—my only family. I'd walk through fire for him."

"Of course you would. That's what you do for family," Bert agreed, and the other men nodded. "Anything and everything."

"Yes." Harper's eyes glimmered, and Colson took his hand.

Sal said, "Seeing you with your brother makes me think maybe the world ain't such a crappy place after all. So many people would put your brother in a home and just visit him. You walk the walk, not just talk the talk."

"I'm trying."

"You succeed." Colson squeezed his hand.

"So long, Colson. Harper." And to Colson's surprise, all three men surrounded David's chair and waved to him.

"Bye, David."

When David smiled sweetly in response, the men couldn't stop talking about it.

"Did you see? He smiled back at us," they all chattered among themselves.

Harper nudged him. "Your pizza's cold."

"Yeah, but my heart is warm. There really are some good people in this world."

Harper leaned in and kissed him. "Yeah, there are. Let's take the rest home, and we can heat it up. I'll go get a box."

He left them alone, and Colson tidied up around the table. He sat in front of David. "I hope you had fun today. Do you like that I was here all weekend? I care for your brother...I love him. I want that to be okay with you."

David grunted, hands twitching, and his head swayed back and forth. Afraid he'd done something wrong, Colson rushed to reassure David. "Don't worry. Nothing is going to change. You and Harper will always be together."

"What's wrong?" Harper set the pizza box on the table.

"I don't know. I was just asking David if he enjoyed himself and assured him that nothing was going to change between you and him."

Harper crouched by David's chair. "That's right, buddy. I'm still going to be there for you. Me and Luis. But now Colson too."

David's fingers curled, and Colson's heart shriveled.

"He doesn't want that. I see it now. He's upset that I've stayed all weekend."

"I don't believe that. Let's go home. It's been a busy day."

The ride was quiet, and while Harper took care of David, Colson packed up his bag. He sat on the bed, wondering if their relationship was over before it had a chance to get off the ground. He sighed and went downstairs.

Harper and David were in the kitchen, and Harper's gaze zeroed in on his overnight bag. "Going somewhere?"

Colson set it on the floor and pulled out a chair. "I think it's probably best if I leave now. It's been a full weekend, and I'm sure David wants to spend some alone time with you."

Harper's smile was frozen. "Is that really the reason, or is it that you've had enough of playing caretaker and you're ready to leave?"

His heart sank as his anger rose. "Don't be ridiculous. I loved every minute of the weekend, including all my time with David. But..." He faltered, his heart as cold as Harper's empty eyes.

"But what?" Harper pressed.

"You saw when we were at Spumoni Gardens and I talked to David about how much I loved spending time with him. How I hoped he was okay with me being here all weekend with you." He cast his eyes to the shadows on the floor. "When you went to get a box, I told him I loved you. He became agitated and upset. I figured it was better if I left and let you have some time together. Alone." When Harper didn't respond, Colson picked up his bag and rose from the chair. "Bye, David. Harper...call me?"

He'd crossed the kitchen, heading to the door, when he heard David cry out. He turned and saw that David's hands were twitching, and he was swaying side to side. Harper had jumped to his side.

"It's okay. Don't worry. Everything's fine."

But David grew more agitated, his voice growing louder, his mouth twisted as if he were in pain. Tears flowed from his eyes. Despite his words only moments ago, Colson stopped.

"What's wrong?" he asked Harper, who was frantically trying to calm David.

"If I didn't know better, I'd think he didn't want you to leave." Harper beckoned him. "Come here, please."

Colson approached David, who watched him, and as he drew close, David quieted. Colson sat on the other side of his wheelchair. "Is Harper right, David? Do you want me to stay? Is that what you're trying to tell me?"

Whimpering escaped from David's lips, and...he smiled and made kissing sounds. Colson thought his heart would explode, and when he glanced at Harper, he knew the tears rolling down his face matched his own. Harper held out his hand in front of David's chair and Colson took it, then placed them on top of David's.

"Don't leave us," Harper whispered. "We both love you and want you to stay."

"If that's what you want."

"We want it." Harper turned his hand palm up, and squeezed his. "I need it."

"I guess we should think about dinner, then?"

David's hand twitched beneath theirs.

CHAPTER TWENTY-FOUR

Waking up Monday morning with Colson naked and warm next to him made the start of the week a pleasure. It also wasn't an impetus to get him out of bed. It was only a few minutes after five.

"Plenty of time," he murmured, and when Colson sighed and snuggled in closer, Harper kissed his neck.

"What time is it?" Colson muttered.

"Time for me to make you feel good before I have to leave." He swept his hand along the curve of Colson's back and cupped a cheek. "I like this."

Colson chuckled. "What? My butt? I know."

Harper nibbled at his ear and throat while his fingers played along the cleft of Colson's ass. "That's a given." He continued to trail kisses over Colson's neck. "I meant waking up with you. Next to me." He gripped Colson's hard cock, and his fingers played up and down the hot shaft. "And this. I like this a lot. I'd like it in my mouth."

"Oh Jesus," Colson choked out as Harper followed his words with action. "Yeah, I think we like the same things."

With his lips wrapped around Colson's rigid length, Harper slid lower until his nose touched Colson's wiry pubic hair. He rose up, his tongue working the smooth crown, lapping up the precome and tickling into the slit. Colson writhed under him, fingers clutching at the bedsheets.

"God, I love seeing you like this." Harper sucked him to the root. Colson's hips bucked, and Harper increased his pace, feeling Colson's dick swell between his lips. Saliva dripped from his mouth, and his heart thundered. "You're gorgeous in my bed."

"Fuck, Harper," Colson groaned and thrust up. "I need you."

Harper released him with a juicy *plop*. "Yeah? You want this?" He rubbed his aching dick and reached for the condoms and lube on the bedside table. He slicked himself up, Colson watching him with avid, hungry eyes.

"Yeah, come on." Colson widened his legs, but Harper grabbed them and pushed them to his shoulders.

"Don't rush me." He rubbed the sheathed head of his dick over Colson's hole and around the rim. Colson's moans filled the air, and a flush rose over his body. "This has to last us the whole day."

Harper eased inside Colson, inch by inch, the tight walls sucking him in. "Fuck, every time is like the first with you." Teeth bared, he rolled his hips, and Colson hissed.

"God."

"Not even close." Harper thrust hard and pulled out, then drove in, Colson catching his rhythm. Harder and faster, his push to Colson's pull, the clutch of muscle on his dick sending jolts of electricity to his balls every time he moved. "What you do to me." Harper leaned in, increasing his pace.

"Harper, *Harper.*" Colson's head thrashed side to side, his hand fast and furious on his dick. "Oh God," he gasped, his body growing stiff as his dick pumped out a stream of come, landing between them. The sweat from their bodies mixed with the sticky release, and Colson's hair lay plastered to his brow.

Seeing Colson fall apart under him drove Harper to the brink, and though he wanted this to last longer–fucking hell, he wanted to feel like this forever–his orgasm smashed through him, splitting him into a thousand flaming pieces that burned to fiery ash. His blood beat hot and his dick throbbed as Colson's ass squeezed him. Harper's head spun, and he lost his breath. The next thing he knew, he was facedown on top of Colson, lips buried in his damp curls.

"Are you alive?" Colson murmured, and Harper caught the edge of laughter in his voice.

"Barely. Maybe I should call in sick. Have you play my nurse." Even though he lay in a puddle of bliss, he wanted Colson, and he trailed his fingers over Colson's face. "Tend to my every need."

Colson snorted. "You wish. And I'm the one who needs help. You wrecked me." He rubbed their scruffy cheeks together. "And I loved every moment of it."

"I know." Harper's smile was smug, and he slowly withdrew and got rid of the condom. "And I love you. And every delicious inch of your beautiful skin with all that ink. What're your plans for the day?"

"Your ego is only surpassed by how much I love you. It's why I let you get away with saying that."

Colson stretched, and Harper eyed his sinuous body. How could he want him again even as his body thrummed with pleasure? He should be satisfied, but Harper knew the more of Colson he had, the more he'd want him.

"As to plans," Colson said, "I'm in the home stretch of this book. I have to start wrapping up the detective solving the murder and figuring out how he and his love interest are going to handle being together."

"Like us?" Harper left the bed and took out his clothes for the day.

Colson's brow furrowed. "I thought we had that settled."

On his way to the bathroom, Harper paused. "We do. I'm not having second thoughts. But there are some odds and ends to think about."

"Such as?" Colson swung his legs over the edge of the bed and brushed the hair out of his eyes.

"We live in two very different houses. I couldn't possibly get David into your place, and I know you love your home, so I'm not asking you to leave it." Seeing Colson's face fall, Harper came to sit by his side. "Hey. It's not anything we have to worry about. We'll work it all out."

"It's true, I love my house." Colson's cheek pressed to his, and Harper drew in his scent and felt the brush of those long lashes against his skin. "But I love you more."

"And I'm not going anywhere, so there's no problem. Now, how about you come shower with me?"

Colson slung an arm around his neck. "I don't know. I kind of like smelling like you all day."

Groaning as desire flooded him again, Harper pulled him down for a kiss. "Maybe I need to get a little dirtier first."

He walked into the precinct and saw Nolan already at his desk. "Good morning. How was the weekend?"

Nolan eyed him, and a tiny smile played on his lips as he drank his coffee. "Fine, but I'm thinking yours was better."

Harper clicked on his computer and signed in. "Yeah? And why's that?" He took out his coffee from the brown paper bag and took a long, satisfying drink. Round two with Colson had cost him the opportunity for breakfast, but would he rather have had Colson sucking his brains through his dick or a bowl of cereal? Not exactly a choice.

"Well…" Nolan stretched out those long legs and laced his fingers over his flat stomach. "Number one, I'm in the office first. Number two, you walked in happy. On a Monday."

Harper pulled out a bagel and took a bite, chewed, and swallowed. "Yeah? That's not such a big deal. It happens."

"In all our years of being partners I can count on one finger the day you came in after me, and it was because David wasn't feeling well. Since you're smiling, it's not that. But number three, and most importantly…" Nolan's grin broadened to shit-eating status. "I spy with my little eye a bunch of red marks on your neck that weren't there on Friday."

"I knew I should've stopped at CVS for some cover-up," he grumbled, but he couldn't pretend to be too pissed when he felt so damn good.

"So..." Nolan crossed his arms. "You and Colson Delacourt had a good weekend."

"You could say that." As much as he disliked talking about his personal life, he was too happy to hold it inside. "We're...together."

True happiness shone from Nolan's face. "I am so glad you took my advice."

Laughter bubbled up. "You? You're going to take credit for my relationship?"

"Why not? I saw it right away at the old lady's house. You couldn't keep your eyes off him." Nolan smirked. "Lie all you want to yourself, but you can't hide from me."

"Apparently not." Harper chuckled. "My luck, to get partnered with the best detective on the force." He paused. "And a best friend. You were right. I was pushing Colson away because of what happened with Ronnie, but they're nothing alike. Ronnie ran away from responsibility and family—Colson runs toward us. We spent the entire weekend together, and there wasn't a single second I felt like Colson wasn't totally in the moment with us. And David loves him."

Nolan leaned in close. "So you say. As do you."

"Are you finished with the Dear Abby schtick now, you two?" Poole's growl from behind had them jumping. Red-faced and annoyed at getting called out, Harper directed a death glare at Nolan before answering.

"Sorry, Cap. What's up?"

"What's up is I need you to review the weekend reports of break-ins and robberies to see if any of them match our guys."

"Break-ins?" Harper frowned. "Didn't we get that crew?"

Captain Poole's smile was thin. "Surprise, surprise, Rose. Bad boys like to copy each other. We have another. Except this time it's a little different."

Poole now had their undivided attention. "How?"

"It's not a group of men this time. It's women."

He and Nolan exchanged shocked glances. "That's unusual. But not unheard of. We once collared a group of women running a neat little shoplifting ring."

"Yeah, I remember. Both of you, go through the reports and start the process. You know the drill."

"You got it," Nolan said. "And unfortunately, we do."

They set up interviews all morning and afternoon and received the same story from each victim. They would ring the bell or knock, and when the person opened, they would push in the door and punch the owner in the stomach or the face. Once they were down, their hands were tied, and they were left on the floor while the house was ransacked.

At a coffee shop near the precinct, they went over their notes. Harper chewed on some fries. "So here's what we've got so far. Apparently, they hang out at the grocery store or outside banks and follow their vics home. They target the elderly and sometimes young girls walking home alone after school."

"I swear." Nolan sighed. "If these people would only use their powers for good and not evil, the world would be a better place."

"But no matter that, they choose violence. And we need to deal with them." Harper thought for a moment. "We should go to the supermarkets in the area and do some scouting. Show them the sketches and see if any of the cashiers or regulars noticed anything."

Nolan shoved the last bite of burger into his mouth. "Ready?"

"Yeah." Harper picked up the check. "I got this one."

Nolan grinned. "Having a boyfriend makes you generous. I like it."

Harper put some bills on the table. "You're an idiot."

They struck out at the first supermarket—they showed the police artist sketches but no one recognized the suspects—then struck gold at the bank with a door-holder, a Mr. Alvin Lewis.

"Yeah, I seen these two. They hang around, cramp my style."

"Cramp your style?" Nolan inquired.

"I hold the door for people, and most just ignore me. Sometimes they give me a smile and a thank-you. But a few of the regulars, they give me a little something—a dollar or two, but it helps with the disability check, you know? At Christmas one of the ladies even baked me cookies and gave me a scarf and gloves." His expression became tender. "She's a sweetheart that Ms. Johnson. Always a kind word."

"Millie Johnson? About five two and ninety pounds? White hair?" Harper knew it had to be Millie, but if this was her bank, he was concerned.

"Yeah. That's her. Anyway, I always make sure to hold the door for her and watch when she walks down the block. She's such a bitty thing."

Harper pressed him. "So these two, you've seen them today?"

"Yeah. They been hanging here for hours. I noticed 'cause they're young and I was surprised they ain't in school. Don't they check up on them?"

"We'll alert the truancy division," Nolan said. "Did you see if they paid particular attention to anybody?"

"Nah, I wasn't lookin'." He rushed to open the door for a young woman with a stroller on her way out.

"Thank you." She hesitated, then reached into her purse, which was slung over the back of the stroller, and fished out a dollar.

"Thank you, miss. And if I was you, I wouldn't keep my bag like that. They can just come and rip it right off, ain't that right, Officers?"

Harper nodded. "He is correct, ma'am. It's best to wear it crossbody."

"I usually do. I just threw it there after the bank, but I guess that's not smart." Her brow wrinkled. "Is something wrong? Are you here because there was a problem?"

"We're investigating a string of push-in burglaries. If any young women come to your door, saying they need help or that they need to use your phone, don't let them in."

"I live in a co-op with a doorman, so that's not an issue, but I'll tell my friends who don't." She glanced at her baby. "That's scary. I hope you catch them."

"We do too, ma'am. And if you do hear or see anything suspicious while you're in the neighborhood, here's our card. Please call us. I'm Detective Rose, and this is my partner, Detective Martinez."

"I will." She walked away.

They thanked the man for his help and strolled down the street to the supermarket. School had started earlier in the month, and Harper already mourned the loss of the less crowded streets, as they dodged a large group of kids clogging the sidewalk.

"I'm looking forward to the next holiday. I don't remember there being so many kids around," he grumbled.

"You don't like kids?" Nolan asked.

"I like them fine." Harper became serious. "I remember when David was little—like two. He used to only want me to read him a bedtime story. I knew it gave my parents a break, so I did it for a little while, but then I stopped because it was annoying to sit and read the same stuff over and over every night." He sighed. "I'd give anything for a redo. I could've been a better brother."

"You're an incredible brother." Nolan paused. "And what about being an honorary uncle?"

For a moment he didn't understand, until Nolan's smile grew broad. "What? You and Gina? Seriously?"

"Yeah. We've been trying since we first got married, but nothing happened. Doctors couldn't explain it, so we gave up, figuring it wasn't in the cards. Three months ago she said she wasn't feeling well and felt nauseated. When it didn't go away, she went to the doctor and *boom*. Pregnant."

Harper hugged him. "That's amazing news. You'll be terrific parents. How's she feeling now?"

"Good, but since she's in her forties, she's high risk. Doctor wants her to be real careful."

"Yeah, I bet. Tell her I'm happy for her."

"I will."

They reached the supermarket, and when they showed the sketches to the cashiers, one of them recognized the girls.

"Yeah, they was just here. Like, ten minutes ago."

He and Nolan exchanged glances. "Thanks. Let's go."

For over an hour they searched the streets but found nothing out of the ordinary. They spoke to women on the street, warning them to be vigilant and handed out their cards, asking them to call if they saw anything.

By six o'clock, his feet hurt, and they'd covered every block of Brooklyn Heights from Atlantic Avenue down to Front Street. At the A train station, he and Nolan stopped. "I'm calling it a night. Tomorrow we'll go out earlier. Maybe we'll get lucky."

"Yeah. I'm ready for a foot massage and a hot shower." Nolan rolled his neck.

"Sorry, but it's time for you to go pamper your wife. Be a good husband, Daddy."

His phone buzzed, and it was Colson.

I'm here with David and Luis. We're waiting for dinner.

An automatic smile tipped up his lips, and Nolan jumped all over that. "Yeah, well, you go home and be a good boyfriend. See you *mañana*." He cackled and ran down the subway steps.

"I intend to. Very good."

Laughing to himself, he began the walk home.

CHAPTER TWENTY-FIVE

It was definitely odd to be in Harper's house without him, but Luis assured him it was fine.

"Dude, you're together. Of course you can be here. And let me tell you, I am so damn happy to see it. I was afraid for Harper. I can't say that to him because he refuses to listen, but it's the truth."

"Afraid for him?" He knew Harper had changed from the hard, cold man he'd met months earlier, to someone loving and romantic. But he still didn't like to talk much about the past.

"You see how he is. So overprotective and hovering."

"You mean over David."

Luis nodded. "Now don't get me wrong. David being kept at home was a blessing for both of them. David receives one-on-one care, which he never could in a group setting, and Harper gets the security of knowing David is safe. But it wasn't easy for Harper. He was torn between thinking he had to stay at home with David and leaving him with someone." He brushed at his eyes. "I've been a home care attendant for a very long time, and I've never seen a relationship like Harper has with his brother."

"He feels a heavy weight of responsibility because he's all David has."

"Because he doesn't let anyone in," Luis insisted. "And then he ended up with that Ronnie...I should've known from the start that one wasn't a keeper."

Colson wasn't a gossip, but he couldn't help wanting to hear what Luis—whom he respected—had to say. "How come? I know Harper loved him."

"*Pfft*. Love. That's not what it was. It was good old-fashioned lust. And I had no problem with it. Harper was wrapped tighter than a second skin. He needed an outlet. But he confused lust with love. Ronnie was never into him for anything other than having a gorgeous man in his bed. He preferred to have David out of the way because he didn't want to see him every time he came to the house."

Colson dreaded asking, but he had to know. "So how do you know—"

"Nah, you're not going to ask why you're different, right? Because you are. You want to fit into Harper's life instead of changing it. You look at him, not past or through him. See, I had someone once I loved more than anything." Luis covered his hand and patted it. "And the way you and Harper are? That's how me and Maria were. Like there's never anyone else in the room but the two of you when you're together. And not only physically. You're in tune with each other. In sync."

"I think so."

"I know so," Harper said from behind them, and he peered over his shoulder to see a visibly tired Harper. "I'm glad you're here."

Luis rose to his feet. "I'll go check on David. He was tired after therapy, so he's taking a nap to make sure he can stay up after dinner with you."

After Luis left them, Colson murmured, "You look like you could use a nap too."

Harper's answering grin held a note of wickedness.

"How about we go upstairs and I give you a massage?" Colson wrapped his arms around Harper and kissed him.

"I think that would be a good start."

Chuckling, they took the stairs to his room, where Harper secured his gun, then kicked off his shoes and shucked his pants, socks, and suit jacket. Colson undid his tie and flicked open the buttons of his shirt, stopping to press kisses along the opening.

"There's something about a man in a suit that does it for me." He pushed the undone shirt off Harper's shoulders and rubbed the muscles. "You're so tight. Come lie with me."

Harper held his arm. "I meant it. I can't tell you how good it feels to come home after a long day and have you here to hold on to."

"I wouldn't be anywhere else. Now get on the bed, Detective. I'm not going to ask you twice."

Snickering, Harper followed his order and lay facedown. He groaned as Colson straddled him and dug his thumbs and fingers into the hard muscles across his back. "Goddamn, that feels amazing."

"Just close your eyes and relax. Or, since I know you're never fully off the job, take a deep breath and let it out slowly."

He worked on Harper's tense muscles, running his hands over the broad expanse of his body. Harper lay still with a sleepy smile on his face.

"You could go into business doing this, although I wouldn't want you touching anyone else."

Colson leaned in and kissed his cheek. "No one else gets this but you. What else do you want?"

"Anything you want to give me."

"That would be everything." With the same slow and gentle touch, he removed Harper's briefs, then his own clothes. Colson traced every inch of Harper's spine with his lips until he reached the swell of his ass. A heavy sigh escaped Harper as Colson blew a stream of air along the dip where his ass rose high and smooth. Harper widened his legs, an invitation to Colson, one he was happy to accept. He licked his fingers and teased inside.

"Oh yeah," Harper groaned. Colson lowered his face to Harper and tongued all around his rim. "You should've let me shower first."

"No, I love it raw and real." To prove it, he spread Harper wide and sucked at his hole. "And this is as real as it gets." Harper moaned and raised his hips higher to reach under him and work his dick. Colson lapped at the outside of his hole, then rubbed his erect cock in the cleft of Harper's ass.

"Fuck, I need in you before I explode."

Colson got the condom and lube. "Turn over." Harper rolled to face him, his thick cock almost flat on his belly. Colson tore open the packet and rolled it over Harper's shaft. He slicked him up and grasped him. "I'm going to ride you, baby."

Harper gripped his hips as he lowered himself onto Harper's rock-hard cock. The head popped through the muscled ring, and he hissed but kept pushing on, needing to be filled, craving to be stuffed with Harper's dick.

"Fuck me. You're swallowing me up like I'm part of you."

"You are. The best part of me. The one that let me love again." Colson leaned down to kiss Harper, and the movement lit him up as the head of Harper's cock rubbed his prostate.

"Oh, goddammit."

Harper flexed his hips and thrust up hard and deep, and Colson moved in tune with him. Colson could feel the swell and throb of his dick as they kissed. Harper grew more demanding, licking into his mouth, tugging at his lip, and sucking his tongue. He wrapped his hand around Colson's rigid shaft.

"Harper, please. Do it. Harder, come on."

He ground onto Harper's shaft as Harper jerked his cock in rough, quick strokes. "Yeah, look at that. You love it, don't you?"

"I-I..."

His climax ripped through him, and he lost the ability to speak. Colson fell forward, and Harper held him close. Harper pumped into him, using his shaking body at a punishing pace, and when he came, his loud groan echoed in the room.

They stayed like that, bodies fitting together, until their hearts settled into a natural rhythm and Colson could find his voice. "Feeling better now?"

Harper kissed his cheek. "The best. And just for the record, you are strictly limited to me."

He smiled against Harper's lips. "Duly noted, Detective."

Every day, he would write, his head filled with images of his characters, and the words flowed from his mind to his fingers and the computer. The burgeoning relationship between him and Harper had unlocked his stifled creativity, and with a start, he realized where he used to wake up and want to pull the covers over his head to keep from facing the endless hours of another day, he now couldn't wait to get up and begin writing.

At six o'clock, he would shut everything off and walk over to Harper's. The three of them would have dinner and then watch a movie, a ball game, or he'd read to David, while Harper would lie on the couch with his head in his lap.

Luis would read the chapters he'd written, and while Harper put David to bed, they'd go over his notes and discuss. One thing he never missed was saying good night to David. Colson receiving his kiss had become part of their family routine.

That Friday, after he said good night to David and they left the room, he stopped Harper. "I have an idea. How would you feel about taking a drive tomorrow?"

"Where to?" Harper asked. "You look as though you have a specific plan in mind."

He took Harper by the hand, and they returned to the living room and lay on the couch together. "I have a house—my grandparents left it to me. It's in Connecticut. It's a ranch, so it won't be a problem with David's chair, and it has a pool, tennis courts, and lots of land. When my grandfather had his first stroke, they installed a ramp at the front, so we can use that. I haven't been there since they passed, but I think maybe we should start using it when you have time off. David would love the country. There are deer and rabbits, and we can take him apple picking. He should get out of the city every once in a while, and this is perfect, don't you think?"

Harper played with his fingers. "I never thought of it like that. But you're right. It's bound to be more stimulating for him, and I'd love to see your grandparents' house—I know they meant so much to you. I think it'll be fun."

"We can go after breakfast."

"Perfect."

Saturday dawned bright and crisp, with a sky so blue, it almost glowed against the leaves of the trees, which had begun their slow march from green to russet and gold. Colson drove while Harper spoke to David, telling him where they were going.

It had been too long since he'd come to the house. Time slipped away, and what seemed like only days or weeks was in fact months and years. He paid the taxes and had a gardener take care of the property, but the soul of the house had been his grandparents, and with them gone, he had little desire to be there, alone, wandering rooms that held nothing but memories.

They pulled up to the circular drive, and he stopped the van. "This is it."

"Beautiful property." Harper got out and engaged the electrical ramp for David's chair. "I can see why you liked living here."

Lost in thought, he tipped his head to the sky, listening to the birds. "I had no choice. My grandparents were the only ones I could count on."

Harper slid an arm over his shoulders. "Not anymore."

Colson smiled and kissed him. "Let's go inside." He took out his keys and opened the door, and Harper wheeled David inside. Colson peered around. "That's odd."

"What is?"

"I expected the house to be stuffier from lack of air conditioning all summer and no one living here."

"Maybe the gardeners turned it on?"

"No, they don't have the keys. Only I do. Let's go to the kitchen." It had been his favorite room, where as a child he'd sit with his grandmother at the giant island and help her bake cookies. Unlike the sleek, modern, all-white design in his house in Brooklyn, this was more rustic and homier, with gleaming maple cabinets, a marble inset in the island for baking, and copper pots and pans hanging above. No wine fridge or cooling drawers. He cocked an ear, and frowning, strode across the room to the huge refrigerator and opened it. "See, this is strange. The fridge was supposed to be turned off. I remember because it didn't make sense to have it running if I wasn't here. And yet it's on, and there's ice in the ice maker."

Harper, who'd been making David comfortable, frowned. "I think you should look through the house and see if anything's missing."

He agreed. "Anything of value was sold, or in the case of my grandmother's jewelry, I put it in the safe deposit box, but yeah, I'm going to do that. Come with me?"

To his relief, the living room, library, and family room all looked intact, nothing out of place. Harper ran a hand over the huge fireplace. "This must be nice in the wintertime—a big fire while you watch the snow out of these giant windows."

"I loved having Christmas here." He looped his arms around Harper's neck. "Maybe we should think about spending our holidays here. I think it's time to make this house a home again."

Harper's kiss was all the answer he needed.

"The bedrooms are this way. The house seems big, but compared to some in the neighborhood, it's pretty small—five bedrooms and three bathrooms."

"Oh yeah, that's tiny," Harper joked.

He opened the door to his grandparents' room. "This was their room. I haven't done anything with it except donate their clothes."

Harper walked in, and his expression tensed. "Do you smell that?"

Colson inhaled. "Not really, what is it?"

"A woman's perfume."

"It's probably my grandmother's. She always wore Joy—her favorite. It's still on the dresser, see?" He picked up the bottle. "I didn't have the heart to throw it away."

They finished inspecting the other rooms, and he was pleased to see the house hadn't deteriorated at all despite his neglect. They ended up in the kitchen, and Harper gave David a snack of applesauce.

"Well, what do you both think?" He made sure to include David in the conversation. "Would you like to come up some weekends and spend time here?"

"I think it would be great to get away, right, David?" Harper looked to his brother, who smiled and blinked. "Maybe we should drive around and see if there are some farm stands or a petting zoo for David."

"There used to be one about a mile away. Let's go. I know there are country stores to get fresh pies."

They spent the next two hours exploring the countryside and loaded up on farmers' produce, apple cider, and the promised pies. One country market had a little petting zoo attached, and David was able to spend some time watching the pigs and goats in their pens. A few of the locals remembered Colson, and no one was outright hostile, but he did get some odd stares when he introduced Harper as his boyfriend.

"Colson Delacourt. Thought you disappeared forever," Dan Frick, the owner of Frick's Farms, stated as he checked them out. "Saw you started writing gory books." His eyes twinkled. "You have anyone in mind when you think up those murders?"

Amused, Colson chuckled. "Not really. Just a vivid imagination."

"Good to know. What happened?" Dan tipped his head toward David. "He have an accident or something?"

"Yes. He was injured as a boy." Harper's jaw worked, ready for battle. "I'm his brother."

Dan nodded. "My sister's kid dove into a pool and ended up paralyzed from the neck down. Needs a breathing tube and everything. But he's the happiest kid 'cause he's alive, you know?"

The tense lines in Harper's face softened. "Yeah. I know."

"Good on you, keeping him with you. God bless."

"Thanks." Colson took Harper's hand and squeezed it. "I think we are."

"Are you moving home? Gonna stay in your grandparents' place?"

"We're thinking of using it for the weekends. A nice getaway from the city."

Frick hesitated, as if he were about to say something, then shrugged. "Should be nice for you." He handed them their bags.

On the drive back to the house, Frick's behavior nagged at him. "Did you think he acted weird when I said we were planning on using the house now?"

"Weird, how?" Harper's brows drew together. "He asked a lot of questions, but nothing outrageous."

"Not sure. Just a feeling. Maybe they're not going to be happy having a gay couple in town. They aren't the most enlightened bunch."

But Harper disagreed. "He seemed okay with us. Maybe it's your overactive imagination."

Colson smiled. "You're cute. Wrong but cute." They pulled up the driveway and unloaded the car. "Let's put the stuff in the refrigerator and have a snack before driving home."

"Sounds good. Luis made us sandwiches. I have them in the cooler."

They lugged everything in and placed it on the island. Colson opened the refrigerator.

"Harper?" he called out. "Harper come here."

Harper skidded to a stop at his side. "What's wrong?"

"Look." He pointed to two bottles of champagne. "These were not there this morning. Someone was here."

"Or still is," Harper said, his eyes narrowing. "Let me look."

"It's my house. I'll do the looking."

"But—"

"But nothing. Stay here with David, please. You have your gun?"

Harper nodded. "My off-duty weapon."

"If I hear or see anyone, I'll come back here and let you deal with it."

"All right," Harper agreed reluctantly. "But be careful."

He left Harper and walked into the library, then the living room, seeing nothing awry. In the family room he spied high heels alongside a pair of men's loafers. His heart kicked up a beat. What the hell was going on? He kicked off his sneakers, and barefoot, padded to his grandparents' room, where the door was half-open and he could hear moans and groans of people having sex.

"Oh, baby, you make me crazy. Fuck me harder," a woman gasped. "You're so big. Give me that dick." The bed creaked, and a man grunted.

"Such a sweet, hot pussy."

Christ, was this really how straight people had sex?

"What the fuck!" Colson slammed open the door. "Who the hell are you—" His voice caught as he took in the scene. His father's naked ass pumping up and down on top of a very young woman, whose eyes grew wide when they met his. She began to scream.

His father glanced over his shoulder. "Shit." He withdrew and sat on his heels.

Avoiding the sight of his father naked, Colson crossed his arms. "Is that all you have to say?" He winced as the woman continued to wail.

"Shut up, Alicia." Without remorse, his father wrapped the sheet around his waist. "And what the hell are you doing here?"

"Me? You have the fucking nerve to ask me what *I'm* doing here? This is *my* house. I don't have to ask what you're doing. How long have you been sneaking over here to bring your girlfriends?"

Alicia had stopped screaming, and apparently unaware she sat bare-breasted, glared at his father. "Hammy, you said this was your house."

"Get dressed, sweetheart. I'll be with you in a minute." His father left the bed and put on his briefs. He stalked outside of the room, and Colson followed. "Why are you here, Colson?"

"The hell you think I'm going to answer to you," he sputtered. "You better get your ass dressed and out of here or I'll call the police."

His father sneered at him. "Do that. Alicia is the police chief's daughter. I doubt he'd want the news spread over town she was spreading her legs for a bottle of Dom Perignon and a trip to Tiffany's." His smile was thin. "And don't think you have anything to hold over my head. Your mother knows I have...friends. She doesn't care. In fact, she prefers it. I haven't shared her bed since shortly after you were born."

He heard the wheels of David's chair, and Harper appeared in the hallway. His father's gaze flicked to them. "Who is that?"

"You are in no position to ask me anything. Get dressed and get out of my house." He left his father to join Harper and David. "My father has been bringing his girlfriends here for God knows how long."

Harper's eyes gleamed. "Oh, yeah? The man who called you a degenerate?"

"Imagine that." His lips thinned and his father turned around and slammed the bedroom door. Less than five minutes passed before he emerged, barefoot and in a sweatshirt and jeans, with Alicia, who clung to his arm. "You left your shoes in the family room."

His father and Alicia swept past them without a word, but Harper was right on their heels. "You must've forgotten to introduce yourself. I'm Harper Rose, your son's boyfriend. I thought maybe Colson was exaggerating how horribly cold you were to him, but I can see now it's worse than I even imagined."

His father slipped his feet into his shoes and waited while Alicia put on her heels. "And I'm supposed to care about your opinion, why?"

"Because this is your son," Harper thundered. "You brought him into this world, and you were supposed to care for him and love him. Protect him from harm. Instead, you were his greatest threat."

"I don't have to listen to your bullshit." He jerked his head. "Alicia, let's go. I've called for the car and it's out front." He strode out of the room, Alicia scampering after him.

"But you will listen because I'm not finished." Harper dogged his steps. "Coward. That's what you are. An old fool who could've had a son anyone would be proud of, but you chose hate instead of love."

"That's rich," his father sneered. "Someone like you, preaching about love."

"Someone like me? What the fuck do you know about me?" Harper planted himself in front of Colson's father. "I'm an NYPD detective, and even now I would save your bigoted ass if I had to. Someone like me takes care of his brother who can't walk or talk because I love him. Someone like me, a gay man, loves your son so fucking much, he'd do anything in the world to make him happy. I'd *give* him the world, everything...anything I could. Because he is so damn worth it. But you can't see it because you're too blinded by one thing. Sex. You and your kind think everything revolves around what we do in the bedroom, but you have no idea." Harper paused for breath, his chest heaving, and Colson stood riveted. "It's how he makes me feel inside my heart that matters most."

"I'm not interested." His father knocked Harper aside as he passed by him, and Colson could feel Harper's restraint from across the room. Harper followed him, and Colson was torn between staying in the room with David and leaving him to watch the unfolding drama. He chose a middle ground and stayed in the doorway, where he could keep an eye on David, yet still see Harper, who was far from finished.

"Make sure you look at Colson one last time because as long as I'm here, you won't be allowed near him."

The door slammed, and Colson began to shake. Harper rushed to his side. "I'm sorry." He held him close. "I'm sorry."

Colson clung to him. "No, don't be. I'm not. Everything you said is true. No one can hurt us because we love each other."

After reassuring David that everything was fine, Harper kissed him. "And the best thing of all?" He shook with laughter. "Your father left those bottles of Dom. Now we can celebrate in style. On him."

"Every day is a celebration when I get to spend it with you."

CHAPTER TWENTY-SIX

It had been an emotionally draining day. They returned home and had a quiet dinner—too quiet, in fact. With each mile they'd put between themselves and Connecticut, Harper had sensed Colson withdrawing, so by the time the meal was finished, he was far in his own head. Harper put David to bed, then took Colson upstairs.

He started with a soft kiss, but instead of the usual flare of passion, he was met with hesitancy. He stopped and took Colson's face between his hands. Sadness rested in Colson's eyes. No matter their estrangement, it had to be devastating to be met with such ugly indifference from a parent. But he waited to hear what Colson had to say, knowing that no matter what it was, he'd only love him harder to make the hurt less painful.

"What's wrong? Talk to me."

"I don't think...I mean, I'm...I'm a little tired." His shoulders drooped. "I'm sorry."

Harper skimmed the outline of his lips. "Hey. Remember what I said? It's not the sex. It's what's in here." He placed a hand over Colson's heart and felt the rapid pump. "Let me take care of you tonight."

They undressed and got into the shower, where he shampooed Colson's hair. Harper soaped Colson up and rinsed him off, tracing his tattoos with his lips.

"Harper." Colson sighed, putting his arms around Harper.

"It's okay." Harper tried to rein in his tumbling emotions. His skin was tight, stretched to the limit from all the love and pain he kept bottled up, not only for David, but now for Colson.

Colson's lips moved against his shoulder. "I'm not going to let what happened with my father prevent me from loving you."

"Oh, I know that." His lips kicked up in a quick grin before he became serious. "I love you and meant every word I said to him. You talk about me needing someone to take care of my needs. Tonight, and every night afterward, I'm here for you."

On the outside he remained calm, but inside he raged at a parent who so callously tossed away a beautiful person like Colson.

"I know you are. You're more of a family—a home—in this short time together than I ever had with my parents."

Dried off and in bed and under the covers, Harper snuggled Colson in close. "Never let anyone make you feel like you don't deserve to be happy." He traced the tattoos of the birds and butterflies. "There's no need to fly away anymore. Not when you have a safe place to call home."

"As long as I'm with you, I'm home."

Sunday was, by unspoken agreement, a family day. Colson picked up bagels, and Harper smiled to himself as they all—Luis included—sat around the table for a late breakfast. Colson broke out a bottle of Dom Perignon and toasted.

"To our family."

He could see them, years into the future, enjoying mornings like this. His family. Forever. Now they had Connecticut too, and he looked forward to creating new memories. Nolan and Gina with their baby could come visit, and Colson's friend Hogan with his family as well. A full house filled with so much laughter and love. Knowing how Colson's grandparents cared so deeply for him, he imagined it would be exactly what they wished for.

"You'll love the house, Luis," Colson said, piling his bagel high with lox. "Tons of room, and there's a pool. I'll have to get someone in to put in a chair lift so David can use it. I bet aqua therapy would be good for him."

"It is, yeah." Luis's eyes shone bright. "He gets it once a week and it helps to massage his leg muscles, but having a whole pool would be amazing."

After they'd eaten, Colson sat with Luis and discussed the book, while Harper put on a movie for David and lay on the couch to work on his notes for the push-in robberies.

Warm breath tickled his ear.

"Huh?" His eyes fluttered opened. "What's wrong?"

"Nothing. You fell asleep." Colson stuck his tongue in Harper's ear, and blood rushed to his dick.

"Troublemaker." He rubbed his eyes. "How long was I out?"

"About two hours. Luis wants to order Chinese. He said David loves lo mein. He's just changing his ostomy bags. And you like my kind of trouble."

"Chinese sound good to you, Harper?" Luis pushed David into the room.

"Yeah, sure. Order me some chicken in black bean sauce, please. And spareribs."

"All right." Luis nodded and pulled out his phone. "What about you, Colson?"

"An egg roll and Hunan chicken."

Harper sighed and picked up his legal pad. He liked to write everything down and draw diagrams to see if he could pick up any patterns. Tomorrow would be another day of canvassing the area, speaking to people in the neighborhood and maybe getting lucky. So many days he was left feeling like he was one step behind the bad guys, spinning his wheels.

"Problems?" Colson slid in next to him. "Care to talk about it?"

"Another day, another group who preys on the elderly and the vulnerable. This time it's female perps, so it's even more dangerous."

Colson looked perplexed. "Why? I'd think the opposite."

Harper tapped his pad with his pencil. "Exactly. Most people, if they see a young, distraught female on their doorstep, wouldn't hesitate to help. These women count on that inherent good nature and capitalize on it for their bad acts."

"That's so sad. People can't trust anyone anymore." Colson frowned. "I'm going to text Hogan that Bea shouldn't open her door, even if it's a woman."

"As much as I hate being negative, I agree."

Colson kissed him on the nose. "You? Hate being negative? You're funny."

The notes and criminals forgotten, Harper wrestled him to the couch for a kiss. The doorbell rang, and Luis walked by, snickering.

"Don't mind me. You can always reheat the food if you need to get busy."

"Are you kidding?" Harper pushed Colson off him. "I'm starving."

"It's already come to this, huh?" Colson lay on the couch, face flushed and eyes dancing. "Second fiddle to spareribs."

Harper held out his hand. "Don't be such a drama queen." He pulled Colson up and kissed him. "I'll save my personal sparerib for you later."

"Oh, for God's sake, do not give up detective work for stand-up."

"I'm standing up right now. Want a peek?" Harper snickered.

"What's gotten into you tonight?" Colson groaned. "It's like you're intent on reviving bad jokes."

Harper lifted a shoulder and gazed across the room. "I don't know. I guess I'm just happy. And I'm not used to it, so I'm being silly."

Colson held his arm. "Hey. I'm just kidding. I love it. And you. You can be as silly as you want as long as it's with me."

Harper leaned in and kissed Colson's smile. "There's nothing silly about how I feel when I'm with you." How was it possible this man lit up all the dark, lonely spaces of a heart he'd given up on? Like everything else in his life, Harper wasn't about to question his good fortune. He'd found someone to share his demons with, someone who didn't run from the storm of Harper's complicated life but rather toward the chaos, embracing the rain.

"I love you too, baby."

"Flattery will get you an extra bite of my sparerib." Snickering, he waggled his brows.

Together, hand in hand, they went to dinner.

"Another Monday, another happy Harper. I don't know if I can stand it," Nolan razzed him.

"Well, get used to it, *Daddy*," Harper teased right back, and Nolan's eyes grew soft.

"I can't wait."

"What can't you wait for, Martinez?" Poole interrupted. "Not the next push-in, because we had a couple over the weekend. Check with Jankowitz and Leeds. They were on duty."

"Will do, Cap."

Poole frowned. "The neighborhood block association is very unhappy, and you know there are lots of judges and politicos who live in and around the area. The mayor is feeling the heat, which means they're stepping up the pressure at One PP, and it all falls on us." His smile was thin. "Let's get moving."

Harper spied Jankowitz coming into the bullpen from the bathroom and waved him over. "Bring your partner. We need to talk about the push-ins."

Twenty-year veteran Detective Jeff Leeds made a face as he settled into a chair opposite them. A grumpy bear of a man, he had instincts that couldn't be taught and a gut that rarely pointed him in the wrong direction. "I gotta tell you, what's the world coming to when we got girl gangs roaming the streets?"

Jankowitz set his hard jaw and rolled his eyes behind black-framed glasses. "I tried to tell Jeff here that it doesn't matter—man or woman, thugs are gonna thug. They hit one old man on Columbia Heights off Cranberry. He was wheeling his little grocery cart to his front door, and when he opened it, this girl conked him on the head and took his wallet. Poor slob had over a hundred bucks in it. He'd just been at the bank."

"Only one perp this time?" Harper asked, surprised.

"Yeah, looks like they're splitting up because about five minutes later another vic—a woman in her sixties—opened the door and got the same treatment, only this time her house was ransacked. No prints, nothing." Jankowitz made a disgusted sound.

"Getting brazen," Leeds added. "But that's when they usually slip up."

"We hope," Nolan said. "But if they're splitting up, that means they feel emboldened because we haven't been able to catch them."

"Yet. I think they're getting cocky and greedy, not bold," Harper insisted. "I agree with Leeds."

"One thing you're gonna find interesting"—Leeds pulled his notepad closer—"is that the lady told us the one who popped her over the head had a tattoo of the devil on her arm. So these are the same people doing the e-scooter robberies."

"Fucking hell," Harper cursed. "It never occurred to me to connect them. Makes it harder, but it's all good info."

"All right." Jankowitz rose to his feet. "I'm going home to remind my wife I'm alive. See you in a couple of days."

"Thanks, guys." Nolan raised a hand in a salute. "We're going to head out in a few."

That proved to be delayed, as they got tied up with phone calls and leads calling in from all the cards they'd handed out. It wasn't until the afternoon that they escaped the squad room and got to the street. They interviewed the elderly man, who couldn't remember a thing, and several of the neighbors on the street, but no one had seen anything. The woman who'd been burglarized had left to go to Long Island and stay with her daughter for a while, so that was a bust.

"A whole lot of nothing," Nolan groused.

He agreed and was about to suggest a cup of coffee when his phone rang with an unidentified number.

"Rose," he answered.

"Is this the detective I spoke to last week? The one at the bank? I was holding the door. You gave me your card."

"Yes." He searched his memory. "Mr...Lewis?"

"That's me."

"How can I help you?"

"Well, I think I'm the one who's going to help you. Ms. Millie Johnson was here, and I didn't think nothin' of it, but then I noticed this girl followed her down the block. Now, I couldn't go far 'cause this gentleman was paying me fifteen dollars to watch and make sure his car didn't get no tickets. But I saw Ms. Johnson go into the fruit stand, and this girl waited, then followed her. Like a lion stalking her prey."

"Thank you very much." He shoved the phone in his pants. "Let's go." He waved to Nolan and took off. "That was the door opener from the bank. Said some girl was following Millie Johnson home."

They tore through the quiet streets, zipping past dog walkers, delivery people, and the stroller brigade. At the approach to Millie's house, he drew his weapon, as did Nolan. The front door sat ajar, and he raced up the brownstone's stairs. He heard voices—female and a male—and ran inside.

"Freeze, police." He pointed his gun...at Millie, who stood unfazed in her foyer.

"Detective Rose. We were just about to call you."

He spied Colson standing over a girl on the ground. She was holding her face and moaning.

"Anyone else here, or is she alone?"

"No," Colson answered.

Nolan scanned the room and holstered his gun. "What happened?"

"I was just about to ask that," Harper growled. "Will someone tell us?"

"Please come sit, Detectives." Millie twittered around them. "Can I get you some tea?" Her birdlike gaze twinkled at him. "Although you'll have to wait for more water to boil. My uninvited guest is wearing my first cup."

He raised his eyes to the ceiling. "Help me, Lord." Hearing smothered laughter in the background, he glared at Colson. "No tea. Thank you." His patience was wearing thin. "The facts?"

"Well, I came home from the bank and the market—they had strawberries on sale, and I knew they'd be the last ones of the season—"

"Ms. Johnson, please?"

"Colson and I were going to have some cookies, and I made a cup of tea. Then the bell rang. This young woman was crying, saying her boyfriend beat her up and could she come in and call her mother."

He frowned. "And you opened the door, even though you know there's been a rash of break-ins. I thought we had this discussion already about you checking the camera."

"That's where I come in." Colson joined the story. "I was already here in the house when she received a call from the bank that they needed her to come in and verify signatures. I offered to stay because she had cookies in the oven."

"All this is very interesting, but can we get to the point where this all happened?" Nolan made a let's-move-on gesture.

Colson continued. "Knowing that Millie was too trusting, once I heard the front door open and this one"—he poked the girl on the floor with his foot—"started with a nasty mouth, I ran in with the cup of tea. When I saw her with her fist cocked to punch Millie, I threw the hot tea in her face."

"He burned me," the girl cried out. "I need a doctor."

"Yeah, sure, honey, we'll get right on that," Harper drawled. He got on his phone and called for backup. In five minutes, two officers were in the house and hauled the girl to her feet. Harper checked her out. "Don't worry. You're not burned. Just wet."

She spit in his face, and though he ducked, some caught him on his cheek. "Bastard," she screamed.

"Aw, crap," he said tiredly. "What'd you do that for?" He tipped his head to one of the uniformed officers, who stared at her in horror. "Add on assaulting an officer to the charges."

"You got it, Detective," the officer answered, and after placing her in handcuffs, led her, still screaming profanities, out of the house.

Colson rushed up to him with a wet washcloth. "Here. Let me." He suffered through having his face washed, while Nolan raged.

"That's disgusting. How dare she do that to you? You should go to the hospital and get checked out. Get a tetanus shot or something."

"She didn't cut me. I'll live." With only the four of them there, Harper was comfortable enough to put his arms around Colson. "Thank you."

Visibly upset, Colson pressed him. "Are you okay? Maybe Nolan is right and you should go see a doctor."

"Nah. I'm fine. Most of it missed me." He made a face. "It's probably more in my hair than anything. I'll take a shower when I get home."

Colson leaned in close and whispered, "I'll make sure you clean it all off."

"Excuse me," Millie interrupted. "Now that we've gotten that unpleasantness out of the way, is there something you haven't told me?"

A cute blush rose over Colson's face, and Harper grinned. "What would that be?"

She wagged her finger at him. "Detective Rose, you're teasing me. Did you take my advice?"

His arm tightened over Colson's shoulders, and his gaze found Nolan, who was trying–and failing–not to laugh out loud.

"I guess you could say so. I listened to my heart."

EPILOGUE

Eight months later

He woke to Harper kissing his neck.

"*Mmm.* Good morning to you too."

"I've never kissed a triple *New York Times* best-selling author." Harper teased his ear. "It's sexy. You're sexy." He continued to trail kisses up and down his neck. "How does it feel?"

Colson turned to face him. "Like a dream. I had no idea people would respond so positively to the story. I just went with my gut." He kissed Harper. "And my heart."

"Hasn't steered you wrong yet." Harper sat up. "Are you ready for the signing today?"

Colson joined him against the headboard. "It's funny. When I was first published, I did tons of them, all across the country. But for some reason, I'm nervous."

"Considering how long it's been, it's natural. But your agent has everything in place."

"Yeah, Ned's a pro. First stop is Brooklyn, then the city. He said they've had a lot of interest at both locations."

"You'll have your own personal security there at your side." Harper grinned. "The best of the best."

"Modestly, he says." Suddenly unsure, Colson bit his lip. "Thanks for taking the day off to be with me. That was a nice surprise."

Harper's brows drew together. "Surprise? Really? Where else would I be?"

Colson cast his gaze at his lap and twisted his fingers together. "Well...my ex never came to any signings. Only the parties celebrating the publishing wins. He felt that signings were part of my job, and he didn't need to hang out and watch me."

Harper's pale eyes darkened to stormy gray. "Watching you is my favorite thing in the world. But seriously? That's what people do for their partners. Be there to support them."

Colson leaned in close. "That's what the right partner does. I love you."

Harper kissed him. "I love you too. And I'll always have your back." With a wink, he rolled on top of him. "And your front, and your..."

Colson covered Harper's mouth with his, pushing his tongue past his lips. "Like I said, don't give up the day job."

Harper reached underneath and squeezed his ass. "You're even hotter now that you're a number one bestseller."

Laughing, he pushed at Harper's shoulder. "Move, you big lug."

"And getting bigger, but I'll save it for later." With a smirk, Harper jumped out of bed. "Let's shower and get dressed. I want to make sure David understands what's happening, since he hasn't been to the city in a long time."

At breakfast, Colson sat beside David to explain. "I wrote a book. Luis helped me. Today I'm going to meet a lot of people who want to buy this book." He held up a paperback copy of *Hunted Heart*. "I'm going to sign the books and talk to them and take pictures. Harper and Luis will be there too. I wanted all my family there. So that's why I asked Harper to bring you and Luis." He caught Luis's excited face. The man was in a suit and tie, and it touched Colson that he'd gone to so much trouble. "And both of you look very handsome." They'd bought David a shirt and a tie, and maybe Colson was mistaken, but he thought David's smile was a bit brighter and his eyes more focused.

Harper finished loading the dishwasher and checked his watch. "We'd better get going. This store we can walk to."

Colson checked his phone. "Ned's there, setting up."

They made a procession and showed up at the Book Nook to see a crowd already gathered. Ned spotted him and waved him over.

"Glad you're early. This is Miles Halloran, the owner."

A good-looking blond man shook his hand. "Great to meet you. My co-owner is a huge fan, and I've just started getting into your books." His big, bright-blue eyes crinkled shut with laughter. "My husband, on the other hand, is also an avid reader of your books and very annoyed he can't be here, so I promised him a signed copy of each one." He glanced behind him and pulled over a younger man hovering in the background. "This is Gordon, my co-owner."

"H-hi, Mr. Delacourt. Miles is right. I'm a huge fan."

"Great to meet you too. This is my family—Harper Rose, my boyfriend; his brother, David; and Luis, who helps with David and is also my personal assistant."

He'd asked Luis to take on that role when the work on the publishing side of the book had begun to take on a life of its own. It was a perfect partnership as Luis could help him while David was at therapy or had downtime.

Miles shook everyone's hand, and to their surprise, crouched next to David's chair. "Hi, David. I'm Miles. Would you like some books to look at while Colson is signing? I think I have some things you might like."

David's head bobbed side to side. Harper turned away and brushed at his eyes, and Colson put a hand on his shoulder.

"He's so happy to be here, I think." To Miles, he said, "Thank you. David is very special to us."

Miles's smile was sweet. "I understand. I have some books for children with sensory issues. Do you think he might like that?"

"He can try and hold them. We've been working on his hand coordination." Always vigilant concerning David, Harper answered before Colson had a chance to.

"I'll go get them."

Miles hurried away, and Ned led Colson to where a huge backdrop of his book stood behind a table set high with stacks of paperbacks and special edition hardcovers.

"Dude, what a turnout."

Hogan and Bea stood with the two little boys by their sides. He hugged them. "Thanks for coming."

"We wouldn't miss it," Bea pronounced. "I bring the kids here at least once a week. Miles and Gordon know them by name, and they have a great selection of children's books. Hi, Harper." Bea waved, and Harper kissed her cheek. She leaned in and gave David a kiss as well. "Hello, handsome. Don't you look good."

David eyes were big and bright.

A line began to form, and Colson wiggled his fingers.

"Okay. Let the fun begin."

Two hours later, only a few books remained, and Colson's hand was cramped. But he'd smiled and taken pictures with innumerable people and discussed the romance angle of the book, which surprisingly, most liked and wanted to see developed further. Hogan had, under his protest, bought the book along with a slew of children's puzzles and stickers and other things to keep the boys entertained.

"We've got the potential for a series, here, Colson." Ned took down the banner. "Think about it for the next book. Detective Rosa and Chief of Forensics Diller could be a three-book series, at the minimum."

"Let's get through one at a time," he joked. "We'll meet you in the city."

This next signing, at a big national chain, was more formal than at the Book Nook. The lines were longer, but he kept up the happy persona and glad-handed everyone. There were almost as many women as men, the former quick to tell him they loved the romance and were hoping for more books with the gruff detective and the shy chief of forensics.

He took a break for a sip of coffee and spotted the three men he'd met the past summer—Sal, Arnie, and Bert. He waved them over.

"How are you? Great to see you here."

"You remember us?" Sal asked. "We weren't sure."

"How could I forget? Three of my biggest fans." He shook their hands.

"We had to come tell you that we all thought the book was great." Bert looked to the other two, who nodded in agreement. "And the romance was good. Not overdone."

"Yeah. It was real natural," Arnie added. "I could see it."

"I'm really glad you enjoyed it." He grabbed three of the special edition hardcovers. "These are for you, on the house."

"Wow, thanks. We were gonna buy them." Sal motioned to the crowd still gathered. "And we're not the only ones, it looks like. Great turnout."

"No way," he brushed them off. "Not for the guys who came all the way from Bensonhurst. Ned," he called out, "this is Sal, Arnie, and Bert, and they have a Sunday book club and talk about my books. Put them on a list to always get my early releases, okay?"

Ned pulled out his phone. "Give me your names, addresses, and emails, and I'll make sure you also get the hardcovers."

He signed each book and gave it to them, with a hug and a promise to let them know the next time they stopped by Spumoni Gardens. Warmth spread through him as he watched them greet Harper and David and introduce themselves to Luis. Adding more people to his new and growing circle.

The next hour flew by, and while he enjoyed the meet and greet, he couldn't deny breathing a sigh of relief at the end. As they were packing up, Harper put his arms around him.

"You must be exhausted. I was tired just watching you."

He tried—and failed—to hide a yawn. "I'm okay. And I don't mind. But I'm looking forward to tonight."

Harper's grin was wicked. "You mean the dinner with Millie, Hogan and his family, and Nolan, Gina, and the baby?" He pulled him closer. "Or *later* later, when it's you and me?"

He put his lips to Harper's ear. "Guess."

"Cole?"

He froze. Only two people called him that, and one of them was Ned, who'd already left.

"Evan?"

He stood there, handsome and put together as always. His face gleamed a rich, russet brown as if he'd recently returned from a sunny vacation. Onyx-black eyes reflected a healthy appreciation as they slowly traveled over him. Harper's grip tightened on his shoulders.

"Looking good. Congrats on the book. Guess you broke out of your slump."

"You could say that. In more ways than one." He smiled into Harper's eyes. "This is my partner, Harper Rose."

"Partner?"

"What're you here for?" Harper's belligerent tone wasn't missed by Evan, whose brows rose.

"Whoa, I'm just here to wish Cole well."

Colson didn't believe that for a hot second and folded his arms. "Is that so? How nice of you, considering I haven't heard one word from you since you walked out. Where's your better half? You know, the one you have your best days ever with?"

Evan flushed. "Uh, we broke up about two months ago. He's still in Paris."

Luis came up to him with David. "We're going to go to the garage. I think David's a little tired. Meet you there?"

"In a minute, yeah."

Colson knew it would be longer than a minute.

Evan gazed after Luis and David. "What's with him?"

Colson could feel Harper draw a deep breath, and he took his hand and squeezed it. Hard.

"*Him* is David. Harper's brother. Which makes him my brother as well. I have a new life, and I've never been happier." Trying to soften the blow, he gentled his tone. "Look, Evan, it's nice that you came by, but I'm not interested in renewing an old acquaintance or being friends or seeing you at all. Harper is all I need." He lifted his and Harper's hands.

Evan's jaw worked hard, and then he walked away.

"He had a lot of fucking nerve showing up here," Harper grumbled.

"Funny. I haven't thought about him in a very long time. I have such a full life, filled with so much positivity, I don't have time for the negative." He laid his head on Harper's shoulder. "It's been a hell of a day. I'm ready to go home and just be with you."

"Me too." Harper nudged his cheek with his nose. "Do you know, that's the best part of my day? Just being with you, knowing you're there and that we have each other...it helps me get through it."

"I'll always be there with you and for you."

Harper kissed his cheek. "Ready?"

At one time, he'd believed he'd never have what so many took for granted. He'd covered his body with tattoos of beautiful, winged creatures, wishing he could disappear and leave the ugly loneliness behind. Now he soared high. There was no longer any need to fly away. He had it all. A home. Family. Love.

He and Harper had love so strong, he woke up every day believing in miracles because he was living his truth and it wasn't a dream. It was real and everything he'd ever wanted.

"I'm ready. Let's go home."

Thank you so much for reading Harper and Colson's story. I hope you loved reading their story as much as I loved writing it. I based their book on the neighborhood I live in, so if you have any questions, I'd love to hear from you! Just email me at felice@felicestevens.com. And yes, Truman Capote did live on Willow Street and wrote Breakfast at Tiffany's there.

FELICE STEVENS writes romance because what is better than people falling in love? Her favorite part of a romance novel is that first kiss...sigh. She loves creating stories of hopes and dreams and happily ever afters. Her stories are character-driven, rich with the sights, sounds, and flavors of New York City, and filled with men who are sometimes deeply flawed but always real.

Felice writes gay romance because she believes that everyone deserves a happily ever after. Having traveled all over the world, she can safely say that the universal language that unites people is love.

Felice has written in a variety of sub-genres, including contemporary and paranormal, and she has a mystery series as well. You can find all her books listed on her website.

Felice is a two-time Lambda Literary Award nominee and a Lambda Award winner in Gay Romance for her book *The Ghost and Charlie Muir*.

BOOKBUB
https://www.bookbub.com/profile/felice-stevens

NEWSLETTER
https://tinyurl.com/y85e69ab

READER GROUP
https://www.facebook.com/groups/FelicesBreakfastClub/

FACEBOOK AUTHOR PAGE
https://www.facebook.com/felicestevensauthor/

INSTAGRAM
https://www.instagram.com/felicestevens

GOODREADS
https://www.goodreads.com/author/show/8432880.
Felice_Stevens

WEBSITE
felicestevens.com

PAYHIP STORE
https://payhip.com/FeliceStevensAuthor